# In Bed with the Devil
## by Susan Mallery

To The Samurai –

If you're all reading this, it means you survived your month here at the lodge. I bet you thought it was going to drive you crazy, right? None of us were ever the type to settle down for long. That's why I made those twenty million dollars dependent on your sticking around. Money talks, brothers. I'm glad you all made it.

Meri always said I was the guy who kept you all together, and she was afraid that after I was gone, The Samurai would be no more. Well, I wasn't about to let that happen. When I got sick I discovered what really mattered. Have *you* worked it out yet?

Yeah, I thought so.

*Hunter*

D0293697

# High-Society Mistress
## by Katherine Garbera

## *He was all arrogant male.*

Totally sure of himself and his impact on her.
And she wished she could prove him wrong.
Wished she could take a step away from him
and dismiss him with a snooty comment that
would put him in his place.

He smelled even better up close than he had
when she'd shaken his hand. He crowded
closer to her and she fought not to back up.
But in the end her need for personal space
won out and she inched away from him.

"You're crowding me," she said carefully.
She was completely out of her element with
this man.

"Good."

"Why good?"

"I like it when you get your back up."

"I don't 'get my back up.' I'm a well-bred
young lady."

"I'm not a well-bred man," he said.

# Available in August 2008 from Mills & Boon® Desire™

*In Bed with the Devil*
by Susan Mallery
&
*High-Society Mistress*
by Katherine Garbera

ᎧᏫᎾᏫᏫᏋ

*A Convenient Proposition*
by Cindy Gerard
&
*A Splendid Obsession*
by Cathleen Galitz

ᎧᏫᎾᏫᏫᏋ

*Playboy's Ruthless Payback*
by Laura Wright
&
*Like Lightning*
by Charlene Sands

# In Bed with the Devil
## SUSAN MALLERY

# High-Society Mistress
## KATHERINE GARBERA

MILLS & BOON®

*Pure reading pleasure*™

*First published in Great Britain 2008*
*by Harlequin Mills & Boon Limited,*
*Eton House, 18-24 Paradise Road, Richmond, Surrey TW9 1SR*

The publisher acknowledges the copyright holders of the individual works as follows:

In Bed with the Devil © Susan Macias Redmond 2007
High-Society Mistress © Katherine Garbera 2007

*ISBN: 978 0 263 85909 6*

*51-0808*

*Printed and bound in Spain*
*by Litografia Rosés S.A., Barcelona*

# IN BED WITH
# THE DEVIL
## by
## Susan Mallery

Dear Reader,

I've always believed that friends are the family we make. That belief carries over to my writing, where I tell stories about friends.

The MILLIONAIRE OF THE MONTH series has been about friends. In my book, Jack and Meredith were once good friends. Then time and distance got in the way. Meri thinks she's back to get closure and maybe a little revenge, but she's wrong. She's back because she's still in love with her friend.

*In Bed with the Devil* wraps up the series, but don't worry if you've missed the other books. I wrote it to stand alone. However, if you've become a fan of the series, you'll enjoy catching up with all the previous characters. And meeting Hunter...

One of the coolest parts about being a romance writer is meeting other writers. These women are intelligent, caring and incredibly funny – qualities I want in my friends. It was a pleasure to work with them.

Happy reading,

*Susan Mallery*

## SUSAN MALLERY

is a bestselling and award-winning author of over fifty books. She makes her home in the Los Angeles area with her handsome prince of a husband and her two adorable-but-not-bright cats.

To the fabulously talented authors in this series.
Thank you so much for inviting me along for
the ride. It was wonderful fun and I would
do it again in a heartbeat!

# One

*Eleven years ago…*

Meredith Palmer spent the afternoon of her seventeenth birthday curled up on her narrow bed, sobbing uncontrollably. Everything about her life was a disaster. It was never going to be better—and what if she was one of the unlucky people who peaked in her teenage years? What if this was the *best* it was going to be?

Seriously, she should just throw herself out her dorm room window and be done with it. Of course, she was only on the fourth floor, so she was not going to actually kill herself. The most likely event was maiming.

She sat up and wiped her face. "Given the distance to the ground and the speed at impact," she murmured

to herself, then sniffed. "Depending on my position…"
She reached for a piece of paper. "If I fell feet first—
unlikely, but it could happen—then the majority of the
stress would be on my…"

She started doing the calculations. Bone density
versus a hard concrete landing or a softer grass landing.
Assuming a coefficient of—

Meri threw down the pencil and paper and collapsed
back on her bed. "I'm a total freak. I'll never be anything
but a freak. I should be planning my *death,* not doing
math. No wonder I don't have any friends."

The sobs returned. She cried and cried, knowing that
there was no cure for her freakishness. That she was
destined to be one of those scary solitary people.

"I'll have to get cats," she cried. "I'm allergic to cats."

The door to her room opened. She kept her face
firmly in her pillow.

"Go away."

"I don't think so."

That voice. She knew that voice. The owner was the
star of every romantic and semisexual fantasy she'd
ever had. Tall, with dark hair and eyes the color of the
midnight sky—assuming one was away from the city,
where the ambient light emitted enough of a—

Meri groaned. "Someone just kill me now."

"No one's going to kill you," Jack said as he sat
next to her on her bed and put a strong, large hand on
her back. "Come on, kid. It's your birthday. What's
the problem?"

How much time did he have? She could make him a
list. Given an extra forty-five seconds, she could index

it, translate it into a couple of languages, then turn it into computer code.

"I hate my life. It's horrible. I'm a freak. Worse, I'm a fat, ugly freak and I'll always be this way."

She heard Jack draw in a breath.

There were a lot of reasons she was totally in love with him. Sure, he was incredibly good-looking, but that almost didn't matter. The best part of Jack was he took time with her. He talked to her as if she was a real person. Next to Hunter, her brother, she loved Jack more than anyone.

"You're not a freak," he said, his voice low.

She noticed he didn't say she wasn't fat. There was no getting around the extra forty pounds on her five-foot-two-inch, small-boned frame. Unfortunately he also didn't tell her she wasn't ugly. Jack was kind, but he wasn't a liar.

Between her braces and her nose—which rivaled the size of Io, one of Jupiter's moons—and her blotchy complexion, she had a permanent offer from the circus to sign on up for the sideshow.

"I'm not normal," she said, still speaking into her pillow because crying made her puffy and she didn't need for Jack to see her looking even *more* hideous. "I was planning my death and instead I got caught up in math equations. Normal people don't do that."

"You're right, Meri. You're not normal. You're way better than that. You're a genius. The rest of us are idiots."

He wasn't an idiot. He was perfect.

"I've been in college since I was twelve," she mumbled. "That's five years. If I was really smart, I'd be done now."

"You're getting a Ph.D., not to mention your, what, third masters?"

"Something like that." Unable to be in the same room with him and not look at him, she flipped onto her back.

God, he was so amazing, she thought as her chest tightened and her stomach turned over a couple of times. Technically the organ in question couldn't turn over. What she felt was just—

She covered her face with her hands. "I have to find a way to turn off my brain."

"Why? So you can be like the rest of us?"

She dropped her hands to her side. "Yes. I want to be a regular girl."

"Sorry. You're stuck being special."

She loved him so much it hurt. She wanted him to think she was more than his best friend's kid sister. She wanted him to see her as a woman.

Right, and while she was having a fantasy moment…

maybe he could see her as a beautiful woman he ached for. As if!

"I don't have any friends," she said as she did her best to ignore the need to tell him she would love him forever. "I'm too young, especially in the Ph.D. program. They all think I'm some upstart kid. They're waiting for me to crash and burn."

"Which isn't going to happen."

"I know, but between my academic isolation and my lack of a female role model since the death of my mother, the odds of my maturing to a normal functioning member of society grow more slim each day. Like I said—I'm a freak." Tears rolled down her temples to get lost in her hair. "I'll never have a boyfriend."

"Give it a couple of years."

"It's not going to happen. And even if some guy does take pity on me and ask me out, he'll have to be drunk or stoned or something to want to kiss me, let alone have sex with me. I'm going to d-die a virgin."

The sobs began again.

Jack pulled her into a sitting position and wrapped his arms around her. "Hell of a birthday," he said.

"Tell me about it."

She snuggled close, liking how strong and muscular he felt. He smelled good, too. If only he were desperately in love with her, the moment would be perfect.

But that was not meant to be. Instead of declaring undying devotion and ripping off both their clothes or even kissing her, he shifted back so they weren't even touching.

"Meri, you're in a tough place right now. You don't fit in here and you sure don't fit in with kids your own age."

She wanted to protest she was almost his age—there were only four years between them—and she fit with him just fine. But Jack was the kind of guy who had dozens of women lining up to be with him. Pretty, skinny girls she really, really hated.

"But you're going to get through this and then life is going to be a whole lot better."

"I don't think so. Freakishness doesn't just go away."

He reached out and touched her cheek. "I have high hopes for you."

"What if you're wrong? What if I do die a virgin?"

He chuckled. "You won't. I promise."

"Cheap talk."

"It's what I'm good at."

He leaned toward her, and before she knew what he was going to do, he kissed her. On the mouth!

She barely registered the soft, warm pressure of his lips on hers and then the kiss was over.

"No!" She spoke without thinking and grabbed the front of his sweatshirt. "Jack, no. Please. I want you to be my first time."

She'd never seen a man move so fast. One second he was on her bed, the next he was standing by the door to her dorm room.

Shame and humiliation swept through her. She would have given a hundred IQ points to call those words back. Heat burned her cheeks until she knew she would be marked by the embarrassment forever.

She'd never meant him to know. He'd probably guessed she had a massive crush on him, but she'd never wanted him to be sure.

"Jack, I…"

He shook his head. "Meri, I'm sorry. You're…you're Hunter's little sister. I could never… I don't see you like that."

Of course not. Why would he want a beast when there were so many beauties throwing themselves at him?

"I understand. Everything. Just go."

He started to leave, then turned back. "I want us to be friends. You're my friend, Meri." And with those horrifying words, he left.

Meri sat on the edge of her bed and wondered when she would stop hurting so much. When would she fit in?

When would she stop loving Jack? When would she be able to walk in a room and not wish for the floor to open up and swallow her whole?

Automatically she reached under her bed and pulled out the plastic storage container filled with her snacks. After grabbing a frosted cupcake, she unwrapped it.

This was it—she'd officially hit bottom. Nothing would ever be worse than this exact moment. It was like dark matter in the universe. The absolute absence of anything. It was the death of hope.

She took a bite of the cupcake. Shame made her chew fast and swallow. When the sugar and fat hit her system, she wouldn't hurt so bad. She wouldn't feel so lonely or totally rejected by Jack Howington III. Damn him.

Why couldn't he love her back? She was a good person. But she wasn't busty and blond and tiny, like the girls he dated and slept with.

"I have a brain," she murmured. "That scares guys."

She said the words bravely, but she knew it was more than her incredible IQ that chased off boys. It was how she looked. How she'd allowed food to be everything, especially after her mom died four years ago. It was turning down her father's badly worded offer to take her to a plastic surgeon to talk about her nose. She screamed that if he really loved her, he would never, ever talk about it again, when in truth she was scared. Scared of changing and scared of being the same.

She stood and stared at the closed dorm room door. "I hate you, Jack," she said as tears slipped down her cheeks. "I hate you and I'll make you suffer. I'm going to grow up and be so beautiful you have to sleep with me. Then I'm going to walk away and break your heart. Just watch me."

*Present day*

Jack Howington III had driven two days straight to get to Lake Tahoe. He could have flown his jet, then picked up a rental car for the month he was going to be forced to stay at Hunter's house, but he'd needed the downtime to clear his head.

His assistant had been frantic, unable to reach him in the more rural parts of the country, but he'd enjoyed the silence. There hadn't been enough silence in his life for a long, long time. Even when he was alone, there were still the damn ghosts to contend with.

He drove down a long driveway toward a barely visible log house. The place stood surrounded by trees with a view of the lake behind. There were windows and stone steps, along with a heavy double wood door.

Jack parked, then climbed out of his Mercedes. Hunter's house had been built just recently, nearly ten years after the death of his friend, but Jack had a feeling that Hunter had left detailed instructions on what it should look like. The place reminded him of Hunter, which was both good and bad.

It was just a month, he told himself as he walked around to the trunk and grabbed his suitcase and computer bag. If he stayed in here for a month, per the terms of Hunter's will, the house would be converted to a place for cancer patients and survivors to come for

free. Twenty million would be given to the town or
charity or something like that. Jack hadn't paid attention
to the details. All he knew was that Hunter had asked him
for one last favor. Jack had failed his friend enough
times to know that this time he had to follow through.

He took a single step toward the house, then stopped
as the front door opened. The lawyer's letter had promised quiet, an office he could work in and a housekeeper
to take care of day-to-day necessities.

Easy duty, Jack had thought at the time. Now, as
a petite, pretty woman stepped onto the porch, he
wasn't so sure.

Next to Hunter, who was long dead, she was about
the last person he wanted to see.

"Hello, Jack," she said.

"Meredith."

Her blue eyes widened in surprise. "You recognize
me?"

"Sure. Why not?"

She drew in a breath. "It's been a long time. We've
both changed."

"I'd know you anywhere."

Which wasn't exactly the truth. He'd kept tabs on
Meri over the years. It was the least he could do after
he'd promised Hunter he would look after his sister.
Jack hadn't been able to deal with her in person, but
distance made things safer. Easier. The regular reports
from his staff meant he wasn't the least bit surprised by
her appearance. Although she looked more…feminine
than usual. He'd known she'd been working in California on a temporary assignment with JPL—Jet Propul-

sion Laboratory, but not the details. He hadn't known she was *here.*

She muttered something under her breath, then said, "Good to know."

Her eyes were still as blue as he remembered. The same color as Hunter's eyes. The same shape. Other than that and an easy laugh, the siblings had had little in common.

He hadn't seen her in years. Not since Hunter's funeral. And before that—

He pushed the memory of her heartfelt declaration and his piss-poor handling of it out of his mind. Let's just say they'd both traveled a lot of years and miles, he told himself.

She'd grown up, he thought as she walked down the stairs and stood in front of him. The baby fat was gone. She looked like what she was—a beautiful, sexy woman who was confident of her place in the world.

Under other circumstances, he could have appreciated the changes, but not with her. Not with the promises he'd made.

"Obviously you received the letter from the lawyer or you wouldn't be here," she said. "You're required to stay for a month. At the end of that time, there will be a brief but meaningful ceremony deeding the house to the town, handing over the keys and the money. You and the other Samurai are free to mingle and catch up, then you're free to go." She glanced at the single suitcase and computer bag. "You travel light."

"Makes it easier to move around."

"But it doesn't give you many choices for that unexpected costume party."

"Is there going to be one?"

"Not that I know of."

"Then I'm good."

She tilted her head slightly, a gesture he remembered. Funny how he could still see the girl in the woman. He'd always liked the girl. He didn't plan to get to know the woman.

He looked her over, then frowned. Was it just him or were her shorts way too short? Not that he didn't appreciate the display of leg, but this was Meredith—Hunter's baby sister. And should her shirt really be that…revealing?

"I'm staying here, too."

Her voice was low and sexy, and had she been anyone else, he would have welcomed the distraction.

"Why?" he asked bluntly.

"I'm the housekeeper. The one you were promised. I'm here to make your life…easier."

There was almost a challenge in the statement. "I don't need a housekeeper."

"You're not being given a choice. I come with the property."

"That's ridiculous," he said flatly. He happened to know she worked for a D.C. think tank and was currently on loan to JPL and some private company, helping them develop a better solid rocket fuel.

"Such language," she scolded gently, then smiled. "It's what Hunter wanted. We're both here because of him."

He frowned. He didn't buy her story. Why would Hunter want his sister at the house for a month? But then, he'd asked all his friends to spend time here, so it was possible. Besides, it wasn't as if Meri would *want* to be in the same house as him. Not after what had happened on her seventeenth birthday.

He'd hurt her. He hadn't meant to, but he had, and after the fact he'd been unable to figure out a way to make things better. Then Hunter had died and everything had changed.

Or maybe he was making too big a deal out of all this. Maybe Meri didn't give a damn about what had happened…or not happened…between them.

"Let's go inside," she said and led the way.

They walked into a large entryway with a staircase and a stone floor. The place was welcoming and masculine. It might not be the house he would have built, but it wasn't going to drive him crazy with lots of frills and smelly bowls of dried flowers.

"You'll get your exercise climbing the stairs. Your room is on the next floor."

He glanced around. "You're down here?"

She smiled. "No, Jack. I'm on the second floor, next to the master. We're only a wall apart."

Meri deliberately widened her eyes and leaned toward him as she spoke. She wanted the invitation to be clear. After what Jack had put her through eleven years ago, he deserved to squirm.

She started down the hall before he had a chance to respond. "There's an office loft area," she continued. "You can use that. It's set up with Internet access, a fax. I'll be in the dining room. I like to spread out when I work. I tend to get really…involved."

She emphasized the last word, then had to consciously keep herself from laughing. Okay, this was way more fun than she'd thought it would be. She should have punished Jack a long time ago.

She made sure she swayed her hips as she climbed and bent forward slightly so he would be sure to notice her very short shorts. She'd worn them deliberately, along with the halter top that left very little to the imagination. It had taken her nearly two days to come up with the perfect outfit, but it had been worth the time.

The shorts clung to her and were cut high enough to show the bottom of her butt. Tacky but effective. Her sandals had a spiked heel that was practically a weapon, but they made her legs look long—a serious trick for someone as short as her.

The halter was so low-cut that she'd had to hold it in place with double-sided tape. She had fresh highlights, sultry makeup and long, dangling earrings that almost touched her nearly bare shoulders.

If the guys back at her science lab could see her now, they would probably implode from shock. Around them she only wore tailored suits and lab jackets. But for the next month she was dressing as a sex kitten and she planned to enjoy every minute of it.

She deliberately sped up at the end of the hall, then stopped suddenly. Jack ran into her. He reached out to steady himself or maybe her. She'd planned that he would, so she turned and held in a grin as the palm of his hand landed exactly on her left breast.

He stiffened and pulled back so fast he almost fell. Meri tried to decide if she minded seeing him in a crumpled heap on the polished hardwood floor.

"Sorry," he muttered.

"Jack," she purred. "Are you coming on to me? I have to say, that's not very subtle. I would have expected better."

"I'm not coming on to you."

"Really?" She put her hands on her hips as she faced him. "Why not? Aren't I your type?"

He frowned. "What the hell is this all about?"

"So many things. I'm not sure where to start."

"Try at the beginning. It usually works for me."

The beginning? Where was that? At conception, where some quirk of the Palmer gene pool had decided to produce a child with an exceptional IQ? Or later, when Meri had first realized she was never going to fit in anywhere? Or perhaps that long-ago-but-never-forgotten-afternoon when the man she loved had so cruelly rejected her?

"We're spending the month together," she told him. "I thought we could have more fun if we played. I know you like to play, Jack."

He swore under his breath. "This isn't like you, Meri."

"How can you be sure? It's been a long time. I've grown up." She turned slowly. "Don't you like the changes?"

"You look great. You know that. So what's the point?"

The point was she wanted him desperate. She wanted him panting, begging, pleading. Then she would give in and walk away. It was her plan—it had always been her plan.

"I'm not going to sleep with you," he said flatly. "You're Hunter's sister. I gave him my word I'd look after you. That means taking care of you, not sleeping with you."

She'd meant to keep her temper. Honestly she'd even written it on her to-do list. But it was simply impossible.

"Take care of me? Is that what you call disappearing two seconds after Hunter's funeral? All of you left—all of his friends. I expected it of them but not of you. Hunter told me you would always be there for me no matter what. But you weren't. You were gone. I was seventeen, Jack. My father was a basket case, I was a total social outcast with no friends and you disappeared. Because that was easier than facing your responsibility."

He put down his luggage. "Is that why you're here? To tell me off?"

He had no idea, she thought, still furious and wishing she could breathe fire and burn him into a little stick figure, like in the cartoons.

"That's only part of the fun."

"Would it help if I said I was sorry?"

"No, it wouldn't." Nothing would change the fact that he'd abandoned her, just like everyone else she'd ever loved.

"Meri, I know we have some history. But if we're stuck here for a month, we need to find a way to get along."

"Be friends, you mean?" she said, remembering how he'd said he would always be her friend, right after rejecting her.

"If you'd like."

She took a deep breath, then released it. "No, Jack. We'll never be friends. We'll be lovers and nothing else."

# Two

The next morning Meri woke up feeling much better about everything. After leaving out food for Jack, she'd escaped to her room, where she'd had a bath and a good cry. Some of her tears had been about her brother, but a lot of them had been for herself. For the geek she'd been and the losses she'd suffered.

After Hunter had died, their father had totally lost it. He'd been less than useless to her. Within a year he'd started dating nineteen-year-olds, and in the nine years since, his girlfriends had stayed depressingly young.

She'd been on her own and she'd survived. Wasn't that what mattered? That she'd managed to get the help she'd needed to move forward and thrive?

She turned on her clock's radio and rocked her hips to the disco music that blasted into the room. She was sorry she'd missed the disco years—the music had such a driving beat. Of course, she was a total spaz on the dance floor, but what she lacked in style and grace she made up for in enthusiasm.

After brushing out her hair, she braided it, then dressed in a sports bra, tank top and another pair of skimpy shorts. Ankle socks and athletic shoes completed her outfit.

Humming "We Are Family" under her breath, she left her room and prepared to implement the next part of her plan for revenge.

Jack was in the kitchen. She walked up to him and smiled.

"Morning," she said, reaching past him for the pot of coffee. She made sure she leaned against him rather than going around. "How did you sleep?"

His dark eyes flickered slightly, but his expression never changed. "Fine."

"Good. Me, too."

She poured the coffee, then took a sip, looking at him over the mug.

"So," she said. "A whole month. That's a long time. Whatever will we do with it?"

"Not what you have planned."

She allowed herself a slight smile. "I remember you saying that before. Did you always repeat yourself? I remember you being a whole lot more articulate. Of course, I was younger then, and one looks at one's elders with the idealism of youth."

He nearly choked on his coffee. "Elders?"

"Time has been passing, Jack. You're, what, nearly forty?"

"I'm thirty-two and you know it."

"Oh, right. Thirty-two. Time has been a challenge for you, hasn't it?"

She enjoyed baiting him too much, she thought, knowing she was being totally evil and unable to help herself. The truth was, Jack looked amazing. Fit, sexy— a man in his prime. The good news was that sleeping with him wouldn't be a hardship.

"You gave up on seducing me?" he asked.

"Not at all. But this is fun, too."

"I'm not sleeping with you."

She glanced around the kitchen, then looked back at him. "I'm sorry, did you say something? I wasn't listening."

"You're a pain in the ass."

"But it's a darned nice ass, isn't it?" She turned to show him, patted the curve, then faced front again. "Okay, go get changed. I'll take you to the nearest gym. You can get a thirty-day membership. Then we'll work out together."

"There's no equipment here?"

She smiled. "I guess Hunter didn't think of everything after all. It's a good thing I'm around."

He stared at her. "You think you're in charge?"

"Uh-huh."

He put down his mug, then moved close and stared into her eyes. "Be careful, Meri. You're playing a game you don't know how to win. I'm out of your league and we both know it."

A challenge? Was he crazy? She always won and she would this time. Although there was something about the way he looked at her that made her shiver. Something that told her he was not a man to be toyed with.

But he *was* just a man, she reminded herself. The sooner she got him into bed, the quicker she could get on with her life.

Jack followed Meri into the large gym overlooking the lake. The facility was light and clean, with only a few people working out. Probably because it was midday, he thought as he took in the new equipment and mentally planned his workout.

Back in Dallas, he worked out in his private gym, built to his specifications. But this would do for now.

"So we can circuit-train together," she said brightly, standing close and gazing up at him with a teasing smile. "I'm great at spotting."

She was trying to push his buttons. He was determined not to react, regardless of what she said or did. Meri was playing a game that could be dangerous to her. He might not have taken care of her the way he should have, but he *had* looked out for her. That wasn't going to stop just because she was determined to prove a point.

"Want to warm up with some cardio first?" she asked. "We can race. I'll even give you a head start."

"I'm not going to need it," he told her as he headed over to the treadmills, not bothering to see if she followed.

"That's what you think."

She stepped onto the machine next to his and set it for a brisk warm-up pace. He did the same, not bothering to look at her speed.

"You didn't used to exercise," he said conversationally a few minutes later as he broke into a jog.

Meri punched a few buttons on her treadmill and matched his speed. "I know. I was much more into food than anything else. Not surprising—food was my only friend."

"We were friends," he said before he could stop himself. He'd liked Meri—she was Hunter's little sister. She'd been like family to him.

"Food was the only friend I could depend on," she said as she cranked up her treadmill again. She was breathing a little harder but barely breaking a sweat. "It didn't disappear when I needed it most."

No point in defending himself. She was right—he'd taken off right after Hunter's funeral. He'd been too devastated by loss and guilt to stick around. A few months later he'd realized he needed to make sure Meri was all right. So he'd hired a P.I. to check in on her every few months. The quarterly reports had given him the basics about her life but nothing specific. Later, when he'd started his own company, he'd gotten his people to keep tabs on her and he'd learned a lot more about her. He'd learned that she'd grown up into a hell of a woman. Obviously she hadn't needed him around, taking care of things.

"The downside of food as a friend," she continued, "is that there's an ugly side effect. Still, I couldn't seem to stop eating. Then one day I made some new friends and I stopped needing the food so much." She grinned. "Okay, friends and some serious therapy."

"You were in therapy?" The reports hadn't mentioned that.

"For a couple of years. I worked through my issues. I'm too smart and weird to ever be completely normal, but these days I know how to pass."

"You're not weird," he said, knowing better than to challenge her brain. Meri had always been on the high side of brilliant.

"A lot you know," she said. "But I like who I am now. I accept the good points and the bad."

There were plenty of good points, he thought, doing his best not to look at her trim body. She had plenty of curves, all in the right places.

They continued to jog next to each other. After another five minutes, Meri increased the speed again and went into a full-out run. Jack's competitive side kicked in. He increased not only the speed but the incline.

"You think you're so tough," she muttered, her breath coming fast and hard now.

"You'll never win this battle," he told her. "I have long legs and more muscle mass."

"That just means more weight to haul around."

She ran a couple more minutes, then hit the stop button and straddled the tread. After wiping her face and gulping water, she went back onto the treadmill but at a much slower pace. He ran a few more minutes—because he could—then started his cooldown.

"You're in shape," he told her as they walked over to the weight room.

"I know." She smiled. "I'm a wild woman with the free weights. This is where you really get to show off, what with having more upper-body strength. But pound for pound, I'm actually lifting nearly as much as you. Want me to make a graph?"

He grinned. "No, thanks. I can see your excuses without visual aids."

"Reality is never an excuse," she told him as she collected several weights, then walked over to a bench. She wiped her hands on the towel she'd brought.

"I can't be too sweaty," she said. "If my hands are slick, it gets dangerous. About a year ago, I nearly dropped a weight on my face. Not a good thing."

"You should be more careful," he said.

"You think? I paid a lot of money for my new nose. You never said anything. Do you like it?"

He'd known about the surgery. She'd had it when she was twenty. He supposed the smaller nose made her a little prettier, but it wasn't that big a change.

"It's fine," he said.

She laughed. "Be careful. You'll turn my head with all that praise. My nose was huge and now it's just regular."

"You worry too much about being like everybody else. Average is not a goal."

She looked at him. "I haven't had enough coffee for you to be philosophizing. Besides, you don't know anything about normal. You were born rich and you're still rich."

"You're no different."

"True, but we're not talking about me. As a guy, you have different standards to live up or down to. If you have money, then you can be a total loser and you'll still get the girl. But for me it was different. Hence the surgeries."

"You had more than one?" he asked, frowning slightly. He knew only about her nose.

She sat up and leaned toward him. "Breasts," she said in a mock whisper. "I had breast implants."

His gaze involuntarily dropped to her chest. Then he jerked his head to the right and focused on the weight bench next to him.

"Why?" he asked, determined not to think about her body and especially not her breasts, which were suddenly more interesting than he wanted them to be.

"After I lost weight, I discovered I had the chest of a twelve-year-old-boy. I was totally flat. It was depressing. So I got implants. I went for a jumbo B—which seemed about right for my newly skinny self."

She stood and turned sideways in front of the mirror. "I don't know. Sometimes I think I should have just gone for it and ordered the centerfold breasts. What do you think?"

He told himself not to look, but it was like trying to hold back the tide. Against his will, his head turned and his gaze settled on her chest. Meri raised her tank top to show off her sports bra.

"Are they okay, Jack?"

A guy walking by did a double take. "They're great, honey."

She dropped her shirt and smiled. "Thanks."

Jack glanced at the guy and instantly wanted to kill him. It would be fast and relatively painless for the bastard. A quick twist of the neck and he would fall lifeless to the ground.

Meri dropped her shirt. "I love being a girl."

"You're still playing me. I'm going to ignore you."

"I'm not sure you can," she teased. "But you can try. Let's change the subject. We can talk about you. Men love to talk about themselves."

He grabbed a couple of weights and sat on a bench. "Or we could focus on our workout."

"I don't think so." She lay on her back and did chest presses. "What have you been up to for the last ten years? I know you went into the military."

"Army," he said between reps.

"I heard it was Special Forces."

"That, too."

"I also heard you left and started your own company dealing with corporations that want to expand into the dangerous parts of the world."

Apparently he wasn't the only one who had done some research.

"It's impressive," she said. "You've grown that company into quite the business."

"I'm doing okay." Five hundred million in billing in the past year. His accountants kept begging him to go public. They told him he could make a fortune. But he already had more than he needed, and going public meant giving up control.

"Are you married?" she asked.

He looked over at her. She'd shifted positions and was now doing bicep curls. Her honey-tanned skin was slick with sweat, her face flushed, her expression intense. She was totally focused on what she was doing.

Would she be like that in bed? Giving a hundred percent, really going for it?

The thought came from nowhere and he quickly pushed it away. Meri could never be more than Hunter's baby sister. She could dance around naked and beg him to take her—they were never going there.

"Jack? You gonna answer the question?"

Which was? Oh, yeah. "No, I'm not married."

"You're not gay, are you? Hunter always wondered."

He ignored her and the question. If he didn't react, she would get tired of her game and move on to something else.

She sighed. "Okay, that was funny only to me. So there's no wife, but is there someone significant?"

"No."

"Ever been anyone?"

"There have been plenty."

She looked at him. "You know what I mean. A relationship where you're exchanging more than bodily fluids. Have you ever been in love?"

"No," he said flatly. Women tried to get close and he didn't let them.

"Me, either," she said with a sigh. "Which is deeply tragic. I want to be in love. I've been close. I thought I was in love, but now I'm not so sure. I have trust and commitment issues. It's from losing my mom when I was young and then losing Hunter. Isn't it interesting that knowing what the problem is doesn't mean I can fix it?"

He didn't know what to say to that. In his world, people didn't talk about their feelings.

"You lost a brother when you were young," she said. "That had to have affected you."

No way he was thinking about that. He stood. "I'm done. I'm going to take a shower."

She rose and moved close. "Want to take one together?"

He had an instant image of her naked, water pouring over her body. How would she feel? His fingers curled slightly, as if imagining cupping her breasts.

Damn her, he thought. She wasn't going to win. It was time to stop playing nice.

He moved forward, crowding her. She stepped back until she bumped into a weight bench, then she dropped into a sitting position. He crouched in front of her.

"You do not want to play this game with me," he told her in a low voice. "I'm not one of your brainy book guys. I have seen things you can't begin to imagine, I have survived situations you couldn't begin to invent. You may be smart, but this isn't about your brain. You can play me all you want, but eventually there will be consequences. Are you prepared for that, little girl?"

"I'm not a little girl."

He reached behind her and wrapped his hand around her ponytail, pulling just hard enough to force her head back. Then he put his free hand on her throat and stroked the underside of her jaw.

Her eyes widened. He sensed her fighting fear and something else. Something sexual.

He knew because he felt it, too. A pulsing heat that arced between them. Need swirled and grew until he wanted to do a whole lot more than teach her a lesson.

Then she smiled. "I'm getting to you, aren't I?"

He released her. "In your dreams."

*  *  *

Back at the house, Meri went up to her room to change clothes. She didn't offer to help Jack with his. After their close encounter at the gym, she needed a little time to regroup.

There had been a moment when Jack had touched her that had if not changed everything then certainly captured her attention. A moment when she'd been aware of him as being a powerful man and maybe the slightest bit dangerous.

"I'm not impressed," she told herself as she brushed out her hair, then slipped into a skimpy sundress that left her arms bare. "I'm tough, too." Sort of.

Jack was right. He'd been through things she couldn't begin to imagine. While they'd both changed in the past eleven years, she wondered who had changed more on the inside. Was the man anything like the boy she'd both loved and hated?

Before she could decide, she heard the rumble of a truck engine. A quick glance at her watch told her the delivery was right on time.

"It's here! It's here!" she yelled as she ran out of her room and raced down the stairs. "Jack, you have to come see. It's just totally cool."

She burst out of the house and danced over to the truck. "Were you careful? You were careful, right? It's very expensive and delicate and I can't wait until you set it up. You're going to calibrate it, right? You know how? You've been trained?"

The guy with the clipboard looked at her, then shook his head. "You're a scientist, aren't you?"

"Yes. How'd you know?"

"No one else gets that excited about a telescope." He pointed back at the compact car parked behind the truck. "He calibrates it. I just deliver."

Jack walked outside and joined her. "A telescope?"

"I know—it's too exciting for words. It was very expensive, but the best ones are. You won't believe what we'll be able to see. And it's so clear. How long until sunset?"

She looked at the sky. It would be too long but worth the wait.

"You bought a telescope for the house?" he asked.

"Uh-huh."

"We already have one."

She wrinkled her nose. "It's a toy. This is an instrument."

"But you're only here for a month."

Less if her plan went well. "I know, but I want to see the stars. Everything is better when there are stars to look at."

"You're leaving it in place, aren't you?"

"For the families," she said, watching anxiously as the ramp was lowered on the truck. "I'll write up some instructions, although it's computer-guided. They won't have to do anything but type in what they want to see, then stand back and watch the show. Not that we'll be using the program. I can find whatever you want to see."

"I have no doubt."

She glanced at him. "What?"

"Nothing. Just you."

Which meant what? Not that Jack would tell her if she asked.

"Hunter would have loved this," she said absently, knowing her brother would have made fun of her, then spent the whole night looking at the sky.

Thinking about her brother was both wonderful and filled with pain. While she appreciated all the memories she had, she still had a hole in her heart from his passing.

"I think about him every day," she told Jack. "I think about him and wish he were here. Do you think about him much?"

Jack's expression closed and he turned away. "No. I don't think about him at all."

She knew he couldn't be telling the truth. He and Hunter had been close for a long time. They'd been like brothers. Jack couldn't have forgotten that.

Her instinct to be compassionate battled with her annoyance. Temper won.

"Most people improve with age," she said. "Too bad you didn't. You not only break your word but you're a liar, as well."

# Three

Jack spent a couple of hours in the loft office, working. He called his assistant back in Dallas.

"They're building more roads in Afghanistan," Bobbi Sue told him. "They're looking at maybe an eighteen-month contract, but we all know those things take longer. And Sister Helena called. They want to take in another convoy of medical supplies."

His business provided protection in dangerous parts of the world. His teams allowed building crews to get their jobs done and get out. The work was dangerous, often a logistical nightmare and extremely expensive. His corporate clients paid well for what they got.

The corporate profits were channeled into funding protection for those providing relief efforts in places often forgotten. He'd grown up in the shadow of the

Howington Foundation, a philanthropic trust that helped the poor. Jack hated having a number after his name and had vowed he would make his own way.

He had. He'd grown his company from nothing, but he couldn't seem to escape that damn sense of duty. The one that told him he needed to use his profits for something other than a flashy lifestyle.

His critics said he could afford to be generous—he had a trust fund worth nearly a billion dollars. What they didn't know is he never touched it. Another vow he'd made to himself. He'd grown up with something to prove. The question was whether or not he would have achieved enough to let that need go.

"Get Ron on the contract," Jack told his assistant. "The usual clauses. Tell Sister Helena to e-mail the best dates for the convoy and we'll get as close to them as possible."

"She's going to want to leave before you're back from your vacation in Tahoe."

"I'm not on vacation."

"Hmm, a month in a fancy house with nothing to do with your time? Sounds like a vacation to me."

"I'm working."

"Talk, talk, talk."

Bobbi Sue had attitude, which he put up with because she was the best at her job. She was also old enough to be his mother, a fact she mentioned on a regular basis, especially when she hounded him on the topic of settling down.

"Someone else will have to take Sister Helena's team in," he said. "See if Wade's available." Wade was one of his best guys.

"Will do. Anything else?"

"Not from my end."

"You know, I looked up Hunter's Landing on the Internet, and the place you're staying isn't that far from the casinos."

"I'm aware of that."

"So you should go. Gamble, talk to some people. You spend too much time alone."

He thought about Meri, sleeping in the room next to his. "Not anymore."

"Does that mean you're seeing someone?"

"No."

"You need to get married."

"You need to get off me."

Bobbi Sue sighed. "All right, but just in the short term."

Jack hung up. He glanced at his computer, but for once he didn't want to work. He paced the length of the spacious bedroom, ignoring the fireplace, the view and the television. Then he went downstairs to confront the woman who seemed determined to think the worst of him.

Not that he cared what she thought. But this wasn't about her—it was about Hunter.

He found Meri in the kitchen, sitting on the counter, eating ice cream out of a pint-size container.

"Lunch?" he asked as he entered the room.

"Sort of. Not exactly high in nutrition, but I'm more interested in sugar and fat right now."

He stared at her miniature spoon. "That's an interesting size."

She waved the tiny utensil. "It's my ice-cream-eating spoon. I try to avoid using food as an emotional crutch, but sometimes ice cream is the only solution. I use this spoon because it takes longer to eat and I have a better chance of getting disgusted with myself and stopping before finishing the pint. A trick for keeping off the weight. I have a thousand of them."

"This situation required ice cream?"

She licked the spoon. He did his best to ignore the flick of her tongue and the sigh that followed, along with the rush of unwelcome heat in his body.

"You pissed me off," she told him.

Translation: he'd hurt her. Hunter was her brother. She wouldn't want to think his friends had forgotten him.

He leaned against the counter as he considered what to do. His natural inclination was to walk away. Her feelings didn't matter to him. At least they shouldn't. But this was Meri, and he was supposed to be looking out for her. Which meant not making a bad situation worse.

Maybe a small concession was in order. "I don't want to think about Hunter," he admitted. "I've trained myself not to. But he's there. All the time."

She eyed him. "Why should I believe you?"

"I don't care if you do."

She surprised him by smiling. "Okay. I like that answer. If you'd tried to convince me, I would have known you were just placating me. But your stick-up-the-butt attitude is honest."

"Excuse me?"

"You're excused."

He frowned. Had she always been this irritating?

"You getting much work done?" she asked as she checked her watch. "I'm not. There's so much going on right now and I really need to focus. But it's tough. Being here, seducing you—it's a full time job."

He folded his arms over his chest. "You need to let that go."

"The seduction part? I don't think so. I'm making progress. You're going on the defensive. What happened in the gym was definitely about taking charge. So that means I'm getting to you." She held out the ice cream container. "Want some, big guy?"

She was mocking him. She was irreverent and fearless and determined. All good qualities, but not in this situation. She was right. He wanted to get control. And he could think of only one way to do that.

He moved close and took the ice cream from her. After setting it and the spoon on the counter, he cupped her face and kissed her.

He took rather than asked. He claimed her with his lips, branding her skin with his own. He leaned in, crowding her, showing her that she hadn't thought her plan through.

She stiffened slightly and gasped in surprise. He took advantage of the moment and plunged his tongue into her mouth.

She was cool from the ice cream, cool with a hint of fire. She tasted of chocolate and something that had to be her own erotic essence. He ignored the softness of her skin, the sensual feel of her mouth and the heat that poured through him.

She pulled back slightly and gazed into his eyes. "Is that the best you can do?" she asked before she put her arms around his neck and drew him in.

She kissed him back with a need that surprised him. She opened for him and then met his tongue with darting licks of her own.

She'd parted her legs, so he slipped between her thighs. Although she was much shorter, with her sitting on the counter, he found himself nestled against her crotch.

Blood pumped, making him hard. Desire consumed him. Desire for a woman he couldn't have. Dammit all to hell.

Then he reminded himself that his reaction was to an attractive woman. It wasn't specific. It wasn't about Meri. As his assistant enjoyed pointing out, he'd been solitary for a long time. Even brief sexual encounters no longer intrigued him. He'd been lost in a world of work and nothing else.

He had needs. That was all this was—a scratch for an itch.

He pulled back. "Interesting."

She raised her eyebrows. "It was a whole lot more than interesting and you know it."

"If it's important for you to believe that, go ahead."

"I don't mind that you're not making this easy," she told him. "The victory will be all the sweeter." She picked up her ice cream and put the cover back. "I'm done."

"Sugar and fat needs met?"

"I no longer need the comfort. My bad mood is gone."

So like a woman, he thought as he leaned against the counter. "Because I kissed you?"

She smiled and jumped to the floor, then walked to the freezer. "Because you liked it."

He wasn't going to argue the point.

She closed the freezer door with her hip, then looked at him. "Tell me about the women in your life."

"Not much to tell."

"It's tough, isn't it?" She leaned against the counter opposite his. For once, her eyes weren't bright with humor or challenge. "Being who we are and trying to get involved. The money thing, I mean."

Because they both came from money. Because they'd been raised with the idea that they had to be careful, to make sure they didn't fall for someone who was in it for the wrong reasons.

Without wanting to, Jack remembered sitting in on a painful conversation between Hunter and Meredith. He'd tried to escape more than once, but his friend had wanted him to stick around to make sure Meri really listened.

"Guys are going to know who you are," Hunter had told her. "You have to be smart and not just think with your heart."

Meri had been sixteen. She'd writhed in her seat as Hunter had talked, then she'd stood and glared at him. "Who is going to want me for anything else?" she demanded. "I'm not pretty. I'll never be pretty. I'm nothing more than a giant brain with braces and a big nose. I'm going to have to buy all my boyfriends."

Hunter had looked at Jack with an expression that begged for help, but Jack hadn't known what to say either. They were too young to be guiding Meri through life—what experiences did they have to pass on? Doing twins from the law school hardly counted.

"I have it easier than you do," he said, forcing himself back to the present, not wanting to think about how he'd failed both Hunter and Meri. "The women I go out with don't know who I am."

"Interesting point. I don't talk about my family, but word gets out. I've actually reached the point in my life where I have to have men investigated before I start dating them. It's not fun."

"You're doing the right thing." Not that she was the only one checking out her dates. He ran a check on all of them, too. For casual dates, he only bothered with a preliminary investigation, but if it looked like things were getting serious, he asked for a more involved report.

She glanced at her watch again.

"You have an appointment?" he asked.

She grinned. "I have a surprise."

"Another one?"

"Oh, yeah. So there's no little woman waiting in the wings?"

"I told you—I'm not the little-woman type."

"Of course. You're the kind of man who enjoys a challenge. Which is what I am."

Okay, so kissing her hadn't gotten her to back off. He needed another direction. He refused to spend the next three and a half weeks dodging Meri. All he needed was a plan. He'd never been defeated before and he wasn't about to be defeated now.

"But I want something different from the men in my life," she continued. "Maybe my tastes have matured, but I'm looking for someone smart and funny—but normal-smart. Not brainy. I could never marry another genius. We'd have a mutant child, for sure."

He chuckled. "Your own version of genetic engineering?"

"Sort of. I made a list of characteristics that are important to me. I used to have a whole program I wrote one weekend, but that seemed so calculated. A list is more ordinary."

"Not if you wrote it in binary code."

She rolled her eyes. "Oh, please. I'd never do that. C++ maybe."

He was going to guess C++ was another computer language, but he could be wrong.

"Not that I needed a computer program to know Andrew is a great guy."

Jack stared at her. "Andrew?"

"The man I've been dating for a while now. He checked out great, and things are getting serious."

Jack didn't remember hearing about any guy named Andrew. Not that he got personally involved unless things were heating up—which, apparently, they were. Why hadn't he been told?

"How serious?" he asked as he heard the sound of a truck heading toward the house.

"I'm probably going to marry him," Meri said, then ran out of the kitchen. "You hear that? They're here!"

Marry him?

Before he could react to that, he found himself following her to the foyer and beyond that to the front of the house. A shuttle van pulled to a stop in front of the porch, and the door eased open.

"Who's here?" he asked, but Meri wasn't listening. She bounced from foot to foot, then threw herself into the arms of the first person off the shuttle. He was short, skinny and wearing glasses thick enough to be portholes. Nothing about him was the least bit threatening, and Jack immediately wanted to kill him.

"You made it," Meri said, hugging the guy again. "I've missed you so much."

The guy disentangled himself. "It's been a week, Meri. You need to get out more."

She laughed, then turned to the next person and greeted him with exactly the same enthusiasm. Okay. So nerd guy wasn't Andrew. Good to know.

Meri welcomed all eight visitors with exactly the same amount of enthusiasm, then she turned to Jack.

"Everybody, this is Jack. Jack, this is my team."

"Team for what?" he asked.

She grinned. "Would you believe me if I said polo?"

Judging from their pale skin and slightly peering gazes, he was going to guess none of them had ever seen a horse outside of the movies or television.

"No."

"I didn't think so. This is my solid-rocket-fuel team. We're working on ways to make it less toxic and more efficient. There's a technical explanation, but I don't want to watch your eyes glaze over."

"I appreciate that. What are they doing here?"

"Don't freak. They're not all staying in the house. Only Colin and Betina. The rest are staying at nearby hotels."

Jack didn't like the idea of anyone else hanging around. He needed to concentrate on work. Of course, if Meri were distracted by her friends, she wouldn't be such a problem for him.

"Why are they here?" he asked.

"So we can work. I can't leave the mountain, so they agreed to a field trip." She leaned toward him and lowered her voice. "I know you're going to find it difficult to believe, but this is a really fun group."

Most of her colleagues were squinting in the sun and looking uncomfortable. "I can only imagine."

She walked over to the oldest woman in the group—a slightly overweight, stylishly dressed blonde—linked arms with her and led her forward.

"Jack, this is my friend Betina. Technically she's a liaison—she stands between the team and the real world, taking care of all the details the scientifically gifted seem to be so bad with. In reality, she's my best friend and the reason I'm just so darned normal."

He eyed the other woman and wondered how many of Meri's secrets she knew.

"Nice to meet you," he said as he shook hands with Betina.

Betina smiled. "I'm enjoying meeting you, as well," she said. "Finally."

Finally?

Meri grinned. "Did I tell you or what?"

Tell her what? But before Jack could ask, the group went into the house. He was left standing on the porch, wondering when the hell his life had gotten so out of his control.

Meri sat cross-legged in the center of the bed while her friend unpacked. "He's gorgeous. Admit it—you saw it."

Betina smiled. "Jack is very nice-looking, if you

enjoy the tall, dark and powerful type. He wasn't happy about us arriving."

"I know. I didn't tell him you were coming. It was fabulous. I wish you'd seen the look on his face when I explained why you were here. Of course, it was right after I told him I might marry Andrew, so there it was a double-thrill moment for me."

Betina unpacked her cosmetics and carried them into the attached bathroom. "You know you're not marrying Andrew. You're baiting Jack."

"It's fun and I need a hobby." Meri flopped back on the bed. "Why shouldn't I bait him? He deserves it. He was mean to me."

"He was in college. At that age, men are not known for their emotional sensitivity. Actually, they're not known for it at any age. But the point is, you bared your heart and soul and he reacted badly. I agree some punishment is in order, but you're taking it all too far. This is a mistake, Meri."

Meri loved Betina like a sister…sometimes like a mom. There were only twelve years between them chronologically, but in life experiences they were light-years apart.

Betina had been the project manager's assistant at the think tank that had first hired Meri. The second week Meri had been there, Betina had walked into her lab.

"Do you have anything close to a sense of humor?" the other woman had asked. "I don't mind that you're brilliant, but a sense of humor is required for any kind of a relationship."

Meri hadn't known what to say. She'd been eighteen

and terrified of living on her own in a strange city. Money wasn't an issue—the think tank had hired her for more than she'd ever thought she would earn and she had a family trust fund. But she'd spent that last third of her life in college. What did she know about furnishing an apartment, buying a car, paying bills?

"I don't know if I would qualify as funny," Meri had said honestly. "Does sarcasm count?"

Betina had smiled. "Oh, honey, sarcasm is the best."

At that moment their friendship had been born.

Betina had been turning thirty and on her own for over a decade. She'd shown Meri how to live on her own and had insisted she buy a condo in a good part of D.C.

She'd taken care of Meri after both her surgeries, offered fashion advice, love life advice and had hooked her up with a trainer who had pummeled her into shape.

"Why is getting revenge a mistake?" Meri asked as her friend finished unpacking. "He's earned it."

"Because you're not thinking this through. You're going to get into trouble and I don't want that to happen. Your relationship with Jack isn't what you think."

Meri frowned. "What do you mean? I totally understand my feelings about Jack. I had a huge crush on him, he hurt me and, because of that, I've been unable to move on. If I sleep with him, I'll instantly figure out that he's not special at all. He's just some guy and I'll be healed. The benefit is I get to leave him wanting more."

Betina sat next to her and fluffed her short hair. "I hate travel. I always get puffy." Then she drew in a breath. "You didn't have a crush on Jack. You were in love with him then and you're still in love with him.

You're emotionally connected to him, even if you refuse to admit it. Sleeping with him is only going to confuse the matter. The problem with your plan is that, odds are, the person left wanting more could easily be you."

Meri sat up and took Betina's hands. "I love and admire you, but you are desperately wrong."

"I hope so, for your sake."

But her friend sounded worried as she spoke. Meri appreciated the show of support. They were never going to agree on this topic. Better to move on.

She released Betina's hands and grinned. "So Colin is right next door. Whatever will the two of you get up to late at night?"

Betina flushed. "Lower your voice," she whispered. "He'll hear you."

"Oh, please. He wouldn't hear a nuclear explosion if he was focused on something else, and when I walked by his room, he was already booting his laptop. We're safe. Don't you love how I got the two of you into the house while everyone else is far, far away?"

"I guess," Betina said with uncharacteristic indecision. "I know something has to happen soon or I'll be forced to back the car over him. He's such a sweetie. And you know I really like him, but I don't think I'm his type."

Meri groaned. "He doesn't have a type. He's a nerd. Do you think he dates much?"

"He should. He's adorable and smart and funny."

Her friend had it bad, Meri thought happily. And she was pretty sure that Colin found Betina equally intriguing. Usually Betina simply took what she wanted in the man department. But something about Colin made her nervous.

"He's afraid of being rejected," Meri told her. "Something I can relate to."

"I wouldn't reject him," Betina said. "But it will never work. We're on a project together. I'm too old for him and I'm too fat."

"You're six years older, which is nothing, and you're not fat. You're totally curvy and lush. Guys go for that."

They always had. Meri had spent the last decade marveling at the number of men her friend met, dated, slept with and dumped.

"Not Colin. He barely speaks to me."

"Which is interesting," Meri said. "He talks to everyone else."

It was true. Colin was tongue-tied around Betina. Meri thought it was charming.

At first, when her friend had confessed her interest in Colin, Meri had been protective of her coworker. Colin might enjoy the ride that was Betina, but once dumped, he would be heartbroken. Then Betina had admitted her feelings went a whole lot deeper. The L word had been whispered.

After getting over the idea of her friend being in love with anyone, Meri had agreed to help. So far, she'd been unable to think of a way to bring the couple together. Hunter's lodge had offered the perfect opportunity.

"You have time," Meri pointed out. "Jack and I never come down here, so you have the whole floor to yourselves. You can talk to each other in a casual setting. No pressure. It will be great."

Betina smiled. "Hey, it's *my* job to be the positive, self-actualized one."

"I know. I love being the emotionally mature friend. It doesn't happen often."

"It happens more and more."

Meri leaned in and hugged her friend. "You're the best."

"So are you."

Jack looked up as he heard footsteps on the stairs. Seconds later, Meri appeared in his loft office.

She'd changed into a tight skirt and cropped top, curled her hair and put on makeup. Always pretty, she'd upped the stakes to come-get-me sexy.

A quick bit of research on the Internet had told him that the guy she'd mentioned wasn't one of her scientists. Instead he worked for a D.C. lobbyist and was safely several thousand miles away. Not that Jack cared one way or the other. The only issue for him was researching the man more thoroughly. If things were getting serious, it was his job to make sure Meri wasn't being taken.

His low-grade anger was something he would deal with later. He didn't know why he minded the thought of her marrying some guy, but he did.

"We're going to dinner," she announced when she stopped in front of his desk. "You might not believe this, but we're actually a pretty fun group. You're welcome to join us."

"Thanks, but no."

"Want me to bring back something? The fridge is still fully stocked, but I could stop for chicken wings."

"I'm good."

She turned to leave. He stopped her with, "You should have mentioned you were engaged."

She turned back to him. "Why? You claim you're not sleeping with me. What would an engagement matter one way or another?"

"It makes a difference. I wouldn't have kissed you."

"Ah. Then I'm glad you didn't know." Her blue eyes brightened with amusement. "Does the fact that I belong to someone else make me more tempting? The allure of the forbidden?"

He had to consciously keep from smiling. She'd always been overly dramatic.

"No," he told her. "Sorry."

"You're not sorry. And, for what it's worth, the engagement isn't official. I wouldn't be trying to sleep with you if I'd said yes."

A cool rush of relief swept through him. "You said no?"

"I didn't say anything. Andrew hasn't actually proposed. I found a ring." She shifted on her high heels. "I didn't know what to think. I'd never thought about getting married. I realized we had unfinished business, so here I am. Seducing you."

He ignored that. "You're sleeping with him." The point was obvious, so he didn't make it a question.

She leaned forward and sighed. "It bothers you, doesn't it? Thinking about me in bed with another man. Writhing, panting, being taken." She straightened and fanned herself. "Wow, it's really warm here at the top of the house."

He didn't react, at least not on the outside. But her words had done what she'd wanted them to do. He reacted on the inside, with heat building in his groin.

She got to him. He would give her points for that. But she wouldn't win.

"So no on dinner?" she asked.

"I have work."

"Okay. Want a goodbye kiss before I go?"

He hated that he did. He wanted to feel her mouth on his, her body leaning in close. He wanted skin on skin, touching her until he made her cry out with a passion she couldn't control. "No, thanks," he said coolly.

She eyed him for a second, then grinned. "We both know that's not true, don't we, Jack?"

And then she was gone.

# Four

Meri arrived home from dinner with her team feeling just full enough, with a slight buzz. They'd taken the shuttle van into town, and that had meant no one had to be a designated driver. Wine had flowed freely. Well, as freely as it could given no one drank more than a glass, preferring the thrill of intellectual discussion to the mental blurriness of too much alcohol.

But just this once Meri had passed up the wine and gone with a margarita. That was fine, but she'd ordered a second one and was absolutely feeling it as she climbed the stairs to her bedroom.

As she reached the landing, she saw two doors and was reminded that it was also the same floor with Jack's bedroom.

What an interesting fact, she thought as she paused

and stared at the firmly closed door. He was in there. By himself, she would guess. So what exactly was he getting up to?

She was pretty confident he was stretched out on the bed, watching TV or reading. But this was her buzz, and she could imagine him waiting for her in the massive tub in front of the fireplace if she wanted to. Because in her fantasy, he wanted her with a desperation that took his breath away. In her fantasy, he was deeply sorry for hurting her and he'd spent the past eleven years barely surviving because his love for her had been so great it had immobilized him.

"Okay, that last one is total crap," she whispered to herself. "But the other two have possibilities."

She walked to his door, knocked once, then let herself in before he could tell her to go away.

A quick glance around the room told her that he wasn't about to fulfill her bathtub fantasy. Probably for the best. She was really feeling the margarita, and drowning was a distinct possibility.

Instead of being naked and in water, Jack sat in a corner chair, his feet up on the leather ottoman, reading. At least he'd been reading until she'd walked in. Now he set the book on his lap and looked at her expectantly.

She swayed as she moved toward the bed and sank down on the edge. She pushed off her sandals and smiled at him.

"Dinner was great. You should have come."

"I'll survive the deep loss."

She smiled. "You're so funny. Sometimes I forget you're funny. I think it's because you're so intense and macho. Dangerous. You were always dangerous. Before, it was just about who you were as a person, but now you have access to all kinds of weapons. Doubly dangerous."

His gaze narrowed slightly. "You're drunk."

She waved her left hand back and forth. "*Drunk* is such a strong term. Tipsy. Buzzed. Seriously buzzed. I had a second margarita. Always a mistake. I don't drink much, so I never build up any tolerance. And I'm small, so there's not much in the way of body mass. I could figure out the formula if you want. How many ounces of alcohol per pound of human body."

"An intriguing offer, but no."

She smiled. "It's the math, huh. You're scared of the math. Most people are. I don't know why. Math is constant, you know. It's built on principles, and once you learn them, they don't change. It's not like literature. That's open to interpretation and there's all that writing. But math is clean. You're right or you're not. I like being right."

"It's your competitive streak," he said.

She swayed slightly on the bed. "You think I'm competitive?"

"It's in your blood."

"I guess. I like to be right about stuff. I get focused. I can be a real pain." She grinned. "Doesn't that make me even cuter? How can you stand it?"

"I'm using every ounce of willpower not to attack you this very moment."

"You're so lying, but it's sweet. Thank you."

She stared at him. If eyes were the windows to the

soul, then Jack's innermost place was a dark and protected place.

Secrets, she thought. They all had secrets. What were his?

Not that he would tell her. He kept that sort of thing to himself. But if he ever did decide to trust someone, it would be forever, she thought idly. Or maybe that was another of her fantasies.

"You need to help me with Betina and Colin," she told him. "We're going to get them together."

One dark eyebrow rose. "I don't think so."

"Oh, come on. Don't be such a guy. This could be fun. Just think of it—we could be part of a great love match."

"Colin and Betina?" He sounded doubtful.

"Sure. Betina has a serious thing for Colin. I was skeptical at first because Betina changes her men with the rhythm of the tide. A long-term relationship for her is a week. But that's because she's afraid to really care about someone. She had a bad early marriage years ago. Anyway, she's liked Colin for a long time, and that liking has grown into something more. Something significant."

She paused, waiting for him to grasp the importance of the information. Obviously he missed it, because he said, "I'm not getting involved."

"You have to. It's not like you're doing anything else with your time."

"We're going to ignore my work and the effort I put into avoiding you?"

"Oh, yeah. There's hard duty. A beautiful single woman desperately wants you in her bed. Poor Jack. Your life is pain."

She could think of a thousand ways he could have reacted, but she never expected him to smile.

"You think of yourself as beautiful?" he asked quietly, sounding almost pleased.

Meri shifted on the bed. "It was a figure of speech."

"The last time we talked about your appearance, you said you were a freak."

She didn't want to think about that, but if he insisted… "The last time we talked about my appearance, you emotionally slapped me, trampled my heart and left me for dead."

His smile faded. "I'm sorry. I should have handled that differently."

"But you didn't. I wasn't asking for sex right that moment." She didn't want to be talking about this. It was too humiliating. "My point is, Betina is crazy about Colin and I'm pretty sure he likes her. Which is where you come in. I want you to find out for sure."

"What? No."

"Why not? You're a guy, he's a guy. You can ask him if he likes Betina."

"Should I pass you a note in homeroom?"

"I don't care how I get the information, I just need confirmation."

"You're not getting it from me."

She remembered his being stubborn but never this bad. "Have I mentioned you're annoying? Because you are."

"I live to serve."

"If only that were true. Look, they're both great people. They deserve to be happy. I'm just giving them a little push."

"Did you need a push with Andrew?"

She sighed. "I wondered when you'd bring him up."

"You're nearly engaged. Why wouldn't I be curious?"

She tried to figure out what he was thinking from his tone of voice, but as usual, Jack gave nothing away. It was one of his more annoying characteristics.

"We met at a charity auction," she said. "There was a pet fashion show to start things off. Somehow I got tangled up in the leashes and nearly fell. Andrew rescued me. It was very romantic."

"I can only imagine."

She ignored any hint of sarcasm in his voice. Maybe knowing there was another man in her life would make him a little less arrogant.

"He was funny and charming and I liked him right away. We have so much in common. What movies we like, where we go on vacation. It's been really fun."

It *had* been fun, she thought, remembering all the good times with Andrew. But she'd been on this coast for nearly six months. They'd had a chance to get together only a few times, although they talked regularly. Their relationship seemed to be on hold and she obviously didn't mind. Something she was going to have to think about.

"Is he a genius, too?" Jack asked.

"No, he's delightfully normal. Smart but not too smart. I like that in a guy."

"What do you know about him? Did you check him out?"

"Of course. He's just a regular guy. Not in it for money." Her good mood faded. "Is that your point? That no one could possibly want me if it wasn't for the money?"

"Not at all. I just want you to be happy."

"I am happy. Blissfully so. Andrew's the one. We'll be engaged as soon as I get back to D.C." Which wasn't actually true but it sounded good.

"Congratulations."

Jack had ruined everything, she thought bitterly as she stood. Her buzz, her great evening.

"Just because you don't believe in letting yourself care about people doesn't mean the feelings aren't real," she told him. "Some of us want to connect."

"I hope you do. I hope this is everything you want."

"Why don't I believe you? What aren't you saying?"

"That if Andrew was so important to you, you wouldn't stay away from him for six months."

She walked to the door. "Who says I have?"

With that, she walked out and closed the door behind her.

It was only a few steps to her room, and she was grateful for the solitary quiet when she entered. After flicking on a few lights, she crossed to the window and stared out at the night sky.

It was a perfect night for viewing the stars, but she wasn't in the mood. Not even on her brand-new telescope. She hurt too much and it was hard to say why.

Maybe because Jack was right. If Andrew was that important to her, she wouldn't stay away from him for six months. But she had, and it had been relatively easy. Too easy. If she were really in love with him, wouldn't she be desperate to be with him?

Finding the engagement ring had shocked her. She hadn't known what to think about his proposing. She'd been happy, but a part of her had known that it was time to put off the inevitable. That closure with Jack was required.

She'd known about Hunter's friends coming to stay at the house. She'd taken the consulting job in California, hired on as the caretaker of the house and had waited to confront the man who was holding her back. Once she got her revenge on Jack, she would be fine.

"That's what's wrong," she whispered to herself. "I'm still waiting to punish him. Once Jack is reduced to dust, I'll be able to give my whole heart to Andrew. It's just going to be another week or so. Then I'll be happy."

Jack spent a restless night. He told himself it was because he'd had coffee too late in the day, but part of the problem was Meri's words. Her claim that he didn't connect.

Late the next morning, he saved the files on his computer and opened the top desk drawer in his temporary office. There was an envelope inside, along with a letter.

The letter had been waiting for him the first day he'd arrived. He'd recognized the distinctive handwriting and had known it was from Matt. The battered appliances in the kitchen had been another clue. His friend might be able to program a computer to do heart surgery, but Matt couldn't do something simple like work an electric can opener.

For some reason, Jack had avoided the letter. Now he opened the envelope and pulled out the single sheet of paper.

Jack—

When I read Ryan's note that called this place a "love shack," my first thought was, what a load of BS. But now I think he may have been onto something. He was also right about how wrong we were when we compiled our universal truths about women. Remember those? Yeah? Well, now you can forget 'em. We had no idea.

As for me, here's what I learned during my month at the cabin: the most important work you'll ever do has nothing to do with the job. And it's work you can't do by yourself. But when you find a partner you can trust and the two of you do that work together, it pays better than any career you could imagine. And the perks? You have no idea....

Have a good month, pal.

Matt.

Jack read the letter again. He'd figured out a long time ago that he didn't know squat about women. Not that it mattered, as he never got involved. As for Matt and his other friends, sometimes he allowed himself to miss them. To wonder what it would have been like if Hunter hadn't died. Because Hunter was the one who had held them all together. Without him, they'd gone their separate ways. There were times when he—

He stood and shook his head. Okay, he needed more coffee or something, because there was no way he was spending the rest of the morning in his head.

He went downstairs and poured himself coffee. He could hear Meri and her team talking in the dining room.

"String theory is ruining theoretical physics," one of the guys said. "Everything has to be defined and explained, which is wasting a lot of time. Sure there's a why and a how, but if there's no practical application, then why bother?"

"Because you can't know the practical application until you understand the theory."

"It's not a theory. It's equations. Compare string theory to something else. Something like—"

They kept on talking, but even thought Jack knew they were probably speaking English, he had no idea what they were saying. He knew string theory had nothing to do with strings and maybe something to do with the universe. The word *vibrating* was attached to the idea in his head, but whether that meant string theory was about vibrations in the universe or just so above him that it made his teeth hurt, he wasn't sure.

"All very interesting," Meri said loudly over the argument. "But it has little to do with the project at hand. Get back to work. All of you."

There was a little grumbling, but the discussion shifted back to something that sounded a lot like solid rocket fuel. Not that Jack could be sure.

After grabbing his mug, he stepped out onto the deck. Hunter would be proud of Meri. She'd turned into a hell of a woman.

He pulled out his cell phone and hit redial. Bobbi Sue answered on the first ring. "You've got to stop calling me," she told him by way of greeting. "I swear, you're starting to get on my nerves. We're all capable here. We can do the job. You're just bored, and let me tell you, I don't like being punished for your mood swings."

He ignored her. "I want you to check out someone Meri's seeing. Andrew Layman. His address is on file. I want to know everything about him. Apparently it's gotten serious, and I want to make sure Meri isn't getting involved with a guy after her money."

"I swear, Jack, you have got to stop spying on this girl. If you're so interested, date her yourself. Otherwise get out of her life."

"I can't. She's a wealthy heiress. That makes her a target. Besides, I gave my word."

"I wish you were here so you could see how unimpressed I am by you giving your word. This just isn't healthy." Bobbi Sue sighed. "I'll do it, but only because it's my job and, for the most part, I respect you."

He grinned, knowing Meri would adore his secretary. "Your praise is all that matters."

"As if I'd believe that. This'll take a couple of days."

"I'm not going anywhere."

"I hear that. You need to get out. Find a woman. I mean it, Jack. Either get involved with Meri or leave the poor girl alone. You have no right to do this."

"I have every right." Meri might not know it, but she needed him. Someone had to keep her safe.

He hung up and returned to the kitchen for more coffee. Meri entered from the dining room.

"Hi. How's your day going?" she asked as she pushed past him and walked into the pantry. "Have you seen the box of pencils I put in here? Colin insists on fresh pencils when he works. Betina thinks it's charming, but I have to tell you, his little quirks are a pain in the butt. There was a whole new box. I swear."

He heard her rummaging around, then she gasped. He stepped to the pantry door and saw her crouched by the bottom shelf.

"What?" he demanded. "Did you hit your head?"

"No," she whispered and slowly straightened. She held a box in her hand, but it wasn't pencils. Instead it was a shoe box covered with childish stickers of unicorns and stars and rainbows.

"This is mine," she breathed. "I haven't seen it in years. I'd forgotten about it. How did it get here?"

As he didn't know what "it" was, he only shrugged.

Meri looked up at him, her eyes filled with tears. "It's pictures of Hunter and my mom and all of us."

She set the box on the counter and opened the top. There were old Polaroid photos of a very young Hunter standing in front of some church. Probably in Europe. He looked about fourteen or fifteen. He had his arm around a much younger Meredith.

"God, I miss him," Meri whispered. "He was my family."

Betina walked into the kitchen. "It's pencils, Meri. You're supposed to be the smart one. Are you telling me you can't find a—" Betina stopped. "What happened?" She turned on Jack. "What the hell did you do to her?"

"Nothing," Meri said before he could defend himself. "It's not him. Look."

Betina moved close and took the photo. "That's you. Is that Hunter?"

"Uh-huh. I think we're in France." She pulled out more pictures. "I can't believe it. Look at how fat I am. Did anyone stop to say, 'Gee, honey, you should eat less'?"

"Food is love," Betina told her and fanned out the pictures on the counter. "You're adorable and Hunter is quite the hunk."

Several more members of Meri's team wandered into the kitchen. Soon they, too, were looking over pictures and talking about Hunter as if they'd known him.

Jack hung back. As much as he wanted to see his friend, he didn't want to open old wounds. For a second he wondered if Meri would need comforting, then he looked at all the people around her. She didn't need him at all. Which was for the best. He didn't want to get involved.

Meri paid the driver, then carried the bag of Chinese food into the house. "Dinner," she yelled in the general direction of the stairs, not sure if Jack would come down or not. She was gratified to see him walk into the kitchen a couple of minutes later.

"Why aren't you out with the nerd brigade?" he asked as she pulled a couple of plates out of the cupboard.

"Nerd brigade?" She smiled. "They'd like that. It sounds very military. They're all going to a club in Lake Tahoe and I'm not in the mood. Plus, I knew you were lonely, so I stayed home to keep you company."

"I'm not lonely."

He sounded annoyed as he spoke, which made her want to giggle. Jack was really easy to rile. It was that

stick up his butt—if he would just let it go, he could be
a regular person. Of course, his macho I'm-in-charge
attitude was part of his appeal.

"Can you reach those?" she asked, pointing to the tall
glasses some idiot had put on the top shelf. She could
never have left them there.

While he got them for her, she carried the plates and
food over to the table in the kitchen, then went to the
refrigerator for a couple of beers.

When they were seated across from each other, she
said, "So are we invading you too badly?"

"Do you care if you are?"

She considered the question and went with the honest
answer. "Not really, but it seemed polite to ask."

"Good to know. I'm getting work done."

"Your company specializes in protecting corporations in scary parts of the world, right?"

He nodded.

"An interesting choice," she said. "But then, you have
all that Special Forces training."

Again with the look.

She passed him the kung pao chicken. "I know a few
things," she said.

"Yes, that's what my company does. When I left the
Army, I wanted to start my own firm. Being a consul-
tant didn't give me enough control. Someone has to
rebuild roads in places like Iraq, and our job is to keep
those people safe."

"Sounds dangerous."

"We know what we're doing."

"Weren't you supposed to be a lawyer?" she asked.

"I joined the Army after Hunter died."

An interesting way to cope with grief, she thought. But then, maybe the point had been to be so busy he could just forget.

"What do your parents have to say about all this?"

"They're still hoping I'll take over the Howington Foundation."

"Will you?" she asked.

"Probably not. I'm not the foundation type."

She wasn't either, but so far it wasn't an option. Her father seemed content to spend his money on the very young women in his life. Hunter's foundation ran smoothly. She had her trust fund, which she never touched, and a nice salary that covered all of her needs. If Hunter were still alive...

"You have to deal with your grief sometime," she said.

"About the foundation? I'm over it."

"No. Hunter."

Jack's mouth twisted. "I've dealt. Thanks for asking."

"I don't think so. There's a whole lot there under the surface." He'd let down his best friend. That had to bug him. Jack had let her down, too, but for once she wasn't mad at him. Maybe because she'd had a good cry after looking at all the pictures she'd found and felt emotionally cleansed.

She looked at him. "On my bad days I tell myself you're a selfish bastard who played us all. On my good days I tell myself you wanted to stay but couldn't handle what you were going through. Which is it?"

"Both."

\* \* \*

Meri waited until nearly midnight, then climbed the stairs to Jack's office, prepared to let herself out onto the balcony and enjoy the beauty of the heavens. She didn't expect to find him on his laptop.

"You're not supposed to be here," she grumbled as he glanced up. "It's late. You need your rest."

"I see you've changed your seduction techniques. These are interesting. Less effective, in case you were wondering."

"I'm not here to seduce you. I have more important things to do with my time."

He glanced out the French doors toward the sky. "I see. And I would get in the way?"

"You're going to ask a lot of irritating questions. You won't be able to help it. I'll try to be patient, but I'll snap and then you'll get your feelings hurt. I'm just not in the mood to deal with your emotional outbursts."

Instead she wanted to stare at the sky and let the vast beauty heal her soul. Okay, yes, getting Jack into bed was her ultimate goal, but there was a time and place for work and this wasn't it.

"I suspect my feelings will survive just fine," he said.

"No way. You'll go all girlie on me."

She shouldn't have said it. She knew that. She hadn't actually meant to challenge him—she was simply impatient to get out into the night and use the telescope.

He stood without speaking and moved around the desk until he was standing in front of her. Looming, actually. She had to tilt her head all the way back to see into his eyes.

"You think I'm girlie?" he asked in a low, slightly dangerous voice. A voice thick with power. A voice that made her realize he was a whole lot bigger than her and that there were a couple of floors between her and help.

"Not at all," she said quickly. "I didn't mean to say it. The words just slipped out. Bad me. You should probably stalk out and teach me what for by leaving me alone."

Instead he tucked a strand of hair behind her ear. "Do you play all the men in your life?"

She swallowed. "Pretty much."

"Does it work?"

"Mostly."

"Not this time."

He cupped her cheek with his hand, bent down and kissed her.

She'd sensed he was going to and should have had time to brace herself. It was just a kiss, right? No big deal. They'd kissed before, and while she'd liked it, she'd managed to keep perfect control…sort of.

But not this time. The second his mouth touched hers, she started dissolving from the inside out. Technically that couldn't be true, but it *felt* true. Heat poured through her, making her want to move closer. Again something that didn't make sense. The closer she got to Jack, the more their shared body temperature would rise. Wait—it wouldn't rise exactly, it would…

He moved his mouth against hers. This wasn't the angry, something-to-prove kiss he'd given her at the gym. That had been easy to deal with. This kiss was different. It offered instead of taking. He applied just enough pressure to make her want to lean in and do a little demanding of her own.

Without meaning to, she reached up and rested her hands on his shoulders. He pulled her close until they were touching all over. Shoulder to knee, man to woman. He was hard and unyielding, a combination she found wildly erotic.

One of his hands slipped through her hair, tangling in the waves. The other moved up and down her back. Slowly, so slowly. Not touching anything significant, but still…touching.

He continued to brush his mouth against hers, keeping the kiss chaste yet arousing her until she wanted to grab him, shake him and tell him to get on with it already.

When he licked her bottom lip, she nearly groaned in relief. Fortunately she managed to hold in the sound. She even waited a nanosecond before parting for him. She didn't want to seem *too* eager. But then his tongue was touching hers, and staying cool was the last thing on her mind. Not when her blood rushed through her body at Mach 1 and every interesting female part of her began to tingle and ache and move toward begging to be touched.

He kissed her deeply, exploring, teasing, circling. She met him stroke for stroke, wanting to arouse him as much as he aroused her. Not to prove a point, for once, but because a kiss this good should be shared. Because it felt right.

She breathed in the scent of his body. She wished she were physically capable of crawling inside of him so she could know what he was feeling at that exact moment.

Instead she tilted her head and continued to kiss him as if this had been her plan all along.

She felt the hardness of his arousal pressing into her midsection. He wanted her. There was physical proof.

It should have been a moment of rejoicing. She should have pulled away and crowed about her victory. She was more than halfway there. But while she did pull back, she didn't say a word. Instead she stared into his dark eyes, at the fire there, the fire that matched the one raging inside her.

Then she did the only thing that couldn't possibly make sense. She turned and ran.

# Five

If there wasn't twenty million for charity on the line, not to mention the house itself, Jack would have been on the road back to Texas the next morning. But he was stuck for the month. All the other guys had survived their time at Hunter's Landing, so he would, too. But he would bet a lot of money that their weeks had been a whole lot less hellish than his.

He didn't want to think about his most recent kiss with Meri, but he couldn't seem to think about anything else. It had been different. He'd felt the power of his need for her all the way down to his bones. He'd ached for her in a way that was more than unsettling.

Trouble. Meri was nothing but trouble. She'd been a whole lot easier to handle when she'd been a teenager.

He walked into the kitchen, intent on coffee, only to

find one of her team members pouring a cup. Jack frowned slightly, trying to put a name with the face.

"Morning," the guy said and held out the pot for Jack.

"Morning…Colin," he added, remembering the smaller man from his arrival.

"Right." Colin pushed up his glasses and smiled. "Great house."

"I agree."

"It belongs to your friend, right? Meri's brother? The one who died."

Casual, easy words. *The one who died.* They cut through him like a razor and left wounds only he could see. "Yes. Hunter had this house built."

"Meri said this house was being turned over to the town or something. That it's going to be a place where sick people can recover and regroup. That's cool."

It was pure Hunter. Wanting to make a difference even after he was gone.

"How's the work coming?" Jack asked, not wanting to talk about his friend anymore. "Making progress?"

"Not yet. Theoretically there is a way to increase thrust within the confines of a safe formulation, but the nature of our planet seems to be that going faster and longer always means creating something toxic. Meri is determined to change that. When we consider the finite nature of our resources and the vastness of space, there are going to have to be some spectacular breakthroughs before we'll ever have a chance to explore our solar system, let alone the galaxy."

Colin took a quick gulp of his coffee. "The truth is, the next few generations are going to be like the early

Vikings. Going off on the rocket equivalent of rafts into a great unknown. If you consider their total lack of technology, the analogy is even more interesting. Because we consider ourselves cutting-edge, but compare what we have now to the first Russian launches. It's like they used paper clips and rubber bands to hold the whole thing together. But if they hadn't launched first, would Kennedy have pushed space flight? If you knew the number of modern innovations that came out of the space program..." He trailed off and looked slightly confused. "What were we talking about?"

"How your work was going."

"Oh, yeah. Sorry. I get carried away." Colin shifted slightly. "I like your car."

"Thanks." The sleek sports car wasn't practical, but it was fun to drive.

"Get good mileage with that?"

Jack grinned. "No."

"I didn't think so. I'd like a car like that."

"So buy one," Jack told him. Someone with Colin's brain had to make enough money.

"I'd like to, but it's not a good idea. I'm not a great driver." Colin shrugged. "I get easily distracted. You know, I'll be going along just fine and then I think about something with work and—zap—I'm just not paying attention. I've had a couple of accidents. I drive a Volvo. It's safer for me and the rest of the world."

"Okay, then." A sports car was not a good idea. At least Colin understood his limitations.

"Meri said you own a company that works in dangerous parts of the world," Colin said. "Interesting work?"

"More of a logistical challenge. People need to be able to work in dangerous parts of the world. My teams make sure they stay safe."

"Sounds exciting."

"It's an easy way to get dead. You have to know what you're doing."

Colin nodded slowly. He was blond and pale, with light blue eyes and a slightly unfocused expression. "Military background?" he asked.

"Special Forces."

Colin sighed. "I wanted to go to West Point. At least when I was a kid. But I was already in college by the time I was thirteen. Besides, I don't think I would have survived the physical training."

Jack had spent his six years of service staying out of any kind of officer training. "It's all a matter of discipline."

Colin smiled. "Maybe for you. For some of us there's an issue of natural ability. Or lack thereof. Meri talks about you a lot. I decided she had to be making it up, but she wasn't. You really are dynamic and powerful. Probably good with women."

Colin seemed to shrink as he spoke. Jack wasn't sure how to respond to his comments. What most interested him was the fact that Meri talked about him. Unfortunately that was the one question he couldn't ask.

"You have a thing for Meri?"

"What?" Colin's eyes widened. He pushed up his glasses again. "No. She's great, don't get me wrong, but we're just friends. She's not anyone I would…you know…be attracted to."

Jack's first instinct was to grab the little weasel by

the throat and ask him what the hell he thought was wrong with Meri. Then he got a grip and told himself to back off.

His second instinct was to walk away, because he didn't do personal conversations. But then he remembered Meri's insistence that they help Colin and Betina get together.

He refused to play matchmaker, but maybe a couple of questions couldn't hurt.

"You're a lucky guy," he said. "Surrounded by beautiful women."

Colin blinked. "Betina's beautiful."

"Yes, she is. Meri mentioned she wasn't one of the scientists?"

"Oh, no. She coordinates the project. She's just a normal person. She keeps us on track with our time and our budget. She takes care of things." His voice had a dreamy quality. "She always smells good. It's not always the same scent. Some of it is perfume, but there's an intriguing quality to her skin…."

"Sounds like someone worth getting to know."

"She is," Colin said, then paused. "What do you mean?"

"Is she seeing anyone?"

"What? I don't think so. But Betina has a lot of men. Practically a different man every week. She's always fun. I don't think the two of you would get along at all."

Jack held in a grin. "You're probably right. Have you two ever…?"

"Oh." Colin took a step back. "No. We've never dated or anything."

"Not your type either?"

"Uh, no. Probably not." But Colin sounded more resigned than anything else. As if he'd given up hope on the one thing he wanted.

Jack heard the shuttle van arriving and excused himself. He took the stairs up to his office, but as he passed the landing for the bedrooms, he paused. Meri liked to just pop into his room without warning. Maybe it was time to play the same game with her. Last night's kiss had obviously rattled her. He should press his advantage.

He crossed to her room and opened the door without knocking. Meri stood beside her bed.

The drapes were open and sunlight streamed into the room, illuminating every inch of her. Her hair fell in a wavy mass down her back. Her skin gleamed as if it had been dusted with starlight. She wore nothing but a tiny pair of bikini panties.

He stared at her nearly naked body, taking in the dip of her waist, the narrow rib cage and her perfect breasts. She held a bra in each hand, as if she'd been trying to decide which one to wear.

At last he raised his gaze to her face. She looked confused and apprehensive. There was none of her usual sass or spark.

Wanting slammed into him, nearly knocking him over with its intensity. On the heels of that came guilt. He'd promised Hunter he would keep Meredith safe from predators. Men exactly like himself.

"I'm sorry," he said and backed out of the room.

Meri dressed quickly, then stood in the center of her room, not sure what to do. Last night's kiss had been upsetting enough. She'd reacted to it with a passion that had stunned her. She'd wanted him, and nothing in her revenge plan was supposed to be about wanting.

She'd tried to convince herself that her reaction had been perfectly natural. Jack was a good-looking guy she liked a lot. She used to have a crush on him. It had been illogical to assume she could seduce him and not get aroused herself. End of story.

But she hadn't been able to totally believe herself. Now, having seen the need in his eyes, she knew the wanting wasn't all one-sided.

She left her room and went upstairs to his office. Sure enough, Jack was at his computer, staring at the screen as if it were the only thing that mattered.

"We have to talk," she said.

"No, we don't."

"I'm not leaving. You want me. I saw it in your eyes."

"I walked in on a beautiful naked woman. It was a biological reaction to a visual stimulus. Nothing more. I would have wanted anyone who fit the description."

She considered his words. Was he telling the truth? Was that all it was? Biology at work?

"I don't think so," she said. "It was more specific than that. You don't want any woman. You want me."

He finally looked up from the computer. "I've never understood why anyone would bang their head against a wall to make the pain go away, but I do now."

She smiled. "It's just part of my charm. Come on, Jack. You want me. Why can't you admit it?"

He sucked in a breath. She held hers, waiting for the words that would make her want to party like it was 1999.

"I talked to Colin about Betina," he said instead.

She sank into the chair opposite his desk. All thoughts of wanting and sex disappeared as she leaned forward eagerly. "Really? What did he say?"

"Nothing specific. You're right—he has a thing for her, but he thinks he's totally out of her league."

She groaned. "Of course he does."

"Why?" Jack asked. "He's got a lot going for him. He's smart and he has a good job. He seems nice. He should be like catnip."

"It's not that simple. Colin is like me—book-smart, world-stupid. Betina is one of those funny, social people who makes life a party wherever she goes. Colin bonds with the potted plant in the room. Trust me, I've been there."

"You were never that bad."

"I was worse. I had a wild crush on a guy I could never have. Then he broke my heart."

Jack looked out the window, then back at her. "I've apologized for that. I can't take it back."

"I know, but I like punishing you for it over and over again. The point is, being that smart isn't easy. I always knew I didn't fit in, and Colin feels the same way. We're bright enough to see the problem, but we can't seem to fix it."

"You're saying Colin can't take the steps to tell Betina he's interested?"

"He won't see himself as capable."

"Then maybe they shouldn't be together."

"I don't accept that," Meri told him. "Colin is a sweetie. And Betina is my best friend. I owe her everything. I want her to be happy. I'm going to make this happen."

"You shouldn't get involved."

"Too late. Thanks for your help."

"I didn't help."

She smiled. "You so did. When we go to their wedding, you can tell everyone how you had a hand in getting them together."

He groaned. "Or you could just shoot me now."

"Where's the fun in that?"

# Six

"I have happy news," Meri told Betina that afternoon when they'd finished working for the day.

Betina glanced out the kitchen window to where the rest of the team had walked down to the water. "You're giving up your ridiculous quest to sleep with Jack?"

"Never that," Meri told her. "I'm actually getting closer by the day. He's weak with desire. I'm sure you've noticed him limping."

"You're a nut."

"Maybe, but I'm a nut with fabulous news about Colin. He likes you."

Betina had traveled the world, dated a European prince and had a very wealthy sheik invite her into his harem. She had a tattoo, knew how to do henna and had explained the intricacies of sex to Meri in such detail that her first time had been a breeze. But she'd never once, in all the years Meri had known her, blushed.

Betina ducked her head. "I don't think so."

"He does. He talked to Jack about you. He thinks you're great. He's just lacking in confidence. But you have enough confidence for two people, so you're a perfect match."

Betina raised her head. "You dragged Jack into this?"

"I didn't drag him. He wanted to help. Sort of. That's so not the point. Isn't this fabulous? Aren't you happy?"

Betina didn't look the least bit thrilled. Her friend walked over to the kitchen table and sat down. "I'm not sure I want things to change."

Meri sank down across from her. "What? Are you crazy? We're talking about Colin."

"Exactly. He's really special. Right now he's my friend and I can depend on him to always be my friend. If I change that relationship, there's no going back."

"Is that a bad thing?"

"I don't know and neither do you. Meri, there are consequences for everything we do. What if Colin and I don't hit it off? What if he's not who I think he is? Then I'll lose the friendship and have nothing."

Meri didn't understand. "I thought you were in love with him."

"I am. That's what makes this so hard. I'd rather just be his friend than not have him in my life at all."

"But you could be more. You could have it all. I don't understand. You've always been a risk taker."

"Not when something important is on the line. There I'm nothing but a coward."

This was news, Meri thought, confused by her friend. "I don't get it. You're in love with him. There's a very good chance that he's in love with you. And yet you're not going to do anything about it? You'd rather have a skinny piece of pie than the whole thing?"

"It's better than no pie."

"But if you don't try, you'll always wonder. You'll have regrets—and, believe me—those are the worst."

"How would you know?"

Meri smiled sadly. "I grew up the queen of regrets. There were so many things I wanted to do when I was growing up. But I was always afraid. I didn't fit in and I wasn't willing to risk being rejected. So I never tried. I was miserable in college, so sure no one would ever want to be my friend. Looking back, I can see a few times when people approached me. But I blew them off. It was easier to be right than to risk. But it was a high price. Like you said, there are always consequences."

"What are the consequences of sleeping with Jack?" Betina asked.

"So now we're talking about me?"

"I have more confidence in the subject."

Meri considered the question. "I finally get to move on with my life. He was my first crush and then he hurt me. I've grown up and matured, but I've never been able to let him totally go. He's always lurking in the back of my mind. If I can get over him, I can move on. He's the reason I've never been able to fall in love."

"I thought you were in love with Andrew."

Was she? Meri didn't know what real, adult love felt like. She enjoyed Andrew's company. She liked being with him. Six months ago she would have said yes, she was pretty sure she was almost in love with him. Today she was less sure.

"I haven't missed him enough," she said softly. "I've seen him only a couple of times in the past six months. Shouldn't I be destroyed without him?"

"Nothing about you is normal. Andrew seems like a good guy. You'll hook up again when you go back to D.C. You can figure out your feelings then. Assuming you're not in love with Jack."

What? "No way. I don't love him. I want to hurt him. I want to make him crawl and beg and then I want to walk away."

"That's sure the story," Betina said calmly. "The one you've been telling yourself for years. But is it the truth?" She shrugged. "I have my doubts. I think you've never gotten over Jack. I don't think any of this is about revenge. You can't accept you still love him so this is the story you tell yourself. But be careful. You're not into casual relationships. What happens if you sleep with him and then can't walk away? You want him to break your heart twice?"

In love with Jack? "Never. He can't hurt me. I won't let him. He's little more than a symbol of the issues in my childhood. Once I prove I've outgrown him, I can let my past go."

"An excellent theory. You'll have to tell me how that works out for you."

Meri hated her friend's doubts. Betina was her oracle, the keeper of social and romantic knowledge. They'd never disagreed on anything significant before.

"I have to do this," Meri said. "I've waited too long to walk away now. I have to go for it. You should, too. Tonight."

Betina laughed. "You're a brave woman. Braver than me."

"That's not true."

"It is when it comes to matters of the heart. You're willing to risk it all to get what you want, and I'm not."

Jack walked into his room that night weary from too many hours at the computer. He pulled the hem of his shirt out of his jeans and started unbuttoning it, only to stop when he heard something in the bathroom.

He turned and saw the door was closed but light shone from underneath. What the hell?

But as quickly as the question formed, it was answered. There was only one person who would be hanging out in his bathroom. Meri.

He hesitated as he tried to figure out the best way to handle the situation. With his luck, she was probably naked. Maybe in the tub. Waiting for him. She'd been doing her best to seduce him, and he hated to admit that she'd done a damn fine job. He was primed and ready. It wouldn't take much to push him over the edge.

The question was, did he want to fall?

He owed Hunter his loyalty. He'd given his word and he hadn't done much of a job of seeing it through. All his friend had asked was for him to protect his sister. Instead Jack had cut and run. Sure, he'd kept tabs on Meri from a distance, but that was taking the easy way out.

Which meant now was the time to make good on his

promise. He would walk into the bathroom, tell Meredith to get the hell out of there, explain nothing was ever going to happen between them and grit his teeth for the rest of the time he was stuck up here in the lodge.

A least it was a plan.

He sucked in a breath and walked into the bathroom.

It was as he'd expected. Candles glowing, rose petals scattered, the fire flickering and a very naked Meri in the tub.

She'd piled her hair on top of her head, exposing the sexy line of her neck. Bubbles in the bath floated across the water, giving him a quick view of her nakedness before moving to cover the scene. Her perfect breasts floated, a siren's lure calling to him.

He was hard in a heartbeat. Hard and ready to take her every way he knew how.

It wasn't her pale skin or the music playing in the background that got to him. It wasn't the way she'd set the scene or the fact that he knew she wasn't just willing, she was determined. He could have resisted all of that, even her slightly pouting lips.

What he couldn't resist was the book she was reading. She'd set out to seduce him and had gotten so caught up in a textbook on nuclear fission that she hadn't even heard him walk into the bathroom. That was the very heart of Meri. A walking, breathing genius brain trapped in the body of a centerfold. Who else could possibly appreciate the magic that was her?

Meri sighed as she turned the page. Why did Jerry have to go out of his way to make a perfectly mesmerizing topic boring? She'd been a little nervous when he'd asked her to read his latest textbook, and now that she was into it, she realized she'd been wary for a reason. Nuclear fission was one of the great discoveries of the twentieth century. Shouldn't that be celebrated? Shouldn't it at least be interesting? But noooo. Jerry wrote down to his audience and had taken what was—

The book was ripped from her hands. Meri blinked in surprise to find Jack standing beside the tub. Tub? She was in a tub? When had that happened?

She blinked again and her memory returned. Right. She'd planned on seducing him tonight. She glanced around and saw the candles and rose petals. At least she'd done a nice job.

"Hi," she said as she smiled up at Jack. "Surprise."

"You sure are that."

She braced herself for him to yell at her or stalk off or explain for the four hundredth time why this was never going to work. She didn't expect him to pull her to her feet, drag her out of the bath and haul her against him.

She was stunned. In a good way. She liked how he stared into her eyes as if she were prime rib and he were a starving man. She liked how his hands moved up and down her back, then slipped lower, to her butt.

She was totally naked. A fact he seemed to appreciate.

"But I'm all wet," she whispered.

"I hope that's true," he said before he bent his head and kissed her.

His mouth was firm and sure, claiming her with a kiss that demanded a response. She tilted her head and parted for him, wanting to get the party started with some soul-stirring kisses.

He didn't disappoint. He moved into her mouth, brushing her tongue with his, moving leisurely, as if arousing her was the only thing on his mind. Heat poured through her.

Not that she was cold. Not with the fire to her back and Jack pressing against her front.

As he kissed her over and over again, he moved his hands over her body. He touched her shoulders, her back, her hips, tracing her skin, igniting nerve endings everywhere he went.

She raised her hands to his shoulders, then slid her fingers through his hair. She touched his cheeks, feeling the stubble there, before exploring his chest.

He was strong and masculine. When he cupped her rear, she arched against him and felt the hard thickness of his erection. A thrill of anticipation shot through her. She shivered.

He pulled back a little. "Cold?"

"No."

He stared into her eyes. She stared back, wondering what he was thinking. He'd been resisting her best efforts for a while now. Did he regret giving in? Not that she was going to ask. There were some things it was best not to know.

He didn't act like a man with regrets. He bent down, but instead of kissing her lips, he pressed his mouth to her neck and nibbled his way to her collarbone.

His hands rested lightly on her waist. As he teased her neck, licked her earlobe, then gently bit down, he moved his hands up her rib cage, toward her breasts.

Before her surgery she'd been warned that she might

lose some of the sensitivity in her breasts, but she'd been one of the lucky ones. She could feel everything—every touch, every kiss, every whisper of breath. She tensed in anticipation of how Jack would make her tingle.

When he reached her curves, he cupped them gently. He explored her skin, then swept his thumbs across her nipples. Her insides tightened.

He kissed his way down to her breasts and drew her left nipple into his mouth. She leaned her head back as he circled her, then sucked and licked. Ribbons of need wove through her body, settling in her rapidly swelling center. The dull ache of arousal grew.

He turned his attentions to her other nipple, teasing and kissing until her breathing came in pants and her legs began to tremble.

Even as he continued to tease her breasts, he slipped one hand lower and lower, down her belly, toward the promised land. She parted her legs and braced herself for the impact his touch would have on her. Only he didn't touch her *there*. Instead he stroked her thighs and played with her curls. He ran his fingers along the outside but never dipped in.

She shifted impatiently, wondering if shaking him would get the message across. There! He needed to touch her *there*.

But he ignored that place where she was wet and swollen and desperately ready. He squeezed her bottom, he circled her belly button, he touched everywhere else.

Just when she was about to issue a complaint in writing, he pulled back a little, bent down and gathered her in his arms. Before she could catch her breath, he'd carried her into the bedroom and placed her on the bed. Then he was kneeling between her legs, his fingers parting her as he gave her an intimate, six-second-to-climax openmouthed kiss.

The combination of tongue and lips and breath made her moan in delight. He licked her with the leisurely confidence of a man who knows what to do and likes doing it. She gave herself over to the steady stroking and the easy exploration.

Tension invaded her. Each clench of her muscles pushed her higher and closer. One summer while she was still in college, she'd played with the idea of becoming a doctor, so she'd read several medical textbooks. She knew the biological steps leading to an orgasm—the arousal, how the blood made the area feel hot, the mechanism involved in swelling, the response of the sympathetic nervous system.

But none of those words could begin to describe what it felt like to have Jack suck on the most nerve-filled place in her body. How there seemed to be a direct connection between that engorged spot between her legs and the rest of her. How each flick of his tongue made her stomach clench and her heels dig into the bed.

She felt herself getting closer and closer. He moved patiently, slowly, drawing out the experience. Taking her to the edge, then pulling back just enough to keep her from coming.

Again and again she caught sight of her release, only to have it move out of reach.

Then, without warning, he went faster. The quick

flicks of his tongue caught her off guard. She had no time to prepare, no way to brace herself for the sudden explosion of pleasure that tore her apart.

Wave after wave of release swept through her. She pressed down, wanting to keep the feelings going. He gentled his touch but didn't pull away. Not until she experienced the last shudder and was able to finally draw in a breath.

She opened her eyes and found him looking at her. Under any other circumstance, his smug grin would have annoyed her, but considering what he'd just done, she decided he'd earned it.

She grabbed him by his shirt front and urged him to slide up next to her. When he would have spoken, she touched his mouth with her fingers, telling him to be quiet. While she loved a good relationship conversation as much as the next woman, this was a time for silence.

When he was on his back, she unbuttoned his shirt, then kissed her way down his chest to his belly. He was warm and he tasted sexy and faintly sweet. She nipped at his side, which made him both laugh and groan, then she went to work on his jeans.

He was so hard she had trouble with the zipper but finally managed to get it unfastened. He helped her push down his jeans and briefs.

She knelt between his legs, taking in the beauty that was his aroused naked body. His erection called to her. She reached out and touched him, then stroked his length. He put his hand on top of hers.

"I don't have any protection," he said.

She smiled. "Come on, Jack. It's me. When have I not prepared for every contingency?"

She leaned forward and opened his nightstand, then pulled out the condoms she'd put there before she'd started her bath.

Seconds later, the condom in place, she eased herself onto him.

He was big and thick and he filled her, stretching her inside in the most delicious way possible. She braced herself on her hands and knees, settling in for the ride.

His dark gaze met hers. "You really think I'm going to let you be on top?" he asked.

"Uh-huh."

He reached for her breasts. "You're right."

She laughed, then rocked back and forth, easing herself onto him, then off. At the same time, he cupped her breasts, teasing her nipples and providing a heck of a distraction.

She forced herself to concentrate on that place where they joined, but it got more and more difficult as her body got lost in the pleasure. With each stroke, she drove herself closer to another orgasm.

She felt him tense beneath her. She rode him faster, taking them higher and harder, pushing toward their mutual goal.

He abandoned her breasts and grabbed her hips, holding her tightly enough to control the pace. It was just slow enough to make her whimper.

So close, she thought as she concentrated on the feel of him pushing inside of her again and again. So...

And then she was coming. Her release rushed

through her, urging her on. Faster and faster until she felt him hold her still as he shuddered beneath her.

On and on their bodies joined, until they were both still.

Jack rolled her onto her side and withdrew. They stared at each other in the soft light of the room. He touched her face.

"I wasn't going to let you do that," he murmured.

"I know. You mad?"

"Not at you."

At himself? Because he'd betrayed his promise to Hunter? Meri started to tell him it didn't matter when it suddenly occurred to her that maybe it did. To him, at least. That maybe he regretted letting his friend down and that this had been the last promise he'd been able to keep.

Only he hadn't.

"Jack…" she began.

He shook his head. "Don't go there. Wherever you're going, don't."

She opened her mouth, then closed it. She didn't want to apologize. Not exactly. But she felt as if she should say something.

"I should go," she murmured

"You don't have to."

She stared into his dark eyes and knew she wanted to stay. Even if it was just one night, she wanted to spend the time with him.

"I went to a psychic once," she told him. "She told me that one day I would be in bed with the devil. I always knew she meant you. It's not your fault you gave in. It was destiny."

He smiled faintly. "You believe in psychics?"

"I believe in a lot of things. I'm very interesting."

"Yes, you are."

She sighed and snuggled close. "Are we going to make love again tonight?"

"Yes."

"You can be on top this time if you want."

He chuckled. "You're not in charge."

"Of course I am. I'm also totally irresistible. Right now you're wondering how you resisted me for so long."

"It's like you can read my mind."

She closed her eyes and breathed in the scent of him. Everything about this moment felt right, she thought. As if this was what she'd been waiting for. As if—

Wait a minute. She wasn't supposed to *like* having sex with Jack. She was supposed to be getting her revenge and moving on. They weren't supposed to connect.

They weren't, she told herself. She was just emotionally gooey from the afterglow. It was a biological response. Her body's attempt to bond with a man who was genetically desirable. Come morning, she would be totally over him and this and be ready to walk away. Her plan would go on as scheduled and she would be free to move forward with her life.

"I'm healed," Meri told Betina the next morning as she poured milk over her cereal. "Seriously, if I had a limp, it would be gone."

Betina looked her over. "Based on the smirk and the glow, I'm going to guess you and Jack did the wild thing last night."

Meri sighed with contentment. "We did. It was fabulous. Better than I imagined, which is hard to believe. I feel like a new woman. A new woman with really, really clear skin!"

Betina laughed. "Okay. Good for you."

"Any progress with Colin?"

"No. I watched a movie and he spent the evening on his computer. Then we went to bed separately."

Meri felt her fabulous mood fade a little. "That sucks. You need to talk to him."

"I'm not taking advice from you."

"Why not? My plan is working perfectly. Jack has had me and now he wants more. But he's not going to get any more. I'm walking away."

"Really?"

"Absolutely."

"And you don't feel a thing?"

"I'm a little sore," Meri said with a grin.

Betina slowly shook her head. "Okay. Then I was wrong. I guess you don't have any feelings for him. If you're not thinking about being with him again or wanting to hang out with him, then you are healed. Yay you."

Her friend poured coffee and walked out of the kitchen. Meri stared after her.

She didn't have feelings for Jack. Okay, sure, he was a friend and, as such, she would always have a soft spot for him. She was also willing to admit that not sleeping with him again might be difficult, but only because it had been so darned good. Not because she felt any kind of emotional connection.

But as she thought the words, she felt a little *ping* in her heart. One that warned her something might not be right.

"I don't care about him," she told herself. "I don't."

Which was a good thing, because falling for him would totally ruin her attempts at revenge.

She finished her cereal, rinsed the bowl and put it in the dishwasher. Then she walked into the dining room.

Someone rang the bell at the front door. She frowned. It was too early for the rest of the team, not to mention a delivery. So who on earth…?

She walked to the front of the house and opened the door. Her mind went blank as she stared at the man standing there. The man who swept her into his arms and kissed her.

"Hey, babe," he said.

She swallowed. "Andrew. This is a surprise."

# Seven

When Jack finished getting dressed after his shower, he debated going downstairs for coffee or heading up to the loft to check in with his office.

Coffee won, mostly because he hadn't gotten much sleep the previous night. Sharing a bed with Meri had been anything but restful.

He walked out of his bedroom, then paused at the landing to look at the picture he'd mostly avoided since arriving at the house. It showed him and his friends during college. When everything had been easy and they'd called themselves the Seven Samurai.

Hunter laughed into the camera, because he'd always enjoyed whatever he was doing. Luke and Matt—twins who couldn't be more different—held Ryan in a headlock, while he and Devlin poured beer over the group. He knew that just outside the view of the camera sat a teenage girl on a blanket, her head buried in a book. Because Meri had never quite fit in.

Hunter had worried about her, especially after he'd found out he was dying. That's when he'd asked Jack to take care of her.

"Hell of a job," Jack muttered to himself as he turned away from the picture. Sure, Meri was all grown up now, a woman who made her own choices. That was her excuse for what had happened the previous night. What was his?

He'd wanted her. Who wouldn't? She was smart and funny and pretty as hell. She challenged him the way no one else dared. She was sexy and irreverent and so filled with life and ideas. Hunter would have been proud of her. Then he would have turned on Jack like a rabid dog and beaten the crap out of him. Or at least he would have tried. Knowing it was all his fault, Jack knew he just might have let him.

So now what? Meri had claimed she wanted to seduce him, which she probably thought she had. Did they just move on now? Pretend it hadn't happened? Because it shouldn't have, no matter how good it had been. If he could turn back time…

Jack shook his head. No point in lying to himself. If he could turn back time, he would do it all over again. Which made him a pretty big bastard and a sorry sort of friend.

He glanced back at the photo. Now what?

He heard footsteps on the stairs. But instead of a petite blonde with an attitude, he saw Betina climbing toward him.

"Morning," he said.

She reached the landing and looked at him. There was something in her eyes—something that warned him she was not happy about certain events.

"What?" he asked.

"That would be my question to you." She drew in a breath. "Look, it's not my business—"

Great. She was going to get protective. "You're right. It's *not* your business."

She glared at him. "Meredith is my friend. I care about her. I don't want her to get hurt."

"What makes you think that's going to happen?"

"It's in your nature. You're the kind of man who is used to getting what he wants and walking away."

True enough, he thought, not sure what that had to do with anything. "Meri's not in this for the long term," he said.

"That's what she keeps telling me, but I'm not so sure. I think she's in a position where she could get her heart broken."

"Not by me."

Betina rolled her eyes. "Are all men stupid about women or is it just the ones in this house?"

"You expect me to answer that?"

"No. I expect you to respect someone you're supposed to care about. You've known Meri a long time. She's not like the rest of us. She didn't grow up with a chance at being normal. She managed to fit in all on her own."

"I heard you had a part in making that happen."

Betina shrugged. "I gave her direction. She did the

work. But she's not as tough as she thinks. What she had planned for you was crazy—and I told her that, but she wouldn't listen."

"Typical."

"I know. My point is I don't want anything bad to happen to her. If you hurt her, I'll hunt you down like the dog you are and make you pay."

He gave her a half smile. "Going to hire someone to beat me up?"

"No, Jack. I'm going to tell you exactly how much she's suffering. I'm going to point out that you were her brother's best friend and that he asked only one thing of you and you couldn't seem to do it. Not then and not now. I'm going to be the voice in your head—the ugly one that never lets you rest."

He met her steady gaze with one of his own. "You're good."

"I care about her. She's part of my family. She deserves someone who loves her. Are you that guy?"

He didn't have to think about that. "No." He'd never loved anyone. He refused to care. It cost too much.

"Then leave her alone. Give her a chance with someone else."

"Someone like Andrew?" Jack had a bad feeling about him. He would get his report soon enough and then figure out what to do.

"Funny you should mention him," Betina said, looking amused. "I guess you don't know."

"Know what?"

"He's here."

\* \* \*

Meri pulled back, stood in front of the open door and wondered if she looked as guilty as she felt. While she and Andrew had agreed that they were on a relationship hiatus, saying the words and having him show up less than four hours after she and Jack had made love for the third time of the night was a little disconcerting.

"You're here," she said, feeling stupid and awkward and really, really guilty.

"I missed you." He smiled that easy Andrew smile— the one that had first drawn her to him. The one that told the world he was pleasant, charming and curious about everything. "Did you miss me?"

She'd spent five months working on her plan to seduce Jack Howington III and nearly a week putting that plan into action. In her free time she'd been consulting for two different defense contractors and working on her solid-rocket-fuel project. Who had time to miss anyone?

"Of course," she said, resisting the urge to fold her arms over her chest and shuffle her feet.

"Good." He stepped into the house and put his arm around her. "So this is where you've been hanging out."

"I've actually been down in Los Angeles a lot. Remember? The consulting."

"I know. Is your team here?"

"They'll arrive in an hour or so."

"How fortunate." He pulled her close again. "So we have time to get reacquainted."

Ick and double ick. She couldn't get "reacquainted" with Andrew right after having seduced Jack. It was wrong on many, many levels.

She stepped away and looked at him. Andrew was tall like Jack but not as muscular or lean. His brown hair was longer, his blue eyes lighter. Jack was a sexy version of the devil come to life. He played every hand close and gave nothing away. Andrew was open and friendly. He assumed the world liked him—and most of the time it did.

Which didn't matter, she told herself. There was no need for comparisons. She had a relationship with Andrew and she had nothing with Jack. They'd been friends once, she'd proved her point and now she was moving on. She should be happy Andrew was here. He was part of the moving-on bit, wasn't he?

Andrew's blue eyes clouded. "What's wrong, Meredith? Aren't you happy to see me? It's been weeks since we met at The Symposium in Chicago. I've missed you. You said you wanted time for us both to be sure about our feelings. I'm still sure. Are you?"

Life was all about timing, Meredith thought happily as Colin walked into the room, saw Andrew and grimaced.

"Oh. You're here," he grumbled. Colin had never been a fan.

It wasn't anyone's fault, Meri told herself. Andrew was inherently athletic and Colin…wasn't. She wasn't either, but she tried and she always forced her team to attempt something new a couple of times a year. She ignored the complaints and reminded them it was good for them.

"Colin!" Andrew said cheerfully, ignoring the other man's obvious irritation at his presence. "Haven't seen you in a long time. How's it hanging?"

Colin looked Andrew over with the same enthusiasm one would use when seeing a cockroach in one's salad. "It's hanging just fine."

Colin poured his coffee and left.

"I think he's starting to like me," Andrew said in a mock whisper. "We're really communicating."

Despite everything, Meri laughed. "You're an optimist."

"Hey, you like Colin and I like you. Therefore I must like Colin. Isn't that some kind of math logic? You should appreciate that."

She should, and she mostly did. She appreciated that Andrew was never tense or intense. She enjoyed his humor, his spontaneity and how he seemed to live a charmed life. According to every women's-magazine survey she'd ever taken, Andrew was perfect for her.

So how had she been able to be apart from him for six months only seeing him for a few days at a time and not really mind?

Before she could figure out the answer, she heard more footsteps on the stairs. She turned, expecting to see Betina, who would be a great distraction. Instead Jack walked into the kitchen.

The room got so quiet Meri could actually hear her heart pumping blood through her body. She felt herself flush as she tried to figure out what on earth she was supposed to say.

Andrew stepped forward, held out his hand and smiled. "Andrew Layman. I'm Meredith's boyfriend."

Jack looked him over. "Jack Howington the third. Friend of the family."

Meri stared in surprise. Jack had used his full name, including the number. Why? He never did that.

The two men shook hands. When they separated, it seemed that they were both crowding her a little.

"So you know Meredith's dad?" Andrew asked. "You mentioned you were a friend of the family, but she hasn't mentioned you before."

"I knew her brother. Meri and I were friends in college. We go way back."

"Interesting. You never came to D.C.," Andrew said easily. "I know all of Meredith's friends there."

"Sounds like you keep a close watch on her."

"I care about her."

"Apparently not enough that you mind a six-month absence," Jack told him. "You haven't met all of Meri's friends here."

"I already know them."

"You don't know me."

"You're the past."

Jack's gaze was steady. "Not as much as you might think. Meri and I have a history together."

Meri rolled her eyes. It was as though they were a couple of dogs and she were the favorite tree they both wanted to pee on. While she was sure Jack was more than capable of winning the contest, she was surprised he would bother to play. She also hadn't expected Andrew to get drawn in. Since when had he become competitive?

"There's a little too much testosterone in here for me," she said as she stepped back. "You two boys have fun."

*  *  *

Meri made her way to Betina's room and found her friend typing on her laptop.

"Girl emergency," Meri said as she closed the bedroom door and sat on the edge of the bed. "How could he be here?"

"Andrew?"

Meri nodded. "I had no idea. We've been staying in touch via e-mail and we've talked a little on the phone, but there was no warning. He just showed up. How could he do that?"

"He got on a plane and flew here. It's romantic. Does it feel romantic to you?"

"I don't know," Meri admitted, still unclear how she felt. "It's been weeks and weeks. I thought he was going to propose and I thought maybe I would say yes. Shouldn't I be excited that he's here? Shouldn't I be dancing in the streets?"

"We don't have much in the way of streets, but maybe if you danced in the driveway, it would be enough."

Meri started to laugh, then sucked in a breath as she suddenly fought tears. "I'm so confused."

"You slept with Jack. That was bound to change things."

"It was supposed to make them more clear. I was supposed to be healed."

"Maybe the problem is you were never broken."

Meri nodded slowly. Maybe that *was* the problem. She'd always thought there was something wrong with her and that it could be traced back to Jack's painful rejection. But what if that had just been a normal part of growing up and, because of her freakishness, she hadn't been able to see it? What if she'd made it too big a deal?

"You don't think I needed closure with Jack?" Meri asked. "You don't think getting revenge on him will move me to a higher plane?"

Betina sighed. "I don't think anything negative like revenge is ever healthy. You've felt emotionally stalled and unable to commit. Was that about what Jack did or was it simply that you needed more time to integrate who you were with who you wanted to be? Being book-smart doesn't help you grow up any faster or better. Sometimes it just gets in the way."

"I figured that out a while ago," Meri grumbled. "You'd think I could deal with it by now." She drew in a deep breath. "I was so *sure* that revenge was the right way to go. I knew that if I could just make him want me, then walk away, I'd be happy forever."

"Maybe that's still true."

Meri wasn't sure. "Like you said—it's not healthy to be so negative."

"But it is done," Betina reminded her. "Deal with what you have now. Closure. So on to Andrew—if that's where you want to go."

An interesting idea. The only problem was Meri wasn't sure what she thought about anything anymore.

"I need to clear my head. I'm going to run. Could you get the group started without me?"

Betina grinned. "I love it when you leave me in charge."

Later that morning, Jack went looking for Meri. She wasn't in the dining room with her team, although

Betina had told him she was in the house somewhere. He checked out his bathroom, but no beautiful, naked women waited for him. Damn. There were days a guy couldn't cut a break. Then he saw something move on the balcony and stepped out to find her sitting on a chair, staring out at the view.

She looked up as he joined her. "I was going to use the telescope, but it's kind of hard to see the stars with all the sunshine getting in the way."

He glanced at the bright blue sky. "I can see where that's a problem."

"I thought about spying on our neighbors—you know, catch someone sunbathing nude. But I just can't seem to get into it."

Her big eyes were dark and troubled. The corner of her mouth drooped. She looked sad and uncomfortable, which was so far from her normal bouncy self that he found himself saying, "You want to talk about it?"

She shrugged. "I'm confused. And before you ask why, I'm not going to tell you."

"Makes it hard to help if I don't know what's wrong."

"Maybe you're the problem."

"Am I?"

She sighed. "Not really. A little, but it's mostly me."

He took the chair next to hers and stared out at the lake. It was huge, stretching for miles. "Did you know Lake Tahoe is nearly a mile deep?"

The droopy corner turned up. "Someone's been reading the chamber of commerce brochure."

"I got bored."

She looked at him. "Why aren't you married?"

The question made him shrug. "No one's ever asked."

"Oh, right. Because you're so eager to say yes?"

"Probably not. I'm not the marrying kind."

Now she smiled for real. "Sure you are. You're rich and single. What was it Jane Austen said? Something about any single man of good fortune must be in search of a wife? That's you. Don't you want to get married?"

"I never much thought about it. My work keeps me busy."

"Meaning, if you have too much time to think, you take on another job."

How had she figured that out? "Sometimes."

He liked to stay busy, involved with his business. He had some guys he hung out with occasionally. That was enough.

"No one gets close?" she asked.

"No."

"Because of Hunter?"

He stretched out his legs in front of him. "Just because we slept together doesn't mean I'm going to tell you everything I'm thinking."

"Okay. Is it because of Hunter?"

He glanced at her. "You're annoying."

"So I've been told. Do I need to ask again?"

"I should hire you to do interrogations. And, yes, some of it is because of Hunter."

"People die, Jack."

"I know. I lost my brother when he was still a kid. It changed everything."

He hadn't meant to say that, to tell her the truth. But now that he had, he found he didn't mind her knowing.

"It was like with Hunter," he said quietly. "He got sick and then he died. We'd been close and it hurt like hell that he was gone."

The difference was he hadn't kept his brother from going to the doctor. When Hunter had first noticed the dark spot on his shoulder, Jack had teased him about being a wimp for wanting to get it checked out. So Hunter had waited. What would have happened if the melanoma had been caught before it had spread?

"You didn't kill Hunter," Meri told him. "It's not your fault."

Jack stood. "I'm done here."

She moved fast and blocked the door. She was small enough that he could have easily pushed past her, but for some reason he didn't.

"You didn't kill him," she repeated. "I know that's what you think. I know you feel guilty. So what's the deal? Are you lost in the past? Are you afraid to fall for someone because you don't want to lose another person you love? Or do you think you're cursed or something?"

Both, he thought. And so much more. He wasn't allowed to love or care. It was the price he had to pay for what he'd done. Or, rather, what he hadn't done.

"I'm not having this conversation with you," he said.

"Wanna bet?"

She probably thought she looked tough, but she was small and girlie and he could take her in half a second. Or a nanosecond, to talk like her.

"Get out of my way," he growled.

She raised her chin. "Make me."

She was like a kitten spitting at a wolf. Entertaining and with no idea of the danger she was in.

"You don't scare me," he told her.

"Right back at you." Then she smiled. "But you probably want to kiss me now, huh?"

She was impossible. And, damn her, he *did* want to kiss her. He wanted to do a lot of things to her, some of which, if they stayed out here on the balcony, would violate the town's decency code.

So instead of acting, he went for the distraction. "Andrew seems nice."

"Oh, please. You hate him."

"Hate would require me thinking about him. I don't."

"So macho. What was up with the I-know-Meri-better game?"

"I have no idea what you're talking about," he said, even though he did. Establishing dominance early on was the best way to win.

"And they say women are complicated," she murmured.

# Eight

Meri came downstairs and found Andrew waiting for her in the living room and her team hard at work in the dining room. The choice should be simple. Work or the man who had traveled so far to see her.

She debated, then ducked into the kitchen, found the phone book in the pantry and made a couple of quick calls.

"We're taking the afternoon off," she announced as she walked in on her team.

"Oh, good," Andrew said, coming up behind her and putting his hand on her shoulder. "Alone at last."

"Not exactly," she said with a grin. "Everyone, the shuttle will be here shortly to take you back to your hotel. I want you to put on bathing suits and beach clothes. Plenty of sunscreen."

Donny grimaced. "You're going to make us be outdoors again, aren't you?"

"Uh-huh."

There was a collection of grumbles, but everyone knew better than to argue.

"At least we'll get it over with," someone said. "Then we can work."

"You're taking them to the lake?" Andrew asked when the team had left. "Are you sure about this?"

"They can swim," she told him. "They might not be great at it, but they can. It's not healthy for us to sit in this room day after day. Being outside clears the mind. Physical activity is good for them."

He pulled her close. "You're good for me. Haven't you missed me, Meredith?"

"Yes, but maybe not as much as I should have," she told him honestly.

His blue gaze never wavered. "So I left you alone for too long. I knew I shouldn't have listened to you when you said you wanted to take a break."

"I had some things I had to do." Things she wasn't comfortable thinking about with an actual boyfriend in the wings.

She braced herself for his temper or at least a serious hissy fit. Instead he touched her cheek. "I guess I'm going to have to win you back."

Words that should have melted her heart—emotionally if not physically. Because the temperature required to melt a body part would cook it first, and that was gross, even for her twisted mind. So what was wrong with her? Why wasn't Andrew getting to her?

A question that seriously needed an answer.

\* \* \*

An hour later they were down at the edge of the lake. Meri counted heads to make sure no one had ducked out of what she had planned and was surprised to see Jack had joined them.

"Colin told me I wouldn't want to miss it," he said when she approached.

"He's right." She had a little trouble speaking, which was weird but possibly explained by how great Jack looked in swim trunks and a T-shirt. He was tanned—mostly all over, she remembered from the previous night.

Bad memory, she told herself. Don't think about making love with Jack. Think about Andrew and how sweet he is. Although sweet Andrew had chosen not to show up for her afternoon of fun on the lake.

"So what are we doing?" Betina asked. She wore shorts and a bikini top.

Meri was momentarily distracted by amazing curves a couple of hours of surgery hadn't begun to give her. And Betina's assets were all natural.

"Um, that." Meri pointed out to the water, where four guys rode toward them on Jet Skis.

"Nerds on water," Colin muttered. "What were you thinking?"

"That you'll have fun."

"I'll get a sunburn."

Jack moved close. "I like it," he said. "Will they give them lessons?"

"Yes. And make them wear life jackets. It will be fun."

He raised his eyebrows. "Do you always bully them into some physical activity?"

"Pretty much. I'm not athletically gifted either, but I try. We can't spend out whole lives inside. It makes us pasty. This is better."

"Last year she made us ski," Colin said absently as he eyed the Jet Ski. "Norman broke his leg."

"It's true," Betina said. "To this day, the man walks with a limp."

Meri put her hands on her hips. "But he had fun. He still talks about that day, okay? We're doing this. Don't argue with me."

Jack liked the way she stood up to everyone and how they reluctantly agreed. Meri was an unlikely leader, but she was in charge.

"So where's Allen?" he asked.

"Andrew," she corrected. "He doesn't like group sports."

"Not a team player?"

"He plays tennis."

"I see."

She glared at him. "What does that mean?"

He held up both hands. "Nothing. I'm sure he has a great backhand."

"He belongs to a country club. He nearly went pro."

"Afraid of messing up his hair?"

She sniffed. "No. He wanted to do something else with his life."

"Oh. He couldn't make the tour."

"He came really close."

"I'm sure that brings him comfort."

"Look," she said, poking her finger at his chest. "We can't all be physically perfect."

He liked baiting her and allowed himself a slight smile. "You think I'm perfect."

"You're annoying. And you're not all that."

"Yes, I am."

She turned her back on him. He liked getting to her almost as much as he didn't like Andrew. Jack was still waiting on Bobbi Sue's report on the man. His gut told him it wasn't going to be good news. Would Meri listen when he told her the truth?

He refused to consider that Andrew might be an okay guy.

The instructors rode their Jet Skis to the shore. "We're looking for Meri," the tallest, tannest and blondest one said.

"I'm here." She waved. "This is my team. They're really smart but not superathletic. Sort of like me."

She grinned and the guy smiled back. He looked her up and down, then whipped off his sunglasses and moved toward her.

Jack stepped between them. He put his hand on the other guy's shoulder. "Not so fast."

Surfer dude nodded and took a step back. "Sorry, man."

"It's fine."

Meri raised her eyebrows. "You're protecting me from a guy on a Jet Ski. It's almost romantic."

"I was impressed," Betina said. "He could have carried you off to the other side of the lake. We might never have seen you again."

He eyed them both, not sure of their point.

"You overreacted," Betina said in a loud whisper. "She could have handled him herself."

"Just doing my job."

"Sure you were," Betina told him with a wink. "You're not subtle. I'll give you that."

"Didn't know I was supposed to be."

Meri sighed. "While this is lovely, let's get on with the activity. You'll take people out with you and make sure they know what they're doing before setting them loose with the moving equivalent of a power tool, right?"

"Sure thing," surfer dude said.

Jack grabbed Meri by the hand and led her over to one of the Jet Skis. "You can go with me."

"Are you being all macho and take-charge? It's un-expected—but fun."

Now she was baiting him. Which was fair, he thought as he put on a life jacket, pushed the Jet Ski back into the lake, then straddled it. If she had been anyone else, he would have thought they were a good team. But he wasn't interested in being on a team, nor was he inter-ested in Meri. Not that way.

She stepped into the lake and shrieked. "It's cold."

"Snow runoff and a mile deep. What did you expect?"

"Eighty degrees. I'll freeze."

He gunned the Jet Ski. "You'll be fine. Hop on."

She slid behind him, put her feet on the running board and wrapped her arms around his waist.

When she was settled, he twisted the accelerator and they took off across the water.

They bounced through the wake of a boat, then settled onto smoother water. Meri leaned against him, her thighs nestling him. The image of her naked, hungry and ready filled his mind. For once, he didn't push it away. He let it stay there, arousing him, making him want to pull into shallow waters and make the fantasy real.

He didn't. Instead he headed back to the beach, where her friends were being shown the right way to board a Jet Ski.

There was also a new addition to the group. A dinghy had been pulled up on the beach, and Andrew stood slightly to the side, staring at Meri.

"How about something with a little more power?" he said, pointing to the twenty-five-foot boat anchored offshore.

She climbed off the Jet Ski and pulled off her life jacket.

"I need to stay here," she told him. "This was my idea."

Andrew glanced around. "The nerd brigade will be fine." He grabbed her hand. "Come on. It'll be fun."

Jack wanted to step between them the way he had with surfer dude. But this was different. This was the guy Meri thought she wanted to marry. And until he, Jack, had proof that Andrew was only in it for her money, he couldn't do a damn thing to stop her.

"Go ahead," he told her, consciously unclenching his jaw. "I'll take care of them."

"We don't need taking care of," Colin protested, then shrugged. "Okay. Maybe we do."

Meri looked at Jack. "Are you sure?"

"Go. We'll be fine."

She nodded slowly, helped Andrew push the dinghy back into the water, then climbed on board. Andrew started the engine and then they were gone.

Colin stared after them. "I hate it when he takes her away. It's never the same without her."

Jack hated that he wanted to agree.

Meri scraped the dishes into the garbage disposal, then stacked them on the counter by the sink. She was pleasantly full from the Mexican food they'd brought in for dinner and just slightly buzzed from the margarita. Hmm, her team had had liquor twice in a week. If she wasn't careful, they were going to get wild on her.

She smiled at the idea, then caught her breath as someone came up behind her and wrapped his arms around her waist. Her first thought was that it was Jack, who'd mostly ignored her all afternoon. But then she inhaled the scent and felt the pressure of the body behind her and knew it wasn't.

"Andrew," she said as she sidestepped his embrace. "Come to help me with the dishes?"

"No. You don't need to do that. Let someone else clean up."

"I don't mind. I was gone all afternoon."

"You say that like it's a bad thing. Didn't you have fun with me?"

"Sure."

They'd taken the boat to the middle of the lake, dropped anchor and enjoyed a light lunch in the sun, then stretched out for some sunbathing. What was there not to like?

She would ignore the fact that she'd kept watching the shore to see what was going on there. To make sure her friends were all right, she reminded herself. She hadn't been looking to see if Jack stuck around. Even though he had.

"Too bad about the cabin onboard," Andrew said.

"Uh-huh."

It had been small and cramped, and when Andrew had tried to take her down below, she'd nearly thrown up. The combination of confined spaces, movement on water and her tummy wasn't a happy one.

"Let's go have more fun," he said, reaching for her hand. "Back at my hotel."

She sidestepped him. "I need to stay here."

"Why?"

"I was gone all afternoon."

"They survived. Meredith, you're not their cruise director."

"I know, but I'm responsible for them."

"Why? They're adults."

True, but they were her team. "Look, I want to stay here."

He stared into her eyes. "How am I going to win you back if you refuse to be alone with me?"

An interesting point. Did she want to be won back?

Of course she did, she told herself. This was Andrew, the man she'd thought she might marry. She'd slept with Jack; she was over him and ready to move on with her life. She could emotionally engage now. Why not with Andrew?

"I have a great suite," he told her. "With a view. If you don't want to go back to my room, we could go to a casino and go gambling. You know how you like to play blackjack."

It was true. She didn't actually count cards, but she had a great memory and there were usually only a half dozen or so decks in play at any one time. How hard could it be to keep track of three hundred and twelve cards?

Jack walked into the kitchen. He smiled pleasantly at Andrew. "You're still here?"

Andrew stepped close to her. "Trying to get rid of me?"

"I'll let Meri do that herself." He turned to her. "We're about to play Truth or Dare. I know it's your favorite. Want to join us?"

"We're going to state line to the casinos," Andrew said.

Meri glanced between the two men. They were both great in their own ways. Different but great.

"I'm tired," she told Andrew. "I'd really like to stay in tonight."

His. expression tightened. "I'm not interested in hanging out here. I'll go to the casino without you."

She touched his arm. "You don't have to do that. You could stay."

He glanced toward the dining room, where she could hear Colin arguing theoretical equations.

"No, thanks," Andrew told her. He started for the door.

She turned to Jack. "This is all your fault."

"What did I do?"

She huffed out a breath, then hurried after Andrew.

"Don't be like this," she told him on the front porch.

"Like what? Interested in spending time with you alone? I haven't seen you in weeks. The last time we talked on the phone, you said everything was fine. But now I find out it isn't. Were we taking a break, Meredith, or were you trying to break up with me? If that's what you want, just say so."

She opened her mouth, then closed it. Andrew was perfect for her in so many ways. He was exactly the man she was looking for. Added to that was the fact that she'd had him investigated and there was nothing in his past to indicate he gave a damn about her inheritance. Men like that were hard to find.

Six months ago she'd been almost sure. So what was different now?

Stupid question, she thought. Jack was different. Being with Jack was supposed to make things more clear, and it hadn't.

"I'm not trying to break up with you," she told him. "I'm glad you're here. I just need some time to get used to us being a couple."

"Hard to do when we're apart."

"So stay."

"Come back to my hotel with me, Meredith."

"I can't."

"You won't."

She wouldn't. He was right.

"Andrew…"

He walked to his car. "I'll be back, Meredith. I think you're worth fighting for. The question you need to answer is, do you want me to keep trying?"

She watched him drive away. The front door opened and Betina stepped out next to her.

"Man trouble?" her friend asked.

"When does my romantic life flow smoothly?"

"Practically never. You're always interesting, I'll grant you that. So what has his panties in a snit?"

Meri looked at her. "You never liked him. Why is that?"

"I don't mind him. I think he's too impressed with himself. But he's good to you and he passed your rigorous inspection, so that's all I need to know."

"But you don't like him."

"Do I have to?" Betina asked.

Meri shrugged. "Do you like Jack?"

"Are you doing a comparison?"

"No. I'm just curious."

Betina considered the question. "Yes, I like Jack."

"Me, too." Meri held up her hand. "Don't you dare start in on me that you knew I would fall for him, blah, blah, blah. I haven't fallen for him. It's just different now."

"What are you going to do about it?"

"Nothing. Jack and I are friends. The bigger question is, what do I want from Andrew?"

"How are you going to figure that out?"

"I haven't got a clue."

She followed Betina back inside, where everyone sat around on the oversize sofas. Two bowls filled with pieces of paper stood in the middle of the coffee table. They would be the "truth" and "dare" parts of the game.

Meri had learned not to mess with dare with this group. Not when they wanted things like mathematical proof that the universe existed. Answering personal, probably embarrassing questions was a whole lot easier.

As Jack was new to the game, they let him go first.

He pulled out a question and read it aloud. "Have you ever gone to a convention in any kind of costume?"

He frowned and turned to her. "This is as wild as you guys get?"

She laughed. "It's not a big deal for you, but—trust me—there are people in this room with guilty *Star Trek* secrets."

Jack put down the paper. "No."

Colin groaned. "You weren't supposed to get that question."

"Which means there's another one in the bowl about doing it with twins," Meri told him with a grin.

She reached into the bowl and pulled out a paper. "Have you ever been stood up?"

The room seemed to tilt slightly. She remembered being eighteen, wearing her prettiest dress, although a size eighteen on her small frame was anything but elegant. She'd had her hair done, actually put on makeup and gone to the restaurant to meet a guy from her physics lab. She'd waited for two hours and he'd never shown up.

The next day he'd acted as if nothing had happened. She'd never had the courage to ask if he'd forgotten or done it on purpose or for sport.

Jack leaned over and grabbed the paper from her. "She's not answering the question. This is a stupid game."

"I don't mind," she told him.

"I do. I'll tell them about the twins."

All the guys leaned forward. "For real?" Robert asked. "Twins?"

She shook her head. "Jack, it's okay."

"It's not. What happened is private."

What happened? How could he know she'd been stood up? He'd been gone for months. Actually, the nondate had gotten her to think about changing. She'd joined a gym the next day.

She started to tell him that, then found she couldn't speak. Her throat was all closed, as if she had a cold…or was going to cry. What was wrong with her?

"Excuse me," she said and ducked out of the room. She hurried into the kitchen to get a glass of water.

It was stress, she told herself. There was too much going on.

She heard footsteps and turned to find Colin entering the room.

"You okay?" he asked. "I'm sorry about the question. It wasn't for you. I was hoping Betina would get it."

Something inside Meri snapped. "I've had it with you," she said. "Look, you're a grown single man interested in a woman who obviously thinks you're hot. For heaven's sake, do something about it."

He opened his mouth, then closed it. "I can't."

"Then you don't deserve her."

# Nine

Meri needed coffee more than she needed air. It had been another long night but not for any fun reasons. She'd tossed and turned, not sure what to do with her life—something she hadn't wrestled with in years.

She was supposed to have things together by now. She was supposed to know her heart as well as she knew her head. Or did being so damned smart mean she was destined to be stupid in other ways?

The coffee had barely begun to pour through the filter when someone rang the doorbell. She hadn't seen anyone else up yet so she walked to the front door and opened it.

Andrew stood on the porch. He held a single red rose in one hand and a stuffed bright-green monkey in the other.

"It's possible I behaved badly yesterday," he said

with a shrug. "More than possible. I want things to work between us."

She didn't know what to say. While she was relieved to not be fighting, she wasn't exactly in the mood to throw herself into his arms. Which meant that there was a whole lot more for them to deal with.

"Andrew, this is really confusing for me," she said. "You're right. We were apart too long. Things have changed."

"Is there someone else?"

"No," she said without thinking, then had to wonder if that was true.

Not Jack, she told herself. Okay, yes, they'd gotten intimate, but just the one time and nothing since. He was her past. The problem was Andrew might not be her future.

He handed her the monkey. "I brought you this. I thought it would make you smile."

She took the ridiculous stuffed toy. "He's adorable. What about the rose?"

"That's for me. I plan to wear it in my teeth."

He bit down on the stem, which made her laugh. Andrew always made her laugh. Wasn't that a good thing? Shouldn't she want to be with him?

"You want some coffee?" she asked. "I have a pot going."

"Sure." He took a step inside, then grimaced as his cell phone rang. "Sorry. I'm dealing with some stuff at work. Give me ten minutes?"

She nodded and stepped inside. Still carrying the monkey, she returned to the kitchen. Only this time she wasn't alone. Colin stood pouring coffee. He wore jeans, an unbuttoned shirt and nothing else. But it wasn't his unusual outfit that got her attention. Instead there was something about the way he stood. Something in the tilt of his head or the set of his shoulders.

"Colin?"

He turned and smiled at her. "Morning."

A single word but in a voice she'd never heard from him. It was low and confident. He was a man at peace with himself and the universe.

She felt her mouth drop open. "You had sex with Betina."

Colin didn't even blush. "It wasn't sex, Meri. It was making love. And, yes, we did. She's amazing. She's the woman I've been waiting for all my life."

With that, he collected two cups of coffee and carried them back to his room.

Meri laughed out loud. She set the monkey on the counter, then turned to find someone to share the good news with.

But she was alone in the kitchen, so she ran upstairs, taking them two at a time, then burst into Jack's office. He was on the phone but hung up when he saw her.

"You look happy," he said. "So it's not bad news."

"I know. It's fabulous. I saw Colin. He's someone completely different. He and Betina slept together and I think they're seriously in love. Isn't that fabulous? Are you jazzed?"

One corner of Jack's mouth turned up. "Good for Colin. I didn't think he had it in him."

"Oh, there was a tiger lurking behind those silly plaid shirts. And we're a part of it. We got them together."

Jack held up his hands in the shape of a T. "There's no 'we' in all this. They got themselves together."

"Don't be silly. We pushed. And I mean *we*. You were a part of it. You acted like a matchmaker. I'm so proud."

He groaned. "Leave me out of it."

She crossed to the window, then turned back to face him. "This is great. They may get married. We can go hang out at the wedding and take all the credit."

"I don't think so."

She wrinkled her nose. "You're not getting in the spirit of this. It's happy news."

She spun in a circle, holding her arms out and tilting back her head. Soon the room was turning and turning. She lost her balance and started to fall. Which should have worried her, except Jack was there to catch her.

She collapsed against him, then smiled up into his face. He had the most amazing eyes, she thought absently, then she dropped her gaze to his mouth. That part of him wasn't so bad either.

"You need to slow down," he told her.

"No way. Light speed isn't fast enough."

"You'll get hurt."

What were they talking about? She found she didn't know and she sort of didn't care. Not as long as he held her.

"Jack," she breathed.

He released her and stepped back. "Meri, this isn't a good idea."

Then it hit her. She'd run to Jack instead of Andrew.

That couldn't be good. Had Betina been right all along? Had there been more on the line that getting revenge or closure or any of the other reasons she'd given herself for wanting to sleep with Jack? Dear God, what had she done?

"I have to go," she whispered and hurried out of the room. She ran all the way to her bedroom, then closed the door behind her and leaned against it. Where did she go from here?

Jack poured coffee. As he raised his mug, Colin walked into the kitchen.

Meri was right—there was something different about the guy. An air of confidence. He wasn't just a nerd anymore.

The love of a good woman, Jack thought humorously. Apparently the old saying about it being able to transform a man was true. Lucky for him, he'd escaped.

"How's it going?" Colin asked.

"Good. With you?"

"Great."

"No one seems to be talking trash in the dining room today," Jack said.

"Meri gave us the day off."

Probably to ensure that Betina and Colin spent more time together. It was just like her.

"Andrew was here before," Colin said.

"What happened?"

"Something with his office. He had to leave."

"You sound relieved."

Colin shrugged. "He's not my favorite."

"Mine either."

They were an interesting group, these scientists, Jack thought. Brilliant and humble, funny, determined and willing to make fools of themselves on Jet Skis. They looked out for Meri. Hunter would have liked them a lot.

"What?" Colin asked. "You have a strange look on your face."

"I was thinking about Meri's brother. He would have liked you. All of you."

"Meri talks about him. He sounds like a great guy."

"He was. A group of us became friends in college. We called ourselves the Seven Samurai. It was dumb but meaningful to us. Hunter was the connection we all had with each other. He brought us together. Held us together."

Then he'd died and they'd drifted apart.

Jack thought about his friends—something he didn't usually allow himself to do—and wondered how they'd enjoyed their months in Hunter's house. Had their worlds been flipped around and changed or had the weeks passed quietly?

"It's good to have friends like that," Colin said. "Meri's a lot like him. She draws people together. Gets them involved. She handpicked the team for this project. They let her do that because she's so brilliant."

Jack nodded. Meri's brain was never in question. "She's more outgoing than she used to be."

"She's grown up. It's hard for us, the freaks." Colin grinned. "That's what she calls us and herself. We all had to deal with not fitting in and stuff. Meri wants us to put that aside and deal with life as it is. Look forward. That sort of thing."

There was affection in his voice, but not the romantic

kind, so Jack didn't have to kill him. He realized that the reports might have told him the specifics but they hadn't allowed him to get to know the woman she'd become.

"I was thinking about your business," Colin said. "There's some new military software that could help with your security issues."

"Military software? Is it classified?"

Colin grinned. "Sure, but I know the guy who wrote it. There's a couple of beta versions floating around. I might be able to get you a copy to test out—you know, as a service to your government."

"Lucky me." Jack eyed the other man. "You're a lot more dangerous than you look."

Colin grinned. "I know.

"Left foot green," Betina called.

Meri looked down at the Twister sheet on the floor and groaned. "I'm not built to bend that way."

"The very reason I don't try to play the game. But so not the point."

"You're basically mean," Meri muttered. "I don't know why I didn't see that before. Sorry, Robert. I'm going to have to slide under you."

Robert arched his back as best he could. "Good luck with that. You do realize you're in danger of hyperextending your shoulder."

Colin looked up from his awkward position. "I'm not sure she would hyperextend it. Technically speaking—"

"Stop!" Meri yelled. "I don't want any technical talk right now. Let's pretend to be normal."

Colin and Robert both frowned at her. "Why?"

She started laughing, which made bending and stretching impossible. But she still tried, because the big green dot was just out of—

She wobbled, leaned, then collapsed, bringing everyone down with her. She landed on Robert, and Colin sank down on top of her.

"I'm not sure I approve of this," Betina said from the sidelines. "Colin, do we need to talk about fidelity?"

"Not really." He grunted as he rolled off Meri, then scrambled to his feet. "Unless you want to spank me."

Meri gagged. "I so did not want to know that about you two."

"I'm surprised," Robert said from his place on the floor. "Usually men who enjoy domination have powerful positions in their work life. It's an attempt to obtain balance and let someone else take responsibility."

Meri looked at him. "Is there anything you don't know?"

"How to get the girl. Any girl."

"We'll talk later," Meri said, offering her hand and helping him to his feet. "I'm on a roll. Are you interested in anyone in particular?"

Before he could answer, Jack walked into the room. There was something about his expression that warned Meri he didn't have good news.

"What's wrong?" she asked. "Is someone hurt?"

"No, but we need to talk."

He took her arm and led her into the kitchen. She didn't like anything about this.

After folding her arms over her chest she said, "So talk."

His dark eyes were unreadable. "Andrew isn't who you think."

She'd thought maybe her father had been in an accident or had a heart attack. But Andrew?

"Not who I think? You mean like secretly a woman?"

"I'm serious, Meri. I have some information on him. His background. He's not the man he's pretending to be. He's in it for the money."

A thousand different thoughts flashed through her brain. At any other time she would have paused to marvel at the exquisite structure of the human mind—of how it could hold so many contradictory ideas at any single moment. But right now all she cared about was being strong enough to punch Jack in the stomach.

"What the hell are you going on about?" she asked, her voice low and cold. "Why would you know anything about Andrew?"

"I had him investigated."

Anger burned hot and bright. "You have no right to get involved in my personal life. Who do you think you are?"

"I know you're upset—"

"Upset? You have no idea. Dammit, Jack, this is wrong on so many levels." She glanced toward the door to the living room and lowered her voice. "Just because we slept together doesn't mean you get to tell me what to do. You gave up that right the day you walked out on me after Hunter died. You were supposed to be there for me and you weren't. So I don't care what you think about anything."

She started to walk away. He grabbed her arm and held her in place.

"You have to listen to me," he said.

"No, I don't. Not that it matters, but I already had Andrew investigated. Thoroughly. He's clean. He comes from a comfortable background. He doesn't have my trust fund, but he's not hurting for money. He's a good man."

"He's married."

Her entire body went cold. She knew intellectually that her core temperature was what it had been five seconds ago, but the sensation of being on the verge of turning to ice was incredibly real.

"You're wrong," she breathed. "My investigator—"

"Did exactly what I did the first time I learned about Andrew. A basic investigation. That's usually good enough. But when you said you were thinking of marrying this guy, I had my people dig deeper. It was eight years ago. They hooked up and conned an old man out of about two million dollars. Three years ago, they took another heiress for the same amount. I'm guessing you were their next target."

She couldn't deal with the news about Andrew, so she turned on Jack. "You dug into his background? What gives you the right?"

"Someone has to look out for you. Your father is useless. With Hunter gone, there was only me." His gaze was steady. "I couldn't do what Hunter asked—I couldn't stay in your life. I was too destroyed by what had happened. Still, I had a responsibility to look out for you. So I did. From a distance."

"You spied on me?"

"Call it what you want. I made sure you didn't get into trouble."

He'd paid people to watch her? To poke into her private life? But he'd never cared enough to get involved himself?

"Bastard," she breathed and raised her hand to slap him.

He grabbed her by the wrist and held her still. "It was for your own good."

"That's a load of crap. You were trying to assuage your guilt by doing the least you could. You weren't a good friend to my brother and you sure as hell weren't a friend to me. You don't get to do this, Jack. You aren't running my life. I'll marry Andrew if I want and you can't stop me."

"Bigamy is illegal in all fifty states."

Andrew—married? She couldn't believe it. He might not be the handsome prince she'd first imagined, but married?

"He's not playing me," she insisted even as she wondered if he was.

"How do you know? At least look at the report. Then make your own decision."

There was nothing to look at, she thought sadly as she pulled her hand free of his grip. Nothing to consider. She wasn't in love with Andrew. She'd been fighting that truth since he'd shown up here. Their time apart had demonstrated that big-time. She hadn't missed him.

Had she ever been in love with him? Did it matter? If he was married and playing her, then he was nothing but a weasel.

"Your gender sucks," she muttered.

"I agree."

"You most of all. I will never forgive you for spying on me. For spending the last eleven years hiding in the shadows."

"I cared about what happened to you."

"Is that what you call it? I would say you were nothing more than a coward trying to quiet a ghost. But I know my brother. I know Hunter would never stop haunting you. He expected more, Jack. And so did I."

# Ten

Meri lay on her bed facedown, fighting tears. Betina sat next to her, lightly rubbing her back.

"I can't believe it," Meri said into her pillow. "I can't believe he did that."

Betina patted her shoulder. "*I* can't believe I have to ask, but who are we talking about? Andrew or Jack?"

"Both of them," Meri muttered, then rolled onto her back and wiped away her tears. "That's my current life. I have two men betraying me."

She could say the words, but she didn't believe them. She couldn't believe any of this. How had everything gone so wrong?

Betina sighed. "I'm shocked by what Jack found out about Andrew. Do you believe him?"

Meri nodded. "He wouldn't lie about that. He said

Andrew and his wife had a whole scam going. I'm not sure what his plan was with me. He couldn't have married me, and I wouldn't have given him money for anything."

Although, now that she thought about it, he had mentioned a few investment opportunities right before she'd left.

Her stomach hurt from all the emotional churning.

"I thought about marrying him," she admitted. "When I found the ring, I knew he was going to propose and I thought about saying yes."

"You didn't."

"He didn't ask. I don't know what would have happened. Maybe he was planning to propose, then tell me I had to pay off his wife so he could get a divorce." She shuddered. "It's awful. I slept with him. I slept with a married man. I would never do that."

"You didn't know. He tricked you. You're the innocent party in all this."

Meri didn't feel very innocent. She felt dirty and gross and confused.

"I liked him," she said. "I don't know if I ever really loved Andrew, but I liked him. Shouldn't I have known? Shouldn't I have sensed something wasn't right?"

Betina shook her head. "Why? He set out to deceive you. You're a decent person who accepts people for who and what they are. You did a regular background check on him and it came back clean."

"I'm never using that investigation agency again," Meri said. "I wonder if Andrew found out the name of the guy and bought him off."

"Very possibly."

"I hate Andrew."

"No, you don't."

Meri wiped away more tears. "I don't. I can't care enough about him to hate him. I feel disgusted and I'm sick that I let myself get played. That's what hurts about him. That he used me and I was too stupid to recognize what was going on. I hate being stupid."

"No one is smart all the time. Meri, it's awful. It sucks big-time. But here's the thing—you escaped Andrew relatively unscathed. Nothing bad happened. The only thing hurt is your pride, and not even very much at that."

Meri knew her friend was right. Still, memories of all the time she spent with Andrew flashed through her head.

"I introduced him to my friends. You guys never liked him. I should have paid attention to that."

"We have amazing insight. What can I say?"

Meri started to laugh, but the sound turned into a sob. She rolled onto her side.

"Jack was spying on me. He watched me from a distance. He never cared enough to even take me to lunch, damn him. How could he do that? It's gross and creepy."

It was more than that. It was painful to think that Jack would keep his word to Hunter enough to pay others to keep tabs on her but that he didn't care enough to do it himself.

"He was wrong to act like that," Betina said soothingly.

Meri raised his head. "You're going to defend him, aren't you? You're going to say he did the best he could with what he had. You're going to say he was hurting, too, that he blamed himself for Hunter's death. He does, you know. Blame himself. Hunter had melanoma. He saw this weird black thing on his shoulder and wanted to go to the doctor. Jack teased him about being a girl and worrying about nothing."

"That can't be easy to live with."

Meri sniffed. "Statistically, getting the diagnosis a few weeks earlier wouldn't have made any difference in the end. Hunter was going to die. Not that Jack would care about that. He would still blame himself, because that's who he is."

"I don't have to defend him," Betina told her. "You're doing it for me."

"I'm not. He's a low-life who cared only about himself. I was totally alone. My mother was dead, my father is possibly the most emotionally useless man on the planet. I was seventeen. I had no one. No friends, no family to speak of. I was alone in the world and he abandoned me."

"He should have stayed," Betina said. "He should have stayed and taken care of you. I wonder why he didn't."

"Guilt," Meri said with a sigh. "Guilt about Hunter and maybe guilt about me. About how he handled things." Betina knew all about Meri's pathetic attempt to seduce Jack years ago and how badly he'd reacted.

"He was twenty-one and nowhere near grown-up enough to be responsible for a seventeen-year-old with a crush on him. So he left and I had to deal on my own."

"You did a hell of a job," her friend told her. "Hunter would be proud."

Meri considered that. "He wouldn't like my plan to get revenge on Jack."

"Brothers rarely enjoy thinking about their sisters having sex with anyone."

That made Meri almost smile. "You don't approve of it either."

"I don't approve one way or the other. I'm worried about you. I think you wanted to sleep with Jack for a lot of reasons, and none of them have anything to do with punishing him."

"You think I'm still in love with him."

"It would explain a lot."

Meri rolled onto her back and stared up at the ceiling. In love with Jack. Was it possible? The way her personal life was going, it made sense. He'd spent the last ten years doing the least he could justify when it came to her, and she might have spent the same amount of time desperate to give her heart to him.

Jack was staring at his computer screen when Colin walked into his office.

"What's up?" he asked.

"You hurt Meri," Colin said. "That's not right. You can't be so insensitive that you wouldn't know how much the information about Andrew would bother her. Not to mention the fact that someone she respected and thought of as a friend had been spying on her."

"You're not telling me anything I don't already know," Jack told him.

Colin moved closer to the desk. "That's not good enough."

Was Colin trying to intimidate him? Jack didn't think it was possible, but Colin was a changed man since his night with Betina.

"She had to learn the truth about Andrew. She said

things were getting serious. Andrew could have taken her for a lot of money."

"It's not about the money," Colin told him. "It's about trust and caring and being there for someone. She expected more of you, and you let her down."

Small words. Unimportant words, yet they made their point, Jack thought grimly.

"I was trying to protect her," he said, knowing it wasn't enough of an answer.

"There were a lot of different ways to do that. Did you have to pick one that hurt?"

"How the hell was I supposed to tell her the truth about Andrew without hurting her?"

"I'm not talking about Andrew."

Jack nodded slowly. "You're right. I should have thought through telling her that I'd been keeping an eye on her. I did it for her own good."

"No one believes that. You did what was easy, and that's not allowed. You can't go around hurting people like that. It's wrong. Meri matters to me, and I'm going to protect her—even from you."

Jack stood. He was a good half head taller than Colin and about thirty pounds of muscle heavier. He wanted to tell himself that Colin's threats were pitiful. The man couldn't hurt him if he were armed and Jack was unconscious. But he was oddly touched by Colin's bravery in the face of certain defeat. The man took care of the people who mattered, no matter what it might cost him personally.

"It wasn't my intention to hurt Meri," Jack said slowly. "But I'm going to have to do it again."

Colin narrowed his gaze. "What do you mean?"

"I'm going to make Andrew go away."

Colin nodded slowly. "I'd like to be there when that happens."

Andrew's hotel room overlooked the lake. All the right trappings were there—the computer, the lobbying magazines. He looked the part and he played it well. He'd fooled a lot of people.

"This is a surprise," Andrew said as he held open the door, a tacit invitation to Jack and Colin. "To what do I owe this honor?"

"I'm here to run you out of town," Jack said, his voice calm and pleasant. "Colin's going to watch."

Nothing about Andrew's expression changed. "I have no idea what you're talking about."

"Sure you do. I don't know how you passed the preliminary background check. Maybe you're that good at covering your tracks. You might have paid off Meri's investigator, although you couldn't have paid off mine. So I'll give you credit for creating a good front."

Andrew sat on the sofa across from the small fireplace. He waved at the two chairs opposite.

"I'll stand," Jack said.

"Me, too," Colin told him.

"As you prefer," Andrew said. "I have to tell you, this is all fascinating. So what do you think you've found out about me?"

"That you're married. That you and your wife con people for money. You know Meri is worth nearly a billion dollars. She must have been a hell of a prize for the two of you."

Andrew's expression never changed. "I have no idea what you're talking about. I've never been married."

"I have copies of the certificate in the car. Do I have to send Colin to get it? I also have the police statements from the people you two duped. Lucky for you, you didn't break any actual laws. It's not a crime to be stupid."

"You have me confused with someone else," Andrew said calmly. "I care about Meredith. We've been dating for a long time. The relationship is serious. As for your ridiculous claims, ask her yourself. I've never once talked to her about money."

"It was all just a matter of time until you did. Or it would have been."

Andrew was a pro—Jack would give him credit for that. But he was still a rat rooting in garbage.

"It's all just your word against mine," Andrew said. "I'm assuming you told Meredith all this?"

Jack nodded.

"She won't believe you."

"You sound confident," Jack said. "Funny she hasn't phoned you."

"She will."

Would she? Was she mad enough at Jack to want to get back with Andrew? How far would she take things?

He didn't have an answer, so he did the only thing he could think of to protect her.

"How much?" he asked. "Give me a number."

Andrew smiled. "You want to pay me off."

"If that's what it takes. How much?"

The other man hesitated, and in that moment Jack knew he'd been right. If Andrew had been who he claimed, he would have refused any payment.

"Ten million," Andrew said. "Ten million and I'll sign anything you want."

"Five million and you'll still sign."

Andrew smiled. "Done."

Twenty minutes later Jack and Colin were back in Jack's car.

"You paid him off," Colin said. "I thought you'd just beat the crap out of him and be done with it."

"That would have been my preference. But he's good at what he does. He could have gone back to Meri and convinced her I was the jerk in all this. This way, she'll never want him back. He can't ever hurt her."

He had a copy of the check he'd written to Andrew, along with a signed letter saying Andrew was freely taking the money in exchange for never seeing Meri again. Just to be safe, Jack had insisted on a thumbprint under the signature.

"So it's done," Colin said. "She's safe."

"It's not done," Jack told him. "Now I have to tell her what happened."

The house was quiet when they returned. Colin disappeared downstairs, probably to fill Betina in on what had happened. The nerd brigade hadn't shown up for work, which had probably been previously arranged to give Meri some time alone. Better for him, he thought.

He walked up the stairs to the bedroom level and

walked to her closed door. After knocking, he pushed it open.

She'd pulled a chair over to the window. She sat curled up in the chair, staring out at the lake.

"Go away," she said without looking at him.

"How do you know I'm not Betina or Colin?"

"I recognized your footsteps."

"Not my 'foul stench?'"

She turned to look at him. Her face was pale, her eyes red and swollen. "Don't you dare quote *Star Wars* to me, Jack. You haven't the right."

She was hurt. He could see it, but worse, he could feel it. Her pain was a tangible creature in the room. It didn't attack him. Instead it lived and breathed, reminding him that he'd let her down…again.

"We have to talk," he told her.

"No, thanks. I have nothing to say to you."

"That's okay. I'll do the talking. You just listen."

She shrugged, then turned her head back so she was facing the window. He didn't know if she was looking out or not. He had a feeling she was crying, which made him feel like crap.

"Andrew's gone," he said.

"Let me guess. You bought him off."

"I didn't trust him to leave any other way."

"And you didn't trust me to be able to resist him? Do you think he's that charming or that I'm that weak?"

"You're pissed at me. I didn't know how far you'd go to punish me."

She drew her knees to her chest. "I wouldn't give myself to a man who lied to me or tried to play me. You're not worth that."

"I wasn't sure."

"How much?"

He could have lied. He could have said there wasn't money involved. But he wanted to be honest with her.

"Five million."

She didn't react. "I'll have my accountant send you a check."

"You don't need to pay me back. I wanted to keep you safe. That's what I've always wanted."

"Because of your promise to Hunter?"

"Yes."

"But not because of me."

He didn't know what she was asking so he couldn't respond. She looked at him again.

"How many others have you paid off?" she asked. "How many other times have you gotten involved in my life?"

"Twice before."

She sucked in a breath. "The ones who just disappeared? Who broke up with me for no reason?"

"I guess. I wasn't involved in the details."

She stood and faced him. "Of course not. Why would you bother when you have a staff? It must have been desperately uncomfortable to be so close now. Distance makes things tidy. You don't have to deal with emotion."

She put both her hands flat on his chest and shoved him hard. He didn't move.

"Damn you," she cried. "I hate this. Do you know how

much I hate this? I wasn't even a person to you. I was a project. You couldn't be bothered to get involved yourself."

"It wasn't like that. I wanted you to be safe. I didn't want you with the wrong guy."

"And you know who that is?"

"Yes."

She dropped her arms to her sides, then stared up at him with tears in her eyes. "So who's the right guy? Or does he exist?"

"I don't know."

"It's not you."

She wasn't asking a question, but he answered it anyway. "No. I'm not him."

"Just the devil?"

"I'm not that bad."

"You are to me," she said and turned away. "You shouldn't have done it, Jack. It's a zero-sum game. All or nothing. You can't hide in the middle. Hunter would be disappointed, and so am I. It would have been better to just disappear. At least that would have been honest. I could have respected that."

"I don't need your respect," he said, then realized that maybe he did. For some reason, Meri's opinion mattered. As did Hunter's.

He started to leave, then paused at the door. "I didn't know how to be there for you, Meri. I didn't know how to look at you from across Hunter's grave and tell you I was sorry. I didn't know how to be what you needed. So, yeah, I left. But you were never alone. I was always looking out for you."

"That wasn't much consolation when I sat by myself

in a dorm room on Christmas Eve, with nowhere else to go," she said. "And it was more than feeling guilty about Hunter's death. You hated that I had a crush on you."

He thought about that afternoon when she'd turned seventeen and had cried her heart out.

"I didn't know how to help. I couldn't be the guy you wanted me to be."

Her mouth twisted. "Tell the truth, Jack. You couldn't stand me because I was fat and ugly."

Her pain had grown until it threatened to suck all the air out of the room. He felt it and ached for her. He'd always had a rule of never letting anyone get close. Never letting anyone see the truth about him—not the emptiness of his heart or the darkness of his soul.

He walked over and grabbed her arms, forcing her to face him. "Did it occur to you that I liked you a lot? That I saw the woman you would become and knew that I would never measure up? Did you ever once think that by letting Hunter down I knew I'd lost both of you forever?"

Tears filled her eyes. "Don't be cruel. Don't pretend I mattered."

"You did matter. We were friends. Could there have been more as you'd gotten older? I always thought so. Until it was impossible because of what I'd done. I let him down. I let you down. I knew it and I couldn't face either of you."

He turned away and walked to the door. "I lied to you before. About Hunter. I think about him every damn day."

He reached for the door handle but instead felt something warm. Somehow Meri had gotten in front of him. She touched his face, his shoulders, his chest.

"Jack, you have to let it go. You didn't do anything wrong. Hunter would never want you to suffer like this."

"I don't know how else to make it right," he admitted.

"So you're going to punish yourself forever?"

He nodded slowly.

"You're right," she whispered. "I am the bright one in this relationship." Then she leaned in and kissed him.

He told himself to resist. That being with her was the last thing he had the right to do. But her mouth was soft and insistent, and her hands urged him forward. She was beautiful and caring and sexy and smart. How was he supposed to resist her?

She touched her tongue to his bottom lip, then nipped at his flesh. Fire shot through him. Fire and need and the knowledge that for a few minutes he could forget the past and live only in the present.

"You're a hard man to convince," she murmured as she grabbed his hand and placed it on her breast.

He caressed the curve. "But at least I'm hard."

# Eleven

Meri laughed softly as Jack swept her into his arms, then carried her to the bed. He set her down, bent over her and kissed her with a hot need that made her want to forget everything but the moment, the man and how he made her feel.

His mouth was firm, his tongue insistent. He touched her everywhere, his hands tugging at clothing, pulling it off until she was naked. He stroked her body, caressing her bare skin, arousing her with a quick touch of her breast, fingers teasing the curve of her hip, dipping between her legs, then moving away.

It was like being attacked by a sensual, marauding beast who took what he wanted in sneak attacks. A tickle at the back of her thighs, a quick lick on her nipple, a puff of hot breath against her neck. Over and over he touched her, then moved on before she could get lost in the moment.

She writhed beneath him for several minutes, alternately laughing, then moaning. She finally drew him to a stop by wrapping her legs around his hips and holding him in place on top of her.

He braced himself above her, his dark eyes bright with passion, his mouth tempting.

"You're playing with me," she murmured.

One corner of his mouth turned up. "Tell me you don't like it."

"I can't."

"Meredith."

He breathed her name like a prayer. The sound caught her off guard, seeping inside of her, making her strain toward him. But for what? Sexual release? Or something far more dangerous?

Before she could decide, he bent down and kissed her. She parted for him, welcoming the stroke of his tongue and the arousal his touch brought. She reached between them and tugged at his shirt. She unfastened the buttons and he shrugged it off.

His jeans went next, and his briefs. He'd walked in barefoot. When he was as naked as she, he leaned toward her nightstand and opened the drawer. The condoms she'd bought were under the book she'd been reading.

But instead of putting one on, he dropped the protection on the corner of the nightstand, then shifted onto his side. He bent down and took her right breast in his mouth, at the same time reaching between her thighs to tease the most sensitive part of her.

She parted her legs and tried to catch her breath as he explored her swollen center, then dipped inside. He mimicked the act of love with his fingers before easing up to that one important spot and circling it.

He rubbed her gently, then harder and faster. He moved so he was kissing her mouth, even as he continued to touch her there. Around and around, taking her higher with each stroke, keeping ahead of her somehow, so she was the one chasing him. Chasing the sensations that made her body tense and promised a release that would shatter her world.

She tried to catch her breath, but there was a tightness in her chest that made it hard to breathe. The closer she got, the more her heart seemed to squeeze until, as she reached the point of no return, the pain gave way.

She shattered, both inside and out. Her orgasm claimed her in a rush that erased every thought in her head but one: she loved Jack.

Through the waves of pleasure, that single truth grew until she wondered how she'd ever convinced herself otherwise. Of course she loved him. She'd loved him from the first moment she'd met him and for all the eleven years they'd been apart. She'd never loved anyone else.

Her body slowed and relaxed, but not her mind. Not even when he put on the condom, then eased between her legs and filled her until she knew she was going to come again.

He made love to her with a steady rhythm designed to spin her into madness, and she went willingly, wanting to get lost in the sensation.

But the feel of his body on hers wasn't enough to clear her mind. Nor were the waves of release, the heat, the sound of his gasps for air or the pounding of *his* heart.

Meri clung to him for as long as he would let her, holding him close, wanting time to stand still. If only she could believe that was possible. But it wasn't. She knew enough about the universe to know all things were in motion—at their most basic level. That nothing was static.

Which meant, in time, with luck, her pain would fade. Because the other thing she knew down to the cellular level was that Jack would never love her back.

Jack breathed in the scent of Meri's body as he stroked her face. She was so beautiful. She'd always been beautiful.

He slid off her so he wouldn't snap a rib, then propped his head up on his hand and wondered what the hell he was supposed to say. What happened now?

She sat up and reached for her clothes.

"Where are you going?" he asked. "An appointment?"

He smiled as he spoke, but when she looked at him, his smile faded. There was something wrong—he could see it in her blue eyes.

"What?" he asked.

"I have to go."

"Where?"

"Away. We both know this is not what you want or need. You've never been the guy to settle down. I don't know if you can't or you won't. Some of it is your guilt over Hunter and some of it is…honestly I don't have a clue what it is."

She blinked several times, then swallowed. "I can't stay with you, Jack."

He hadn't thought about her leaving until she said she had to, and now he didn't want her to go.

She scrambled out of the bed and pulled on her clothes. "This is crazy. All of it. I don't know what I was thinking. I had this great plan. Betina warned me, but did I listen? And I'm supposed to be the smart one."

"What are you talking about?"

She slid on her T-shirt, then looked at him. "You have to stop it, Jack. You're not allowed to spy on me anymore. I know you'd call it looking after me. Whatever it is, you have to stop. I'm a grown woman and I can take care of myself. If there are mistakes to be made, then I'll make them. Stop protecting me."

"I don't want to."

"This isn't about you."

He didn't understand. They'd just made love. It had been great. So why was she leaving? And when the hell had it gotten so cold in this room?

"Just like that?" he asked, getting angry because it was easy and something he could understand.

She slipped her feet into her sandals. "Just like that. Goodbye, Jack."

Then she was gone.

He stared at the door. What was going on? What had just happened? She couldn't leave. Not like this.

He swore, then scooped up his clothes and put them on. He had no idea what she wanted that she hadn't gotten. Was she still pissed about Andrew? About the fact that he, Jack, had watched out for her?

She should be grateful, he told himself as he stalked up the stairs to his office. He'd taken care of her. He'd kept her safe. That had to be worth something. She was just too stubborn to admit it.

Still angry, he opened his computer and did his damnedest to get lost in work. It was the only safe place he could think to go.

Meri burst into Betina's room without knocking. It was only after she heard scrambling that she realized she might have interrupted something.

"I'm sorry," she said, turning away. She hadn't seen anything—the tears had blinded her.

"Wait," Betina said. "You don't have to go."

"I'm in the way."

"You're not."

Her friend grabbed her and pulled her close. Meri went willingly, needing the support. She had a vague impression of her friend in a robe and a guy hovering in the background, then the tears began again.

"What happened?" Betina asked as she stroked Meri's hair. "What did Jack say?"

"Nothing. He didn't have to. I get it. I've been so stupid. You were right about everything. I didn't want revenge or closure. I'm in love with him. I have been for years. He's the reason I can't seem to commit to anyone else. I love him. I was afraid to admit that, so I came here with my crazy idea of showing him. I think I secretly thought he'd take one look at the new and improved me and be struck by lightning or something."

Meri sank onto the floor and let the tears flow. She

hurt so much. It felt as if someone had cracked open her chest and ripped out her heart.

"How can I be so smart and so stupid at the same time?" she asked.

"Because you're human and no one is smart when it comes to matters of the heart."

Made sense, she thought, wishing it were a year from now and the pain had lessened. Not that she expected it ever to go away. She had a bad feeling she would love Jack forever.

"He doesn't want me," she whispered. "He never did. I thought it was about the age difference or how I looked, but now I'm not so sure. I think maybe it was just me."

Which made it hurt. She couldn't change who she was any more than she already had. He didn't want the very essence of her being. What else was left?

"He's an idiot," Betina murmured.

"No. He's just a man who can't pretend to be in love with me." Meri sucked in a breath. "I have to go. I can't stay here. We'll need to regroup somewhere else. Maybe down south. Pasadena or something."

"Don't worry about it. Do you want me to go with you?"

Meri managed a smile as she looked at her friend. "No. I want you to stay with Colin and be in love for the both of us."

Jack worked until dark. When he finally realized he couldn't see anything other than his computer screen anymore, he stood and stretched. It was only then he noticed the silence of the house.

Uneasiness slipped through him as he went down-stairs and pushed open the door to Meri's room.

The furniture was exactly as he remembered—with the exception of the bed. Someone had stripped off the sheets and left the blankets neatly folded. The closet was empty, as were the drawers. She was gone.

He raced down to the main floor, where he found Betina packing up the notes from the dining room.

"What are you doing?" he demanded.

"Leaving." She didn't bother to look at him.

"All of you?"

She nodded. "We'll finish the work elsewhere."

Work? He didn't care about the work. He cared about Meri. "Where is she? She can't leave. She has to stay the month."

He'd known that from the beginning. That she was stuck here, too. Just like him. They couldn't escape each other. Hadn't that been the point?

Betina looked at him. "She doesn't have to stay here. That was just something she told you. Hunter's donation has nothing to do with her. It was always about his friends."

She'd lied about having to stay? Why? So he wouldn't force her to leave? To make him think he had time?

"Where is she?" he asked again.

"I'm not going to tell you. If she wants you to know, she'll get in touch with you herself."

He didn't understand any of this. Why had Meri been here in the first place? What had she wanted? Why leave now?

"Is it Andrew?" he asked. "Is she upset because I told her what he was?"

Betina's expression was almost pitying. "It's a guy thing, right? This failure to comprehend the most basic of human emotions? It has to be. I can't believe you're honestly that stupid." She smiled, then shook her head. "It always comes down to smart and stupid. How strange."

"What are you talking about?"

"Nothing," she told him. "Meri came here because she thought she wanted closure. She got it, in a way. She's been in love with you all these years. But the man wasn't really you. He was someone better. The person she thought you would be. Meri embraces life. She loves and is loved. She cares about people. She thought you were all those things, too. But she was wrong. And now she's gone."

Meri loved him? She couldn't. Not after what he'd done. Not after he'd let her down time after time.

"She can't," he whispered.

"That's what I keep telling her, but does she listen?" Betina closed the box. "I'm done here. Colin and I will be gone within the hour. Then you can have the house to yourself. You've got a few weeks left, right? I hope you enjoy your time here."

She started to leave. He grabbed her arm. "You can't leave it like that. There has to be more."

"Why? You don't want there to be more. It's not like you really care about her. She's just Hunter's little sister, right? An annoying responsibility. Your problem is you didn't know what you had until you lost it, and now she's gone forever. Goodbye, Jack."

He released her and let her go because there was nothing left to say.

Fine. He could be fine his last few weeks here. It was just three weeks, and then he'd go back to Texas and bury himself in his work. He would stay busy and he would forget. He was good at forgetting.

Three days later, Jack knew he was damn close to slipping into madness. The house was empty. Too empty. The silence mocked him. Worse, he found himself missing Meri's nerd friends. He missed the arguments about string theory and the scraps of paper with equations that had dotted every surface. He missed walking into a room and not understanding a word of what was being said despite the fact that everyone was speaking English.

He missed the closeness, the way Meri bullied everyone to get outside, to live life. He missed her insisting on a better telescope because the stars were so beautiful. He missed the sound of her voice, her laughter, the way her body moved. He missed her quirky sense of humor, her brilliance and how her smile could light up a room. He missed *her.*

She wasn't the teenager he'd known all those years ago. The young woman who had intrigued him and at the same time scared the hell out of him. Not just because she was Hunter's sister but because there was a quality about her that warned him she would expect only the best of herself and those in her world.

For a while he'd thought maybe he could live up to those expectations, but then Hunter had gotten sick and he'd known he would only hold her back.

He'd let her go for a thousand reasons that made

sense at the time. She didn't need him. She had to grow up on her own. She was better off without him. He was afraid. They'd both been so young and his feelings for Meri had been confused. So he'd walked away and stayed away. He'd kept tabs on her from a distance. He'd taken the coward's way out.

He hadn't expected to ever see her again. Then she'd been here and he'd been thrown. She'd wanted to seduce him and he knew he couldn't let that happen. Because of what he owed both her and Hunter.

He walked into the empty living room and stared at the perfectly arranged furniture. It was all so comfortable. He wanted to throw things, break things, mess it all up. Because life wasn't tidy or comfortable. It was a pain in the ass.

He turned to leave, then spotted a DVD case on the floor, by the sofa. Someone had dropped it. Or left it on purpose. Meri? Betina? Hunter?

He picked it up and stared at the plain black cover. Someone had stuck on a piece of paper covered with a single word.

*Hunter.*

Against his better judgment, Jack walked to the DVD player and put in the disk. Then he turned on the television and braced himself for the pain.

Someone had taken the time to transfer Hunter's home movies, he thought as he watched snippets of the first confusing days at Harvard. There were shots of Hunter's friends. All of them. And Meri. She was always hanging on the fringes.

She'd been the one to show them around, list the

best places to get pizza at three in the morning. She'd been there since she was a kid.

There were shots of snowball fights and a late-night party by a bonfire.

He leaned back against the sofa and lost himself in the images. A vacation here, a camping trip there. Seven guys who had become friends. No. Brothers. Brothers he hadn't seen or talked to in years.

The scene shifted to a yacht vacation they'd all taken one spring break. The camera panned to show the guys stretched out in the sun after a very late night. Meri walked on deck and paused, looking awkward and un-happy. She turned her gaze to him. He had his eyes closed and didn't see the look on her face. The one that clearly showed she loved him.

He felt it then, the cold slice of pain that was almost familiar. It took him a second to place it and then he re-membered the knife attack in a Central American jungle. At first there had been nothing—just a breath of expectation, followed by the warm sensation of liquid as his blood flowed out. Then there had been the sharp sting that had quickly grown into agony.

It was the same today. As if razors had sliced his heart and his soul, as he realized he'd lost something precious. Something he could never replace.

He picked up his cell phone and pressed the buttons that connected him to his office.

"I don't have anything," Bobbi Sue snapped by way of greeting. "If you'd stop calling me, I might get a chance to find her."

"She has to be somewhere."

"You think I don't know that? She turned in the rental car at the airport in Los Angeles, but she didn't get on a plane. If she's in a hotel somewhere, she's using cash and a false name. I'm checking all her friends to see if they've used their names to register her. It's taking time."

He didn't have time. He had to find her *now*. He'd spent every minute of the past three days thinking he had to go after her himself, but leaving meant blowing the donation, and Meri would hate him for that.

"Keep looking," he said and hung up. To give his assistant the time she needed.

Jack stood and paced the length of the living room. He wanted to be doing the search himself, but he was trapped in this damn house. Trapped with memories and ghosts and a burning need he'd acknowledged three days too late.

He loved her. He had for a long time. In college, he'd assumed she would grow up and they'd get together. The plan had existed in the back of his mind, as if he'd known they were meant for each other. Then Hunter had died and everything had changed.

His cell rang. He reached for it.

"You found her?"

"I'm not looking for her."

The voice was familiar. "Colin?"

"Uh-huh. So you're looking for Meri?"

"I have my entire staff on it."

"You won't figure it out. Besides, what does it matter?"

"It matters more than anything."

"I *want* to believe you."

Because Colin had information. Why wouldn't he?

Meri would tell Betina where she was going and Betina would tell Colin.

"I have to find her," Jack said hoarsely. "I love her."

"What if that's too little too late?"

"I'll convince her."

There was an excruciating minute of silence.

"I kind of believe you," Colin said. "Okay. When your month is up there, I'll tell you where she is."

"What?" Jack roared. "You'll tell me now."

"Sorry. No. You have to stay. It's a lot of money on the line."

"I'll pay them the difference myself."

"Okay, yeah. You're probably good for it. But leaving now violates the spirit of what Hunter was trying to do. You really think Meri will be happy about that?"

"You think she's happy thinking I don't care about her?"

"Good point, but I'm not going to tell you. Not until the time is up."

The call ended. Jack picked up the coffee table and threw it through the sliding glass door. The glass shattered with a satisfyingly destructive sound.

"Dammit all to hell," he yelled into the subsequent silence.

And no one answered.

# Twelve

Meri was thinking maybe she should get a dog. One of those small ones she could travel with. From her corner room at the Ritz-Carlton in Pasadena she could see down into a beautiful grassy area, with plants and paths where people walked their small dogs several times a day. At least then there would be something else alive in the room with her.

She glanced at her watch, then sighed. Her team wouldn't arrive for another half hour, which meant time to kill. Maybe it was just her, but the days had gotten much longer in the past few weeks. The things she loved no longer made her as happy as they once had. She found it more difficult to laugh and sleep and be really excited about Colin and Betina's announcement that they were getting married.

Not that she wasn't thrilled for her friends. There was nothing she wanted more than their happiness. It was just...

She missed Jack. Yes, that was crazy and made her an idiot, but there it was. She missed him—his voice, his touch, his laugh. The way he took charge and wasn't the least bit intimidated by her. She'd loved him most of her life. How was she supposed to stop loving him?

"Therapy," she murmured as she continued to stare out the window. It had helped her before—to figure out what normal was. Maybe talking with a paid professional could help her get over Jack. Maybe she could find a really cute male therapist and do a little emotional transference, because getting over anyone else had to be so much easier than getting over Jack.

She closed her eyes against the pain. He would be gone by now. His month at Hunter's house had ended at midnight. Had he already started back to Texas or was he just getting on the road? What was he thinking of her? Would she ever be the one who got away or was that just wishful thinking on her part? She knew he would come back for the reunion, but for now, he was gone.

There was a knock at the door. Housekeeping, she thought. Okay. That was fine. They could clean while she walked the grounds and made friends with the little dogs. Maybe an owner or two could give her some advice on which kind to get.

Jack would be a big-dog kind of guy, she thought absently. Of course, if she had his feelings to consider, she wouldn't need a dog in the first place. She would have a husband and a family, although a dog would be nice, too. Maybe one of—

She opened the door and stood staring. "You're not housekeeping."

Jack pushed past her into the room and shrugged. "I can go get you more towels if you need them."

"I don't need towels."

She stared at him, unable to believe he was here. He looked good—tired and maybe thinner but still powerful and sexy and the man of her dreams.

"You're supposed to be heading home," she said. "Your four weeks are up."

He looked at her. "Is that what you think? That I'd put in my time, then walk away?"

"Sure."

"Because it's what I've always done. Put in my time, kept my distance, not gotten involved."

Her stomach flipped over a couple of times. Okay, physically it couldn't turn, but the churning caused by anxiety did a really great imitation.

She wanted to throw herself into his arms. She wanted him to hold her and tell her it was going to be all right. Only he wouldn't, because nothing in her life had ever been that easy. She had no idea why he was here. Maybe to offer her some advice or something. She would smile politely, listen, push him out the door, then have a private breakdown. She was getting good at those.

"How did you find me?" she asked.

"Colin told me."

"What? He didn't."

"Oh, yeah. But he did it in a way you can totally

respect. He tortured me first. He called right after you left and said he knew where you were but he wasn't going to tell me until my month was up. Something about a donation and that damn house."

Colin had called Jack? She wasn't sure if she should be happy or planning to return the engagement present she'd already bought.

"You were looking for me?" she asked cautiously.

Jack touched her face. "What do you think?"

"I don't know."

"You must have had an idea. You went to a lot of trouble to stay hidden."

"I don't want your pity," she admitted. "I don't want you watching over me anymore. I don't want to be a project or Hunter's little sister."

His eyes were dark and unreadable. Something flashed through them.

"Would you settle for being the woman I love?"

She heard the words. The vibration of sound worked its way through her ears and was transmitted through her brain via—

"What?" she asked, suddenly not caring about the hows and whys of her body. "What?"

"I love you, Meri. I have for a long time. I always thought…" He shrugged. "I thought there was something between us back then. But you were young and I was young and then Hunter got sick. I couldn't deal, so I ran. You know all this. I ran, but I couldn't let go. I took the coward's way out. I spied on you. You were right to call it that. I kept track from a distance, where it was safe. Where I was safe."

She had to sit down. Her legs felt weak and the room was spinning. Instead she reached for him, and he caught her and held her as if he might never let go.

"I missed you," he murmured, speaking into her hair. "I missed you so much. Not just the past three weeks, although they were hell, but for the past eleven years. I'm sorry I didn't know before. I love you, Meri. I want to be with you. I want to make this right."

He grabbed her by her upper arms and held her in front of him. "Can you forgive me? Can you tell me what to do to make it right? Can you ever care about me?"

She began to laugh and cry and went back into his arms, where he held her so tight she couldn't breathe.

It felt good. It felt right.

"Of course I love you," she said, her voice shaking. "What did you think all this was about?"

"You're a complicated woman. I had no idea. You left. That confused me."

"I wanted to leave before you could dump me. I couldn't have my heart broken again."

"I'll never leave you," he promised. "I love you. I want to be with you always. Marry me?"

It was as if someone had injected fizz into her blood. She felt light and bubbly and more happy than she'd ever been.

"What kind of dogs do you like?" she asked.

"Whichever ones makes you happy."

She smiled. "Good answer."

The first time Hunter Palmer had gone into the light, he hadn't known what to expect. Until he'd been diagnosed and told he had weeks to live, he'd never thought about having a soul or what it meant to die. Now, ten years later, he had all the answers. But there were still questions. Questions only his friends could answer.

He moved through the reception celebrating the dedication of Hunter's House, unseen, unfelt but very much there—for his friends. Once they had been the Seven Samurai—men who had vowed friendship forever. After he'd died, they'd gotten lost. Now they'd found their way back.

Hunter moved close to Nathan Barrister.

Six months ago Nathan had never heard of Hunter's Landing. Now he was married to Keira, the mayor of Hunter's Landing, and dividing his time between a house in Knightsbridge, London, and Keira's house here in the mountains.

His life was rich and full and more than he could have ever imagined. And he owed it all to Hunter. All of them did. Nathan closed his eyes and whispered his thanks to the friend who had somehow made all of this possible. And somehow he was sure Hunter heard him.

"What're you smiling about?" Keira asked, leaning into his shoulder, tipping her face up to his.

"You," he said, wrapping his arm around her and holding on tightly. "I'm smiling because of you."

"Ooh, that's what I like to hear." She turned to look at the remaining Samurai and the women who had saved them—loved them. "It's a wonderful day. I think your friend Hunter would have approved."

"Are you kidding? He would have loved this. All of us together again. Whole again." With Keira in his arms,

Nathan looked out at his friends and the women who had become the heart of the Samurai. They weren't the same, any of them. Somehow, through the magic of this place, they'd all become *more*. Smiling down at his wife, Nathan said, "I just don't think it's possible to be any happier than I am at this moment."

"Wanna bet? I have a surprise for you," she said, wrapping her arms around his middle and staring up into his eyes. "And I think today is the perfect day for this announcement."

"Yeah?" He looked at her and thought about the coming night, when he could hold her close in their bed, lose himself in the wonder of loving and being loved. "I love a good surprise."

"We're going to have a baby."

"We're what?"

"You're going to be a daddy."

"When?" His heart jolted, then kicked into a gallop. "How? What?"

"Surprise!"

She looked so happy. So beautiful. And she'd given him everything.

"I love you," he said, cupping her face between his palms. "Thanks for loving me back."

"My pleasure. Believe me."

He did. He believed her. Just as he believed that his life, his world, was only going to get better and better. Holding on to his wife, he tipped his head back, looked to heaven and said again, "Thanks, Hunter. I really owe you for this."

Hunter touched his friend's shoulder and moved on…to Luke.

It was just the kind of event Hunter would have enjoyed, Luke thought. Plenty of cold beer, good food and beautiful girls.

Make that beautiful *women*. Their time in the house had brought each of the remaining Samurai a lover with whom the men intended to spend the rest of their lives. Hunter couldn't have known that would happen…or could he?

Luke grinned at his fanciful thought, then caught Lauren's eye. "Hey, do you think we'll have time later for a round or two at the Game Palace?"

"Pool during the reunion?" She twisted one of her blond curls around her finger.

"Why not? We'll invite Matt and Kendall along and we can kick their butts. How much do you want to bet she's never played?"

Lauren frowned. "I thought you were giving up your competitive ways."

Luke snagged her in one arm and drew her close. "You know that won't happen. I've just learned to temper them with a little perspective. And with a lotta love from you, honey."

"And from Matt."

Luke gazed over the top of her head at his twin brother, who looked equally relaxed and equally loved by his Kendall. He and Matt had spent a lot of their lives as each other's enemies, but their time at Hunter's House had resolved their conflicts and returned them to a brotherhood that Luke appreciated more each day.

From across the room Matt looked up as if he'd heard

Luke's thoughts. Like many twins, they could communicate without a sound. His brother lifted his sweating beer in a little toast, and Luke returned it. Then he directed another toast heavenward.

*Thank you, Hunter. I vow to live a better, fuller life.*

Then he looked back down at the woman who owned his heart. "Speaking of vows…"

She tilted her head. "What?"

"A little birdie told me that a couple in this room is planning on sneaking off to Reno on Sunday to tie the knot."

"Really?"

He nodded, then captured her left hand so he could rub his thumb over the engagement ring he'd placed there. Yes, he was living a better, fuller life, but oh, how he still enjoyed winning. "Now, if we make a quick dash tonight, my sweet, sweet Lauren, we could just beat them to the altar…."

Hunter laughed quietly as he moved away. Luke would never change. Of course, Lauren didn't want him to, which was why they were so happy together.

He looked around the room and saw Devlin Campbell looking uncharacteristically worried.

As happy as Devlin was to see his old friends, he was more anxious to get home. Nicole's obstetrician had forbidden her to travel by plane with the baby so close to being born, and he missed her.

Ryan wandered over, Devlin's best man and the same guy who had declared he was swearing off women for the month he was to be at the lodge. But the Love Shack had weaved its magic on Ryan as it had the rest of them. He'd found true love, too.

"What's right with this picture?" Devlin asked Ryan as they glanced around the room.

Ryan smiled. "Yeah. Amazing. And you're missing Nicole, I'll bet."

"As much as I've liked getting together with all the Samurai, I want to be home."

"Think we'll do this again sometime? A gathering of the clan?"

"We should. Maybe a golf weekend somewhere once a year."

"It would take some doing, coordinating our schedules."

"One thing I've learned, Ryan—you have to make time for what's important. My wife, the Samurai. You're important."

"Let's go propose the idea while the wives are around to hear. They'll force the issue. Women like that kind of bonding stuff."

As if on cue, Devlin's cell phone rang. Panic struck him full force when he saw it was Nicole. Had she gone into labor without him?

"You okay?" he asked.

"I love you. I miss you. That's all."

He relaxed. She loved him and missed him. *That's all.* Such an elemental part of his life now. His beautiful wife, her love and devotion. But *that's all?*

On second thought, maybe it *was* that simple. Maybe that was the secret of life. The best things weren't complicated.

Hunter nodded. He touched Devlin's arm to ease his worry. Nicole would be fine. Then he followed Ryan across the room.

His arm draped around Kelly's shoulders, Ryan looked around at the Seven Samurai who'd finally gathered together again. He said *seven* because he knew Hunter was here in spirit. In fact, Hunter had brought about this reunion, thanks to his will.

Hunter had always been the glue that had bound them together, and now they were his legacy.

Ryan looked down at Kelly. They'd been married just weeks, but they'd been the best damn weeks he'd had in a long time. Since before his mother and Hunter had died, in fact. He felt alive again.

They'd gotten married in an intimate ceremony in California's Napa Valley. Erica and Greg had served as the matron of honor and best man. Because it was summer break, he'd been able to fly them in, along with their kids, for a family vacation. He grinned thinking about how thrilled Kelly's friends had been to get away to a romantic place, even if it was with the kids in tow.

He and Kelly would be in the same situation in a few years, especially if they kept having the same steamy nights they'd been having the past few weeks.

Kelly glanced up at him. "Why are you grinning?"

He bent and murmured something sinful in her ear.

She went still, looked embarrassed, then swatted him playfully. "Behave."

He laughed as he straightened because she'd given him exactly the reaction he would have predicted.

"Impossible with you, Venus," he responded irrepressibly.

Hunter chuckled, patted his friend on the back, then walked toward Luke's twin.

It was strange, Matthias thought, seeing all six of them together again after so many years. Even stranger that they were here without Hunter. Though, in a way, maybe Hunter *was* here with them. Maybe he'd been with them all along. And it was fitting that Hunter had been the one to bring them all together again, since he'd been the one who'd united them in college. They were still the Seven Samurai, Matthias supposed, but now one was missing. And somehow the Six Samurai just didn't seem right.

Then he realized they weren't six anymore. They were twelve. And they weren't Samurai anymore, either. Samurai were warriors, always prepared for death. Matthias, Luke, Ryan, Jack, Nathan and Devlin were family men now, focused on their lives ahead with the women who had made them complete.

That was what Kendall had done for him, anyway. Completed him. Filled in all the empty places that he hadn't wanted to admit were empty.

As if she'd sensed something, Kendall looked up at him, narrowing her gaze thoughtfully. "What are you thinking about?" she asked. "You look…happy."

"That's what I'm thinking about."

"Not the Perkins contract?"

"Nope."

"Not the Endicott merger?"

"No."

"Not the Sacramento conference?"

He tightened his fingers around hers. "I'm thinking about our life together. And I'm thinking about how we need to get right to work on that."

"You're the boss."

He shook his head. "No. We're a newly announced partnership. One that's going to take the world by storm."

She pushed herself up on tiptoe and brushed her lips over his. "I'll prepare the memo at once."

"We'd better make it a PowerPoint demonstration," he told her. "This is going to be big."

Hunter nodded with pleasure. Everything had turned out the way he'd hoped. The possibilities had been there, of course, but his friends had been the ones to take the right steps.

Last he turned to Meri, his sister. He'd missed her, but he was proud of the woman she'd become. It had taken her and Jack far too long to find each other, but at last they had.

He eased close, wishing he could hug her and tell her how much he loved them both.

"There's something about the house," Meri told Jack. "All these people falling in love. It's almost scary."

"You scared to be in love with me?"

She smiled. "Never. I'm used to it. I've loved you a lot longer than you've loved me."

"Have not."

"Have to."

Jack grinned. "Are all our fights going to be this mature?"

"I hope so." She leaned close to him. "I love you,

Jack. I think Hunter would be very happy to know we're together."

Jack nodded. "I agree. I know it's strange, but there's a part of me that thinks he wanted this all along."

If Hunter had eyes to roll, he would have done it. Then he cuffed his friend on the shoulder. What else would he have been talking about when he'd made Jack promise to take care of his sister?

It had all worked out in the end. For each of his friends. When he'd known he was dying, he'd vowed to find some way to make sure they stayed together—brothers. He'd been afraid that guilt and time and distance would pull them apart. On a sleepless night weeks before his death, the idea of the house had been born.

Now, ten years later, he was content. His sister was finally where she belonged and his brothers had become the men he knew they could be. He would tell them everything…eventually.

He smiled at them. His work here was done. He would wait for them on the other side, in a better place than they could begin to imagine. Hunter turned then, moving into the light…this time to stay.

\* \* \* \* \*

# HIGH-SOCIETY
# MISTRESS

### by
## Katherine Garbera

Dear Reader,

I've always loved romance stories that involved revenge. I think it's because I've dedicated my life to being a good girl and always fair to everyone. I like the thought of plotting revenge, and then going after it in fiction.

Gavin Renard is a man bent on revenge. The course of his life changed when he was on the cusp of adulthood. His safe, affluent family was shattered by the actions of August Lambert, and from that moment on Gavin wanted revenge.

Tempest Lambert has spent her entire life trying to get her father's attention. The heiress has done everything from being a brilliant straight-A over-achiever to turning into the tabloids' favourite subject with her outrageous behaviour. And through it all she's still not done more than get a raised eyebrow from her father.

But from the moment she meets Gavin she forgets about getting a reaction out of her father. Though she knows they are business rivals she falls for Gavin. Their story is one of redemption and second chances.

Please stop by my website at www.katherinegarbera.com for a behind-the-scenes look into *High-Society Mistress*.

Happy reading!

*Katherine*

**KATHERINE GARBERA**

is a strong believer in happily ever after.
She found her own after meeting her Prince
Charming in Fantasyland at Walt Disney
World. She's written more than thirty books
and has been nominated for a *Romantic Times
BOOKreviews* career achievement award
in Series Fantasy and Series Adventure.
Katherine recently moved to the Dallas area
where she lives with her husband and their two
children. Visit Katherine on the web at www.
katherinegarbera.com.

This book is dedicated to all the readers at
katherinegarbera.com. Thanks for always
playing with me at Chatty Kathy!

# One

Tempest Lambert, the tabloid's favorite party girl extraordinaire, stood quietly in the foyer of her condo building, dressed conservatively and trying not to be nervous. It was silly really. She'd charmed heads of state and celebrities. She'd made the world her oyster. But one man still had the power to reduce her to a nervous wreck.

Her father's chauffeur-driven car arrived promptly at 7:35 p.m. Tempest normally would have driven herself to the Leukemia Foundation Gala dinner and silent auction but her father had wanted to speak with her in person. And this was the only time he had in his schedule.

So here she was trying to smile and pretend that

this wasn't a big deal. And when her father didn't get out of the car to greet her she had her first inkling that it really wasn't a big deal to him.

"Good evening, Ms. Lambert."

"Good evening, Marcus." The elderly chauffeur had been with her father for almost twenty years. He gave her a quick smile. "You look beautiful tonight."

"Thanks," she said, her nerves melting away at the compliment. This was her night. She'd just handled a rather messy PR problem for Tempest's Closet. Her father had even e-mailed her a note that said good job. The only note he'd ever sent her.

She slid into the car as the chauffeur held the door open for her. Her father was on the phone and didn't glance up as the car door closed behind her.

She tried to relax against the plush leather seat of her father's Mercedes-Benz E63 AMG Sedan. The driver sat in the front facing forward, all but invisible to them. She wasn't nervous. Well, maybe a little. It had been so long since she'd allowed herself to want her father's approval. At twenty-eight she was well on her own.

August Lambert, the CEO of Tempest's Closet, was an imposing man. Well over six-feet tall he'd always seemed bigger than life to her when she'd been a little girl. He'd revolutionized the way Americans thought about and purchased clothing with his line of high-end retail Tempest's Closet stores that he had started back in the 1970s and named for her after her birth.

He finished his phone conversation and made a

note in his day-planner before looking over at her. Silence grew between them as he studied her face. She wondered what he saw when he looked at her.

Some people said she looked like her mother but Tempest had never really believed that. Her mother had been one of the most beautiful women Tempest had ever seen. And what she saw reflected back in the mirror was never…beautiful.

"Thank you for meeting with me," he said.

"No problem. What did you want to see me about?"

"I'm promoting Charles Miller."

No small talk or chitchat from him. Just the blunt news that she…well, she hadn't expected.

"Charlie Miller? You've got to be kidding me." Dammit, she'd meant to be calm and cool.

"He's the right man for the job."

She gave her father a hard look—one that she'd picked up from him. "Please tell me you didn't promote him over me because I'm a woman."

"Tempest, I'm not a sexist."

She knew that. She was grasping at straws trying to find a reason. "I'm not so sure, Father. I have more experience than Charlie and am better qualified."

August sighed and rubbed the back of his neck. He stared at the car window watching the Lake Shore Drive scenery pass. She loved Chicago. Sometimes she wished she didn't because then she could simply leave her father and Tempest's Closet far behind.

Her father seemed so unapproachable, so alone. Even though only a few inches of space separated them.

And she felt the distance between them widen. No matter what she tried, she could never get his approval. His respect. A few crazy stunts when she was in her late teens and early twenties and he was going to hold that against her for the rest of her life.

"I haven't done anything to draw attention to myself lately," she said, quietly. This job had become the driving force in her life—no longer a party girl, she'd become a businesswoman. Something she was sure her father would notice.

"There was an article in *Hello!* not a week ago about you and Dean Stratford with pictures of you in your love nest."

"Father, please. You know there's nothing between Dean and me. He's recovering from a serious addiction. He needs support from his friends."

He glanced over at her. "It doesn't matter what I know. The world believes you're a party girl."

She couldn't believe what she was hearing. "The board knows I'm not."

He rubbed a hand over his heart before he put his hands in his lap, linking his fingers together. "I'm more concerned with what the public thinks."

Tempest couldn't argue that point. She almost regretted it but she'd made herself a promise long ago not to apologize for her actions. Though they were most times misconstrued she knew that she always only had the best of intentions where all of her escapades were concerned.

"I think we can overcome that. I've been working with the children's foundation, which is helping my image."

"It's not enough, Tempest. Tempest's Closet is facing some tough times."

"What kind of tough times?" she asked. Being in PR, her focus was more on image than on the company bottom line. But she hadn't heard any rumblings of trouble.

"Nothing you need to worry about."

"I'm an employee, Father. Of course I worry about the stability of the company. Tell me what's going on." She worried more about her father. It had always been one of her biggest fears…losing him. And if anything happened to Tempest's Closet he'd have nothing left to live for.

"It's Renard Investments."

*Again?* Gavin Renard had been gunning for Tempest's Closet since he'd come onto the investment scene some ten years earlier. He was always trying to man some kind of takeover.

"And Charlie will be a better VP to help you out?" she asked carefully.

"Yes. I need a public relations vice president who can get out there and give us some good spin."

"I think the articles about me should prove I know something about spin," she muttered.

"That's not the kind of spin we want."

"Father, please."

She'd spent her entire life trying to make sure that no one in the world pitied her. Poor little motherless rich girl. Instead she'd made life her party and now she had the feeling she was paying for it. She'd gone to Vassar and gotten her degree. Though she'd heard rumors that her affair with the dean of students was the only reason she'd passed, she knew she'd done the work and Stan had no control over her grades.

She crossed her legs, feeling the smooth silk of her Valentino gown against her skin. She glanced at him out of the corner of her eye.

He sighed and she had her answer. Why she was surprised, she couldn't understand. She hated that she always wanted something from him that he could never deliver.

"I'm sorry, Tempest. My mind is made up."

"Unmake it," she said, starting to lose her temper. Though she desperately wanted to hang on to it. Desperately wanted to find the cool and calm front that her father always presented. Why hadn't she inherited that?

"I think we're done here."

"Not yet. I want you to tell me exactly why I wasn't promoted."

He looked her square in the eye. "You're not responsible enough. I don't trust you to do the job."

The words hurt worse than she'd expected. And she felt the sting of tears in the back of her eyes but refused to cry in front of him. She had, in fact, never cried in front of him. She knew he considered it a cheap feminine ploy used to manipulate men.

"I don't think I'm going to be able to continue to work for you."

"That's your choice, Tempest."

"No, Father, that's yours."

From across the crowded ballroom Gavin Renard caught a glimpse of Tempest Lambert. The socialite was surrounded by a group of people and didn't look the way he'd expected her to. They'd never met, though they attended many of the same functions. To be honest he never really paid that close attention to her until tonight. Maybe it was the way she'd split from August as soon as they'd entered the room.

In her photos she appeared too thin and her mouth was always set in a pout. Her eyes usually held a vacuous expression. As he maneuvered around for a closer look, he noticed that her wide-set blue eyes weren't vacuous tonight. They seethed with something that was either passion or anger.

She wasn't as scary thin as she appeared to be in her photos. He'd thought her an attractive woman when he'd seen her on the cover of *People* magazine but in person she radiated a kind of beauty that left him speechless.

She was his enemy's daughter. So he knew the details of her life. That her mother had died when she was six of complications due to breast cancer. He knew that Tempest had been shipped off to a boarding school in Switzerland and, from all reports, been an excellent student until she turned eighteen and came into the fortune left her by her grandparents.

She'd dropped out of school and joined Europe's party set and never looked back. For six years she partied hard and with little regard for others. There were rumors of affairs with married men, scandalous photos of her in every paper on the continent and occasionally in the U.S.

Then she'd dropped off the party circuit and returned to the States to go to college. The report he'd read of her transcripts had indicated she was an excellent student. But once again she found herself embroiled in a scandal just weeks before graduation when pictures of her and the dean of students surfaced in a local paper.

She glanced up catching him staring. He arched one eyebrow at her, but didn't look away.

"What are you doing?"

Gavin didn't take his gaze from Tempest as he replied to his brother Michael's question.

"Flirting with a pretty lady."

"She's off limits, Gav. Unless you've changed your mind about…?"

"I haven't." He would never change his mind about going after August Lambert's business. August was the reason that Gavin was so successful. The reason he'd driven himself and his employees to take his company to the top. The reason he was here tonight.

Since he'd been old enough to understand the business world, he'd known who August was. At first Gavin had been in awe of what the man accomplished but seeing his methods up close and personal had changed the admiration to disdain.

He'd never forget the excitement he'd felt when he'd heard that August Lambert was opening one of his innovative Tempest's Closet stores in his home town. But he hadn't understood his father's quiet anger toward the man, and had felt a wave of distain for his father and his small-town mind-set in a way only a twelve-year-old boy could.

But in a short while, as the life his father had provided for the Renard family had fallen apart, Gavin had come to understand why his father hated Lambert. Soon Gavin felt hatred for the man, too, slowly turning to a need for revenge that had never left him. The opening of Tempest's Closet had slowly driven all the Main Street shops out of business. Gavin had watched his father struggle to keep the downtown area vital, even going to August Lambert for help. But Lambert had refused.

"Of course you haven't."

"What's your point?"

"Just that you don't want to get involved with someone who works for a company we're going after."

He glanced at Michael. "Since when do I need advice?"

Michael punched him in the arm. "Old man, you always need advice when it comes to your personal life."

"Yeah, right. I think I see Melinda trying to get your attention."

Michael groaned under his breath but turned toward the woman he'd been dating on and off for the last four years. "When are you going to marry her?"

"When you start taking my advice."

"Never?"

"I don't know," Michael said, but the comment felt as if it were directed more at himself than to Gavin.

"Catch you later, Gav. Remember what I said."

"Later, Michael."

As his brother left, Gavin realized that Tempest was no longer talking with the group. The doors opened for seating in the main banquet room. Gavin held back, hoping for one more glance of Tempest.

He felt a hand on his shoulder. Long manicured fingernails rested on the black fabric of his dinner jacket. A sweet sultry scent perfumed the air and he glanced over his shoulder at Tempest.

"Well, hello," he said.

"I saw you watching me."

"Good."

"In some cultures it's considered impolite to stare."

"Your point is?"

She walked around in front of him, staying close

in the crush of people trying to enter the banquet room. "My point is I don't believe we've met."

"Gavin Renard."

"Ah."

"So you've heard of me."

"Vaguely," she said, with a twinkle in her eye. She took another sip of her drink. "I'm Tempest Lambert."

"I know who you are."

"Because of your business interest in Tempest's Closet?" she asked.

Her boldness surprised him. And he wasn't sure why. "Among other things."

She took a sip of the drink in her hand, tipping her head to one side. "Don't believe everything you read about me, Mr. Renard."

She was an enticing bundle of femininity. "I don't."

She reached up and touched his chin. Just her fingertips against the stubble on his face. "That's good because I have a proposition for you."

"I like the sound of that."

"Not that kind of proposition."

"A man can hope."

She turned away, but not before he saw a flash of desire in her eyes.

Interesting.

"What's your offer?" he asked.

"I'm in the market for a job, Gavin," she said.

Just the sound of his name on her lips made everything male in him come to point. He wanted to hear her say his name, but from the tangled sheets of his bed after they'd had wild sex. Not in the middle of this crowded function while he was trying to follow Michael's advice to keep his hands to himself. "No."

She sighed. "I'm very good at PR and I think I can be an asset to your company."

"I can't hire you." He wondered if August had set his daughter up to come to him for a job—maybe with the intent of using her as a corporate spy.

"Don't say no. Not yet. Let me come to your office tomorrow and talk to you. Once you see my resume you might reconsider."

He took her arm. God, her skin was smooth and soft. Softer than a woman's arm should be. He drew her away from the flocks of people and into a quiet part of the hallway. She didn't hesitate to follow him.

He stopped when they were alone and she leaned back against the wall watching him the way a woman watches a man she wants.

"Don't play with me, Tempest."

"I'm not," she said, quietly.

But he knew she was. Gavin hated to think that he might be falling in lust with the daughter of his enemy. Hated that August might have found the one chink in his otherwise impenetrable façade. But then what kind of man would use his daughter like that?

Suspicion and desire warred inside him and he finally gave into desire. He leaned in over her. So close he could see that her blue eyes weren't a pure color but a combination of several different shades.

And that her lashes were thicker than a mink stole. And her lips, ah, hell, her lips were full and wide and as she drew her tongue over the bottom one he remembered exactly how long it had been since he'd held a woman in his arms.

And he couldn't trust her. His best bet would be to scare her off with a bold pass. From what he'd read of her, she was used to pampered boys who lived off their family's fortunes.

"Gavin?"

"I don't need you in my PR department... but..." he said.

"Don't say it," she warned him.

He didn't voice his request, just tugged her a little closer and brought his mouth to her ear. She shivered as his breath brushed over her and he felt an answering spread of sensation. He felt the first tingling of arousal in his loins.

"It's obvious we're attracted to each other," he whispered.

She pulled back from him. "I am attracted to you, which makes no sense at all."

Hell, he knew that. But he wanted her. More than he should. This wasn't logical or rational but she felt so right.

Too right. It reminded him that the deep freeze he'd carefully existed in while focusing on his plan of revenge was starting to thaw. In her gaze he saw a hint of sadness and the kind of determination that played havoc with his control.

She closed her eyes. He saw her skin flush at his words and her shoulders sank back, lifting her breasts toward him.

He caressed the long line of her cheekbones. Her skin was softer than the sea mist. Her lashes drifted down as he explored the angles and curves of her face. He traced the lines of her lips as they parted under his touch. He stroked his thumb over her full lower lip, watched the natural pink color of her lips darken.

She tipped her head back and leaned the slightest bit toward him. There was a bit of haughtiness in her that intrigued him. He wanted to take her in his arms and see how haughty she looked after he ravished her mouth with his kisses.

She shrugged her shoulder. "I'm not looking for an affair, Gavin. I'm looking for a job."

He knew he'd never hire her but he didn't want to just let her walk away from him. And he knew that was her intent. "I can see you tomorrow at eleven."

"Great. Prepare to be amazed," she said, walking away.

# Two

Tempest had dressed for her interview with Gavin Renard with care. Her black Chanel suit was a classic and she wore it like a security blanket. She loved the feeling of the lined summer-weight wool skirt against her legs. She paired it with a pair of ultra-thin sheer French hose and some Ferragamos that were understated and sophisticated.

But still she was nervous. Her hands trembled as she took a sip of the coffee Gavin's secretary Marilyn had gotten for her. She hated being that betrayed by her own emotions and forced herself to rehearse in her head what she planned to say one more time.

She wasn't only thinking of a new job. She was

thinking of Gavin Renard the man, and that ticked her off. It was one thing to think of him as a way to make her father sit up and take notice of the kind of executive he let slip through his fingers. But who would have thought that this man could mess with her plans? Of course, to be honest, she hadn't had much of a plan when she walked over to him. She'd just wanted to meet the man her father was so obsessed with and get a bead on whether or not there was something there she could use to make her father reconsider her for the promotion. Those plans had gone out the window when she'd realized how attracted she was to Gavin.

"Ms. Lambert?"

"Yes?"

"Mr. Renard will see you now."

She smiled her thanks at the secretary and put her coffee cup on the end-table. She took a deep breath before getting to her feet. Her mother had always said to take her time. That it was better to arrive late and prepared for an event than on time and unrehearsed.

In her mind she cranked up "Welcome to the Jungle" by Guns 'N' Roses. Then she picked up her briefcase and walked into his office.

Gavin stood when she entered. His shirt was a deep blue that made his gray eyes seem even more brilliant in the office lighting. He was taller than she remembered and she realized her heels the other evening had given her an extra inch of height that these didn't. She smiled up at him as the soundtrack in her head changed from energizing rock to Sade's "Smooth Operator."

He smelled really good, too. The spicy male scent enveloped her as he held out his hand. The slow sensuous music in her head made the office background drop away.

"Good morning, Tempest."

She shook her head. His big hand totally engulfed hers. She held on longer than she should have before pulling back and nervously clearing her throat. No, she thought. She wasn't nervous. She was calm, cool, totally collected and together.

"Good morning, Gavin. Did you enjoy the benefit last night?"

"Yes. Please have a seat."

So much for small talk. It was clear to her that Gavin wasn't interested in the social niceties that she'd built her life around. She made a mental note to remember that. She sat down and pulled her resume from her briefcase.

"Thank you for agreeing to this meeting."

"I'm still not sure why I did," he said.

For a minute she thought this was a big mistake and then their eyes met and she realized he'd agreed for the same reason she'd asked. *Mutual attraction.* She knew this was an impossible situation. He'd never be able to forget she was her father's daughter.

But she wasn't one who backed down. She'd

made it her life's goal to always keep moving forward. Never looking back. She wanted Gavin to see her as a prospective employee first and a woman second. And to totally forget she was a Lambert. Today that seemed really important. She was just another out-of-work businessperson.

"Because you're a shrewd businessman who knows a good thing when he sees it," she said, handing him her resume. Stay cool and confident, she reminded herself.

"I definitely liked what I saw the other night."

She smiled at him. This might be easier than she'd expected. She could play on the attraction flowing between them like a high-voltage current.

"Me, too."

He gave her a half-smile. It was an arrogant expression from a man who was confident of his appeal to the opposite sex. But then she wasn't lacking in confidence herself. She crossed her legs letting the hem of her skirt ride up the slightest bit. His eyes tracked the movement.

"What exactly is it that you do, Tempest?"

"I'm in PR. I've been responsible for most of the press you've seen about Tempest's Closet for the last three years."

"What makes you think I've been watching your press?"

"Please, Gavin. I think we both know that you are aware of every move that Tempest's Closet makes."

He shrugged one shoulder and leaned back in his chair. "I am."

He said nothing else, letting the silence build between them. She couldn't stand it because she knew he was building the case against her in his head. Finding the words to tell her to take her brief-case and walk out his door.

And this was her only option. Her only chance to really make sure her father realized that he'd let her slip through his fingers…for good this time.

"Just look at my resume. I think you'll see I'm more than you expected."

"You already are," he said.

She was a little startled by that. She handed him her resume and sank back into the chair.

Her resume was more impressive than he'd expected it to be. He didn't know why he was sur-prised. He'd made a few phone calls this morning and found out more information on his enemy's daughter than she'd probably be comfortable with him having.

Everyone he spoke to mentioned her keen intel-ligence and her ability to put people at ease. She had a knack for finding the morsel of good news in the worst situation and spinning it out until the media was running with the idea she fed them.

In short she'd be the perfect addition to his team if she weren't August Lambert's daughter. But she was. And nothing could change that.

He hadn't been able to get anything from his Tempest's Closet source on why Tempest was job hunting. But he'd figure that out today. See if there was anything in her leaving Tempest's Closet that he could use to his advantage.

She shifted her legs again and he tracked the movement with his eyes. She had dynamite legs. All he could think of was how smooth they'd feel to his touch. The few glimpses he'd had of her thigh were enough to make his fingertips tingle.

He frowned and forced himself to study her resume. He wasn't getting involved with her. He wasn't doing the lust thing with this woman. It had nothing to do with the advice of his brother and everything to do with focus. He couldn't afford any kind of distraction now that he was so close to his goal. Ten years of walking the path of revenge and he wasn't going to lose it this close to the finish line.

"Why did you leave Tempest's Closet?" he asked. No one knew the answer to that.

"I had a differing opinion with my boss."

"You mean your father, right?"

She sat up straighter in the chair and put both of her feet on the floor. Staring him straight in the eye. "I didn't get the job because of nepotism. I worked hard to prove myself within our charitable foundation before making the move to Tempest's Closet."

"Of course you did." He knew she'd gotten the job the same way every other employee had. Through her qualifications and skills. In fact, she'd probably had to work harder.

He knew how contentious her relationship was with August. He also didn't want her to leave his office until he figured out if there was a way that he could exploit that. There had to be something here he was missing.

"I'm not going to argue the point. If you can't see what an advantage I'd be to your organization then you're not the man I thought you were."

He glanced up at her then and realized he felt a grudging respect for her. She fought dirty...well she fought to win. And he always respected winning except when August Lambert won.

And somehow this daughter of his had to be the key to bringing him down. No, she was the key to twisting the pain of losing when August fell. And the old man was going down.

Right now, though, he needed some answer from her. He should be treating this like an interview. Keeping his eyes off her legs and focusing on what she was doing here. "Why did you go into PR?"

She relaxed in her seat, crossing those long legs again. "It seemed like the right fit for me. I know a lot of people in the media."

"Is it only because of your contacts?" he asked. There had to be more. She'd been hounded by the press for years before she'd started working in PR. He thought it was a very shrewd move on her behalf to turn that around. To make dealing with the press her career.

She swallowed hard. "I just wanted to give them something real to print. To move the focus off of me and onto something else. That's why I started with the charity. I knew no one would take me seriously until I changed my reputation in the media."

He respected what she'd done. To some extent he'd made a similar decision when he'd entered the investing world. His family had started with nothing and he'd turned that around. Taking the very thing that had ruined his father and making it his own strength.

"Good move."

"Thanks," she said, flashing him a grin that stopped him in his tracks. She had a wonderful smile.

"Okay, as impressive as your qualifications are, I can't hire you."

Her smile disappeared and she blinked a few times. "Is it because I'm a Lambert?"

Yes, he thought. She had to see he couldn't hire her. But he didn't want her to just walk out his door. He wanted to see her again. "Only partly. I don't have any openings in my PR department."

"But you said partly. Don't think about who my father is."

"It's a big part of who you are, Tempest. Even if I had an opening, I wouldn't hire you."

"You're missing out on one hell of a PR exec, Gavin," she said, standing up and gathering her briefcase.

He stood as well and walked over to the door, blocking her from leaving.

"I think if I hired you, I'd miss out on a hell of a woman, Tempest."

Her eyes widened and he knew she was debating the next move to make. He wondered then if he wasn't the only one fishing for information. If he wasn't the only one who was dealing with emotions he didn't understand exactly.

That's what he wanted to find out. He'd never be able to trust her in his office but in his bed…that was something all together different.

"Are you saying you want to date me?"

He thought about that for a long minute. Dating her really wasn't any different than hiring her. She was still his enemy's daughter…but he'd been focused on revenge for too long.

Barely an inch of space was between their bodies. He smelled even better up close than he had when she'd shaken his hand. He crowded closer to her and she fought not to back up. But in the end her need for personal space won out and she inched away from him.

He was all arrogant male. Totally sure of himself and his impact on her. And she wished she could prove him wrong. Wished she could take a step away from him and dismiss him with a snooty comment that would put him in his place. Remind him that she was the daughter of August Lambert.

"You're crowding me," she said carefully. She was completely out of her element with this man.

She didn't know him well enough to know the best way to deal with him. She only knew one thing for certain. She wasn't leaving this office without some kind of offer. Her pride was on the line, and to be honest, pride was the only thing she'd ever really had that was her own.

"Good."

"Why good?"

"I like it when you get your back up."

"I don't *get my back up*. I'm a well-bred young lady." No one had ever said anything like that to her before. He treated her like he wasn't impressed by her pedigree, which of course he wasn't. He disliked her father. Did that feeling transfer to her, as well?

"I'm not a well-bred man," he said.

She realized she knew practically nothing about Gavin. There was something in his tone that warned her that he hadn't had the same privileged upbringing she had. "Well, for future reference, I get haughty."

"I'll make a note."

She couldn't believe their meeting had come to this. Flirting. She was flirting with a man who had pretty much said he wasn't going to do what she wanted him to. And for some reason that didn't hurt as much as she'd thought it might. But then she was a master at hiding the hurt inflicted on her by the men in her life. And Gavin technically wasn't in her life.

Gavin was a long shot for a job from the beginning. But she wasn't ready to throw in the towel yet.

"I've got a deal for you," she said.

"I'm not interested in making deals."

"You're kidding. Your entire career is based on making deals."

He leaned closer to her, bracing his arms on the wall on either side of her head. Just like that she was trapped. He brought the heel of his hand down on her shoulder and tangled his fingers in her hair.

"Is it a business proposition?" he asked, using his grip on her hair to tip her head to the side. His thumb traced the line of her jaw.

He touched her so carefully. Like she was something fragile and breakable. It wasn't the way people usually treated her. Everyone knew she was tough as nails. Ballsy and brash and haughty. No vulnerabilities.

"Tempest?"

What the heck was he talking about? Then she remembered. She wanted to make a deal with him. She wanted to convince him to hire her. And she'd use whatever she had to get his attention. If that meant playing up the attraction between them then so be it.

"Kind of."

"Kind of?"

She thought quickly, trying to blunt the impact of his body next to hers. She closed her eyes so that she wouldn't have to look into his brilliant gaze. But that just made her more aware of his body heat and the yummy scent of his aftershave.

She cleared her throat. "You give me one media event to handle and if I do a good job you hire me."

He looked her straight in the eyes and she saw his answer before he said anything. She put her finger over his lips. Traced the lower one when his lips parted.

"Tempest…"

"Don't say no."

He leaned down so that when he spoke his breath brushed her ear. She shivered in awareness and had the feeling that Gavin knew exactly what he was about when it came to seducing women. And it had been so long since she'd been with a man. Three years to be exact. Three long years while she'd focused on her career. And look where that had gotten her.

"Tempest…"

"What?" she asked, cocking her head to the side so that her mouth was angled right next to his—a breath away. She wet her lips and watched his eyes following the movement of her tongue.

"I can't hire the daughter of my enemy."

She was afraid he'd say that. She had known this was a long shot, but she'd spent her entire life battling against a man who was resolved to feel nothing for her. She didn't give up easily and she wasn't going to now either.

"I'm not your enemy," she said. "This could work to your advantage."

He shook his head.

"Gavin, this is my last chance to prove to him that he's made a mistake. I'm not leaving your office unless you change your mind."

"An ultimatum?"

"A promise. I'm not the flighty-flirty heiress you've read about in the papers. I'm a well-educated asset that could be working for you."

He sighed and moved back from her. "I'm not making any promises, but I'll consider you if there is an opening."

"That's all I ask."

"Until then…"

"Yes?"

"Dinner?"

"What about it?" she asked. She wasn't going to accept an invitation like that. She was, after all, Tempest Lambert.

"Would you have dinner with me tonight?"

"I'm busy."

"Liar."

"I do have plans. You can join me if you want. I'll pick you up here at seven."

# Three

Gavin had been surprised when he'd gotten the e-mail from Tempest asking him to meet her at the Gillock Gallery on north Ravenswood Avenue. He'd worked later than he'd planned to and then made his way across town to the gallery opening for an artist that Gavin had never heard of before, Pablo Montovan.

He mentioned Tempest's name at the door and was told to go right in. He got a glass of wine from the waiter and walked through the room stopping to study the art. He'd never taken time for the niceties in life. Michael collected sculptures and their mother had an affinity for photography. But Gavin wasn't interested in anything unless it brought him closer to his goal of bringing down August.

For the first time he realized how one-dimensional his life was. How work-centric he was. He took a sip of the California chardonnay and studied the portraiture. It depicted a crowd of people in the center of the canvas on a solid block of color. As he stood there he realized how alone each person was. Isolated in a sea of many.

He glanced back and came face-to-face with Tempest.

A soft feminine hand rested on his shoulder. "Like it?"

"I'm not sure."

"Why not?" she asked. She wore a simple cocktail dress in black and white. But the dress was anything but simple on her.

He shrugged, not planning on answering that.

"This piece—Waiting #7. Makes me feel kind of sad. Not a good feeling of expectation. But like they are all waiting for something they don't want."

He took another sip of his wine.

"Come on, Gavin, tell me what you see."

"I'm not really into art," he said, afraid any comments he made would reveal too much of his own inner turmoil.

He saw the disappointment in her eyes and told himself it didn't matter. He'd only come tonight out of curiosity. Not about the art but about the woman he couldn't figure out.

"Nice turn out," he said.

She sighed and then smiled at him. But it wasn't her usual brilliant expression.

"Yes, it is. I was worried that Pablo wouldn't get the crowds he does in Europe."

"You're a friend of the artist?" he asked. There seemed to be few circles where she didn't know someone. He knew that would be a great asset in a PR director. For a minute he wondered if she had been legit in his office. Was she really just looking for a job? Or was he right to suspect that her father might be using her as a pawn?

"Yes. I want you to meet him. I noticed that the lobby of your building is a little bare. Pablo does some stunning murals."

Gavin followed her through the crowd, stopping when she did and engaging in small talk with people he had nothing in common with. Yet slowly he realized he didn't mind it. He liked listening to Tempest and the way she talked to others.

She effortlessly put everyone at ease. Finding obscure connections between the various groups and starting conversations that weren't frivolous. She introduced him as simply the head of an investment firm and when he noticed a few raised eyebrows from people who'd obviously heard of the feud between him and August, she simply smiled it off.

Was that her intent? To plant the seeds of doubt in public so that his investors would get jittery and pull back?

He pulled her to the side of the crowded room.

The noise of conversation and music filled the air but he found a quiet hallway tucked out of the way.

"What?" she asked.

"Why did you invite me here tonight?"

She lifted one shoulder and glanced back at the crowd. She was ill at ease for the first time since he'd met her, her normal boldness stifled by this quiet hallway and his questions.

"I wanted a chance to get to know you better," she said at last. "I'm not going to lie to you. I'm still hoping to convince you to give me a job."

"Why do you want to get to know me better?" he asked, completely ignoring the job thing. He'd already made up his mind not to hire her, nothing would change it. "Are you spying on me for your father?"

She wrapped her arm around her waist and took two steps away from him. There was such hurt in her eyes that he wanted to apologize but he didn't. He'd made a plausible assumption.

"I'm not like that, Gavin."

She waited and he sensed that she wanted him to say something that would make things right between them. But he didn't have the words.

She turned away but he stopped her with his hand on her elbow, tugging her to a stop. "Don't be offended. It was a logical theory."

"And you're always logical, aren't you?"

"Yes. I don't understand you." He'd learned from watching his father that emotion had no place in the decision-making process.

"What's to understand? I want a chance to work for you and I'm attracted to you. I thought we agreed to at least explore the attraction."

Did they? He wasn't sure now what he'd agreed to. Her skin was ultra soft and he ran his finger over the flesh of her inner arm. He knew he should stop, that the touch was too intimate for a public place, but she felt so good. No one should have skin that soft.

Goose flesh spread down her arm and she turned to face him. "You can't argue the attraction."

"I don't want to," he admitted. Though it wasn't logical, it made no sense to confess to feelings that he knew weren't sensible.

"But you don't exactly want to embrace it, either," she said.

"True."

She turned away from him and this time he let her slip free. He'd seen the hurt in her eyes. What had it been like growing up with August as a father?

Tempest was the first to admit she didn't always handle herself well with men she wanted to impress. But normally she was able to insulate herself enough from them that she didn't allow any of their comments to hurt her.

Gavin was different. She really wanted to make a good impression on him. Yet everything she did he saw as a move in the ongoing business of one-upmanship he had with her father.

"Let me introduce you to Pablo and then we can say our goodbyes," she said. She had the feeling no matter what she did to show him she was qualified to work for him, he wasn't going to change his mind.

"I don't want to meet Pablo."

"I promise you won't regret it."

He wrapped his hand around her neck and drew her back against his body. Lowering his head he inhaled deeply and she held herself still in his embrace, afraid to move.

"I regret everything about this night."

There was a finality to his words that she wished she didn't understand but it was too late. He was saying goodbye. She swallowed and stepped away from him, felt his fingers in her hair until she moved far enough away that the strands fell to her shoulders again.

There were a million thoughts rushing around her head. Regret of her own that she'd never get to know this man she was attracted to. Some anger at her father because if not for him…well, if not for him she wouldn't have approached Gavin so she knew that anger wasn't justified. It was just…oh, man, she wanted him. Him, not any other man, and it had been a long time since that had happened.

How had that happened? She was careful not to let anyone too close to her.

"Tempest?"

She shook her head, realizing she'd been standing there staring at him. "You really need something to soften the austerity of the lobby. Art puts people at ease." She needed to keep talking about his business. To somehow keep that knowledge in the front of her mind. If she stopped and let herself think about the fact that she'd been rejected again, she might break down.

"Okay," he said quietly.

She led him out of the hallway and back into the main gallery room. A buffet table was set against the windows that looked out on the street. There was a small jazz combo in the corner and a postage stamp-sized dance floor.

She moved into the crowd away from him. Trying to not be hyper aware of where he was but it was impossible. As she moved through the room she realized the truth of her life.

People smiled at her, air-kissed her cheek. Complimented her haute-couture outfit and made references to events they had attended together in the past. And the truth of the evening kept circling in her head. She kept hearing that voice that she hated listening to, the one that never let her flinch from the truth. The one that made her want to cry.

The truth was that she had a life filled with things just as her father did. A life filled with acquaintances instead of friends. A life empty of any real joy or real emotions.

And for one moment she'd come close to finding someone who'd maybe fill that emptiness.

She finished her Bellini in one long swallow and deposited the glass on the tray of a passing waiter.

Good God, she was getting depressing. She needed to get out of Chicago for a while.

Chicago was the place where her greatest hurts were. It was the city she'd been living in when her mother had died. And now she had this new one.

"Got a minute, Tempest?"

"Sure," she said, surprised to see Charlie Miller at this event. Though he was a crackerjack PR man, he didn't move in the same circles she did.

"Um, first I want to say, I'm sorry you didn't get the promotion."

She genuinely liked Charlie and with a few more years experience he was going to be exactly what her father needed. He was smart and savvy but a little young and inexperienced.

"As my father said, 'the best man got the job,'" she said.

He flushed. "I hope I can live up to that expectation."

"Of course you will. So what did you want?"

"I was hoping you'd have some time in your schedule to sit down and talk about some of the projects that were pending when you left. Kind of get me up to speed."

She had left abruptly. Like a spoiled child when she'd realized she'd once again let her father disappoint her. "Yes, I can. But I can't come by the office. How about Starbucks on Michigan tomorrow?"

"Fine. Ten would be good for me."

The small talk continued for a few more minutes before Kali interrupted them. Grateful for the rescue,

Tempest smiled at her friend. Kali Trevaine was one of Tempest's oldest friends. Kali's mom, Talia, had been a supermodel, one of the first that Tempest's Closet had used in their American marketing campaigns. In those early days her mother had been very active in the company and had brought Tempest to all the photo shoots.

She and Kali had bonded young. Playing in the clothes and getting into mischief. When Tempest had been a teenager and her father had wanted her to stay at school for the summers, Talia and Kali had invited her into their home. Kali was the closest thing Tempest had to a sister.

"What was that about?"

"He's the guy my father replaced me with."

"Ah, the competition. I think you could have taken him in a physical match."

Tempest laughed as she knew Kali wanted her to. It was true that Charlie was a small man, only five-seven and slim. She probably could take him if she were given to doing such a thing.

"Is that your new reality TV show idea? A corporate version of *Celebrity Death Match?*"

"Ah, no, I hadn't thought beyond you. But that thought has merit."

"Please, I was kidding. I don't want to see something like that on TV."

"Maybe America does," Kali said.

"Excuse me, ladies."

Tempest was surprised Gavin had sought her out

again. But maybe he wanted to meet Kali. At five-nine she was thin and stunningly beautiful. Her coffee-colored skin and exotically shaped eyes drew men to her like bees to honey. But Tempest was also disappointed that she'd been so strongly attracted to a man who could go so quickly from wanting her to wanting her friend.

"Yes, Gavin?"

"Dance with me," he said.

He nodded to Kali as he drew Tempest through the crowd to the dance floor.

"I thought we'd said goodbye," she said, as he drew her into his arms.

"Not yet."

She rested her head on his shoulder as the band played a slow jazzy number. She knew this wasn't real and wouldn't last, but for this instant she felt at home in his arms.

There was no way in hell that this woman belonged with him.

She could never be more than a means to an end. But it didn't feel that way and for just one moment he shut down the logical part of his mind and just held her.

The music swirled around them as did the other couples on the small dance floor, but when Tempest lowered her head to his shoulder the rest of the world disappeared.

He knew this was an emotional reaction. Tried to

justify the feelings with the knowledge that anything he started wouldn't go any further than this dance floor.

And that made the need sharpen inside him. He wanted her. His skin felt too tight and his blood flowed heavier in his veins. He'd been jealous when he'd seen her talking with that skinny man earlier. And he didn't like that.

He wasn't a jealous man—he just never permitted himself to connect to any of the women he'd dated. He reserved those emotions solely for his mother and his brother.

But with Tempest everything was different, dammit. He didn't like it. He wasn't a possessive man but each time Tempest had stopped with a group to chat he'd found himself resentful that he wasn't in the group.

"Did you talk to Pablo?"

"Yes," he said, not interested in discussing another man with her. This covetousness was unfounded. She wasn't his. He shouldn't feel so possessive but he did.

"Did you ask him to do a mural—"

"No, Tempest. I don't want to talk about art tonight."

"Then why did you come to a showing?" she asked. There was something in her voice that stopped his impatient answer. That hint of vulnerability he'd noticed before. It roused more than his possessiveness—it made him want to protect her. To ensure that she wasn't hurt.

"Because *you* asked me to," he said, quietly.

She rubbed her cheek against his shoulder and he

wished they were both naked so he could feel the softness of her skin against his own.

"I think there is more to it than that," she said.

Of course there was more to it. Nothing with Tempest was easy. It was complicated by matters that had been a part of his life for too long now. He almost wished they'd delayed their first date until after the November board meeting of Tempest's Closet. After he'd dismantled her father's empire and finally had the revenge he'd spent years working toward.

He knew that she'd never have anything to do with him once he took over her father's company. Sure, the relationship with her father was strained, but August was all that Tempest had. Though a boy at the time, Gavin could remember the stories of Tempest Lambert…poor little rich girl. The Lambert family had one of those curses that the media liked to play up. And Gavin had learned one thing from all the articles he'd read about her. She was an incredibly loyal woman.

Her loyalty to Lambert was obvious to Gavin even thought she'd come to Renard Investments for a job. She was still a Lambert and still passionate about Tempest's Closet.

He wondered what that felt like. He wondered if August had any idea how lucky he was to have someone so loyal to him that no matter how cruelly he treated her, she'd still be there. And for just a moment he wanted to shake Tempest for always allowing her father to hurt her.

"We already discussed this."

"Yes, we did and I thought we'd found closure but somehow I'm back in your arms again."

His gut clenched at her words. He wanted her in his arms. Really in his bed. Naked and willing under him. Only then would he be able to find any closure to the relentless need that kept hammering through his body.

He tightened his grip on her back, slowly sliding his hands to her hips. His fingers flexing and sinking into her soft curves. He drew her nearer to him until her breasts rested against his chest.

Her breath caught in her throat and she tipped her head back, looking up at him with those wide blue eyes of hers. He saw the answering need in her gaze. Saw that she wanted him with the same insane passion. Saw that this wasn't going to be easy for her to walk away from either.

And strangely that was just what he needed to justify lowering his head to hers right there on the crowded dance floor. He forgot that public displays of affection were taboo for him because they made the public and the stockholders doubt his ability to run his business. He forgot that she was the daughter of his rival. He forgot everything except the fact that he hadn't tasted her lips and he wanted to.

Needed to. He wasn't going to last another second until he knew if her kiss was as flat-out hot as he expected it to be.

He lifted one hand from her hips, tangled his fingers in her softer-than-sable hair and tilted her head back.

She gasped as he lowered his mouth over hers and he wasn't tentative in taking her. He thrust his tongue deep into her mouth. He gave her no chance to respond, just wielded his will over her.

She tasted of the slightly sweet drink she'd had earlier and raspberry lip gloss. She wrapped both her hands around his shoulders and shifted in his embrace, her tongue sliding against his. Her hands tangling in the hair at the back of his neck.

Blood roared in his ears as he rubbed his hand up and down her back. He felt the fragility of her spine, the fineness of her slim body. He lifted his head and rubbed his lips along the line of her jaw and down to her neck.

She tasted again of that essence of woman that he was coming to associate only with her. She moaned deep in her throat as he thrust his tongue into her mouth. Her tongue stroked tentatively against his.

Sliding his hands down her back he cupped her hips and pulled her more firmly against his body. He'd meant to keep the embrace light because they were in the middle of the dance floor.

He rubbed his growing erection against her and she made a soft sound in the back of her throat. Her nails dug into his shoulders through the layer of his shirt. She undulated against him.

He lifted his head. Her eyes were closed and face was flushed with desire. He knew that it would take very little for him to persuade her to have sex with him tonight. And part of him wanted to do that, to take what he needed.

His heart beat too quickly in his chest and the lust that had taken entire control of his body abated at the fear that was slowly creeping through him. He wanted her more than he should.

He had to stop this insanity and leave. He rubbed his finger over her wet lips and took a step back.

"Goodbye," he said, knowing that he was going to have a hell of a time forgetting her.

She lifted her hand toward him and he was tempted to stay. Tempted to say the hell with the inappropriateness of their relationship and take something he wanted even thought it didn't fit into his plans.

A camera flash went off to his left. He caught a glimpse of a man running through the crowd. This is what a relationship with Tempest would be like, he thought.

"Gavin?"

He shook his head and walked away without looking back. And it was one of the hardest thing he'd ever done.

# Four

Tempest was tired, cranky and out of sorts when she left her condo the next morning for her meeting with Charlie. And she wasn't very well prepared. She hadn't gone back to the office after she'd decided to quit working for her father, so she had no notes other than the things she'd kept in her head.

And this might not be the best morning for a meeting because all she could think about was Gavin. She hated the fact that they'd both agreed to part ways. She knew it was the most sensible thing to do but she ached for him.

That kiss last night had made it impossible for her to do anything other than moon over the man. And that ticked her off. The only man who'd had the power to completely make her crazy before had been her father. Of course that was an entirely different thing.

All conversations stopped when she entered the Starbucks on Michigan Avenue. She tried to pretend that she hadn't noticed. But she felt like a huge spotlight was on her. She glanced around the barista trying to find something else to engage her attention when she saw a discarded newspaper. She snagged it from the table while she waited to order her coffee.

She skimmed the headlines and then flipped to the society page, hoping her presence at Pablo's opening got him some additional press. Her jaw dropped as she saw the picture of her and Gavin. She hadn't even noticed the flashbulb when he'd been kissing her.

But there they were in the middle of the dance floor. Totally wrapped up in each other. She touched her own lips as they started to tingle. There'd been so much passion in that kiss. She could still feel his body pressed against her. She glanced at the caption and felt the blood drain from her face.

*Sleeping with the enemy? Tempest Lambert never shies away from scandal but cavorting with Gavin Renard the CEO of Tempest's Closet's fiercest competition is a little over the top even by her standards.*

She fumbled in her purse for her sunglasses and donned them quickly. It was too late to really disguise herself but the glasses provided a shield that no matter how false, she needed.

She dug around her bag until she found her cell

phone and dialed Kali's number. She didn't know what to do and needed her friend.

A call beeped in before Kali answered and she glanced down at the caller ID wondering if it would be her dad. It wasn't. The number was one she couldn't identify. She let it go to the voicemail and switched back to Kali's line.

"Hello?" she asked when she heard silence on the open line.

"Tempest?"

Thank God, Kali was home. "Yes, did you see the paper?"

"No. What's up?"

The man in front of her glanced over his shoulder at her and she realized this was not a conversation she wanted to have standing in line at Starbucks. She walked out of the coffee shop and down the sidewalk to a quiet area.

"There's a picture of Gavin and I."

"From last night?"

"Uh…yes."

"From the dance floor?" Kali asked again and the speculation in her friend's voice made her want to cringe.

She'd openly courted the press for years after she'd graduated from finishing school. Used them as a way to make her father notice her even though he'd always made it a point to ignore her. And she'd regretted it for the last few years but it was, of course, too late to go back and change things. But this picture she resented the most.

"Yes," she said to Kali. "What am I going to do? Gavin didn't want to date me for precisely this reason."

"He wasn't exactly an unwilling participant."

"Kali!"

"Well, that's the truth."

"I know. I was just hoping…" she stopped before she said any more. She'd been hoping that Gavin would have a change of heart, but now she doubted he would.

"Oh, honey. I was hoping, too, that this guy would be different."

Sometimes she wished Kali didn't know her as well she did. But right now it was nice to know she wasn't alone. That she had someone in her corner. "There's no way the tabloids aren't going to pick this up."

"You're right. So what's the plan?"

"I don't know. I have to think this through."

"I don't like the sound of that," Kali said.

"Maybe there's a way to make this a win-win."

"For who? You?"

"Me and Gavin."

"Be careful."

"I will be." She hung up the phone and waked slowly back to her car. Her mind was moving swiftly over the possibilities. There had to be a way for this to work to their advantage.

With the press playing up the fact that they were

involved, she might be able to convince Gavin to make their relationship real. She made a quick call to Charlie to cancel their appointment.

She didn't have Gavin's number but knew where his office was so she drove there. She parked and walked into the building wondering what she was going to say to him. But it was nerves ruling her now. It was excitement and the thought that she'd found a way to spend more time with him.

She still wanted a job. A job for her father's rival would anger her father but it was more than that. She wanted the job to prove that someone else had thought her worthy.

She stopped for a minute near the bank of elevators. Nerves simmered again as she realized that Gavin might have had the same thought that the newspaper did. That sleeping with his enemy's daughter would be a nice twist. And she had some doubts for the first time since she'd decided to come to his building.

Then again she'd planned to use him to make her father angry. Could she really begrudge him the same thing?

Tempest heard someone come up behind her near the bank of elevators. Her gut instinct was to try to make herself smaller so she wouldn't be recognized, but instead she put her shoulders back and stood taller

"Tempest?"

Gavin. "Hi. Have you seen the newspaper?"

He nodded. "Let's talk in my office."

* * *

Gavin focused on the fact that he'd correctly predicted that Tempest would come to his office when she saw the photo instead of on the fact that they were alone in the elevator and he wanted to hit the emergency stop button and pull her into his arms.

Only the knowledge that Michael was waiting in his office stayed his hand. He had a vague idea that seducing Tempest wasn't off limits now. Everyone was going to believe they were involved anyway. But the way he felt about her was too intense. Could his logical side stay focused on business if he was involved in an affair with her?

His libido said who the hell cared. But he knew better than to let his groin make a decision.

"Why are you staring at me?" she asked.

There was none of the ballsy attitude she'd had the first time she'd visited his office. "Probably because you're wearing your sunglasses inside."

She flushed a little and shifted her brown Coach bag from her right shoulder to her left. "Oh, I'd forgotten them."

He leaned against the walnut paneling in the elevator and tried to look like he was at ease.

"Why do you have them on?" It was an overcast morning, no sun in sight.

She straightened the large dark glasses on her face and then glanced up at him. "I was in Starbucks when I saw the paper."

"I don't understand."

"Of course, you wouldn't."

He just waited and she sighed and wrapped an arm around her waist. "People stare at me when I'm out. And after I saw that picture of us in the paper I felt…well, I just put the glasses on because it gives me the illusion of hiding."

In that instant he knew whatever else happened between them he wasn't going to be able to just let her walk back out of his door. He wanted to pull her into his arms and hold her tight to his side. But dammit, he wasn't a protector. He was a destroyer. He knew that. Even his success in business had come from buying up failing companies and taking them apart.

He took her sunglasses off and folded them in his hand. She stared up at him and he saw the truth in her gaze. The vulnerability that she never let the world see.

He cupped her face in his palm and tipped her head up so that she could see the truth in his eyes.

"You don't need to hide from me."

She chewed on her lower lip. He lowered his head and brushed her mouth with his. He wanted to deepen the contact but restraint was needed now. Later when they were alone in his office…

"I think I need to hide most of all from you."

"Why?"

"Because you see me in ways that no one else does."

The elevator doors opened before he could respond and his brother stood there in the hallway waiting for them.

"We'll finish this discussion later."

"Will we?" she asked in that sassy way of hers. She was getting herself back from the shock of seeing that photo. He was glad for it. He could deal with the ballsy woman better than the vulnerable one.

"I just said we would."

"Well then I guess your word is law."

"Yes, it is," Michael said.

Gavin gave his brother a hard look but Michael just grinned at him. "Trust me. You can't win when you go up against Gavin."

"I'm not so sure that's true," Tempest said.

"I don't believe we've met. I'm Michael Renard."

"Tempest Lambert."

She shook hands with Michael and made small talk as they walked down the hallway to the executive offices. Gavin envied his brother many things but in this moment he wished he had the ability to loosen up the way Michael did. Then again, Michael lacked the focus and intensity that were so much a part of his own make up.

As they entered his office, Gavin told his secretary they weren't to be disturbed. Tempest and Michael fell silent as they took a seat in the guest chairs.

Gavin walked over to the windows that looked out over Lake Michigan. He'd spent the morning going over different courses of action, trying to find the one that would best suit this situation. The one he could use to his advantage.

For once he didn't trust his own logic. Didn't trust the plan he'd settled on. All because of the one variable he couldn't control—Tempest.

Tempest cleared her throat and he turned around to face her.

"I'm sorry," she said. "You shouldn't have to pay the price just because my life is one big goldfish bowl."

"You don't have to apologize. I'm the one who kissed you."

She flushed and glanced at his brother.

"Um…I'll leave you two to discuss this. Let me know when you need me."

Michael left the office closing the door behind him. Tempest stood up.

"I'm not sure where we go from here, Gavin. Short of me finding another man to go out with—that might draw the press away from you, but I'm not interested in anyone else."

She wasn't going to date anyone else if he had anything to say about it. "That's not necessary. I think the best thing to do would be for us to have an affair. See where this attraction leads."

Gavin stared at her for a moment and realized that the only plan he wanted to enact was one where they were together. There was the added bonus that the press from any type of relationship they had would drive her father crazy.

He wasn't the kind to talk about business outside of the office so even if she were some kind of corporate spy—which he doubted—there was no information she could take back to her father from him.

He didn't allow himself to think of Tempest except in terms of an affair. He hoped like hell that the attraction he felt for her was only a sexual thing and once it ran its course they could both move on.

*An affair*. She wanted one with him but he was so cold when he suggested it. She hesitated. Was she really going to start a relationship with a man who could be so aloof?

"That sounds so romantic," she said hoping she didn't sound too sarcastic. But not really caring if she did.

"It isn't meant to be romantic. We're both attracted to each other. The media will make our lives hell no matter what the circumstances…it's rational."

"Rational? Was that what you felt last night?"

He walked around his desk in long measured strides and she fought to keep her ground. Because there was something about him that intimidated her. Something about his large frame and his stern countenance that made her want to back down. Except she didn't back down for anyone.

He put his hands on her waist, pulling her against his body. "There was nothing sensible or sane about last night. I wanted you and I didn't want to let you go without tasting your kiss at least once."

"Oh."

"I'm not romantic, Tempest. I'm a businessman and for the better part of my adult life I've been focused on only one thing."

"Ruining my father."

He nodded. He didn't even try to deny it which made her respect him just a little more.

"If we decide on an affair, don't expect romance."

"What should I expect?" she asked. No one had ever been as forthright with her as he was now. And in that moment she realized she could really fall for Gavin Renard. She realized that he was the kind of man that she'd been searching for all her life. He was solid and straight forward and he didn't care that she had more money than any one person needed.

"I'll treat you the way that you deserve to be treated in my bed and out of it."

She shivered at his words. She wanted what he'd described but if she said yes to this she'd be little more than his ornament—his date at functions until he tired of her. And a man like Gavin would tire of a woman who allowed herself to only be his bedmate.

"I want you to give me a chance to work for you, too."

He dropped his hands from her and stepped away. "I can't."

"Just let me come up with a PR plan for you. No promises of employment—just a test run to show you what I can do."

"Why is this important to you?" he asked. "You don't need the money."

"No, I don't need the money. But I want to prove to my father that he's wrong."

"What was he wrong about, Tempest?"

Me, she thought. But she'd never said that out loud in the past and she wasn't about to say it to Gavin. She didn't want him to realize that her own father thought she was little more than an ornament for men to use and display.

"That I'm not qualified to run the PR department of a large firm."

He leaned back against his desk, crossing his legs at the ankle. "Why Renard Investments?"

"Because you are rivals," she said, and then wished she hadn't.

"And that will make your success sting a little, right?"

She shook her head. "I know that makes me sound mean and petty but…"

She couldn't go on. Her father did make her want to be petty. Made her want to do ridiculous over-the-top things. Anything that would get his attention. And she was too damned old to still crave his approval. But she'd never had it and would always want it.

"It doesn't sound small at all," he said. "I imagine your relationship with your father is complicated."

"It is. What about you and Michael?"

"We're nothing like you and your dad. Michael knows that I'm here for him. So are we in agreement to an affair?"

"No."

"Why not? It's just the sort of thing you can use to get back at your father."

"He doesn't care who I sleep with."

"I'm not sure about that."

She was. "Trust me. I have it straight from the source."

He'd told her that her cheap escapades were of little consequence to him as long as she didn't bring any of the men home. And she doubted that Gavin would want to come to August's Lake Shore Drive mansion.

"He really said that to you?"

She nodded and shrugged it aside. "Let me do the PR plan…it's obvious to me that your job is your life and it will give us something to do together."

He rubbed the back of his neck. "I could never share any proprietary information with you."

It hurt a little because she knew he was trying not to say that he didn't trust her. But once he got to know her, she was sure she could change his mind.

"I can do something about your reputation as a cold-blooded shark. Someone who goes in for the kill when a company is floundering."

"I like that rep."

"Maybe I can come up with a plan to humanize you."

He stared at her for a long moment and then he shrugged. "Okay, but I'm not hiring you."

"We'll see."

# Five

Tempest was thirty minutes late to her meeting with Charlie. She wasn't exactly sure of what she'd agreed to in Gavin's office but she knew they'd discuss it further when he came to her house tonight for dinner.

She called her housekeeper and informed her she'd have a guest for dinner. Then she stopped in front of the Tempest's Closet corporate offices. Since their earlier meeting at Starbucks had been delayed, Charlie had suggested they try for lunch. He was lounging against a low railing that lined the handicap ramp leading to the entrance, cigarette in one hand, cell phone in the other.

The wind blew his short hair and he stubbed out

his cigarette as he saw her. As he walked toward her, she realized that there was more to Charlie than she'd first thought. He opened the door to her Aston Martin convertible and slid onto the leather seat.

"Sorry I'm late," she said as he slid into the car. He smelled of the summer air and cigarettes. She'd quit smoking almost three years ago but she missed it.

"You're doing me a favor," he said, putting on his seat belt.

"Where to?" she asked, as she eased the car out into the light traffic. It was the middle of the afternoon so they wouldn't have to worry about the lunch crowds.

"Some place quiet so we can talk without worrying if we're overheard."

She chose a small restaurant in the Art Institute that was quiet at this time of the day. They sat in the back corner and she gave him all the information she had on the projects she'd been working on. The part that would be more difficult for Charlie would be using her contacts.

She wrapped things up quickly. "Well, that's it then. Good luck, Charlie." She put her notebook back in the large Coach bag that she'd brought with her and made a move to get up.

"Thank you, Tempest. There's one more thing," Charlie said. His tone of voice made her leery. What else could they possibly have to discuss?

"What?" she asked. She sat back in her chair

almost afraid of where this was going, which was ridiculous because Charlie had nothing over her. He had nothing she wanted, except her father's respect.

"The picture of you and Gavin Renard from today's paper."

"What about it?" She tried not to sound defensive. But she didn't think that Charlie was the right guy to be talking to her about her personal life.

Charlie glanced away from her. "Your father has made that our number one priority."

"I don't see why it's any business of his. I am no longer employed by Tempest's Closet."

"You are still a major shareholder."

Tempest rubbed the back of her neck and really wished she'd stayed in bed this morning. "I always let my father vote my shares. If he has a problem with me he knows how to reach me."

Charlie didn't say anything, just leaned back in his chair. "He's put you back on the payroll. There was an article in the business section tying your departure and your relationship with Renard together."

"No. Tell him no."

"I can't, Tempest. He's not listening to me on this subject."

"Who is he listening to?"

"I have no idea. I got an e-mail from Jean this morning and tried to call him."

Jean was her father's secretary. "I'll take care of it."

"Thanks," he said, getting to his feet. "If it turns

out you're still in my department, I'd like you to handle the new store opening in Los Angeles."

"Better have a back-up plan because I'm nothing more than a shareholder now."

"I do," he said. She followed him out of the restaurant, trying to numb her mind. But it wasn't working. Just when she thought there was no way for her to feel more insignificant to her father, he did something like this. But she'd moved on and was trying to win Gavin's trust. That meant there was no way she could return to work for Tempest's Closet.

She tried to tell herself that it didn't matter what he did, that she'd moved on. And a part of her had moved on. A big part of her was looking forward to a new relationship with Gavin and the new opportunities he offered.

Charlie said nothing as she drove him back to his building. The entire time she stewed over her father and the fact that he thought…who knew what he thought.

"I'm not coming back to work at Tempest's Closet, Charlie. As far as I'm concerned I resigned and no one from HR has contacted me."

Charlie smiled at her as he opened the door. "I understand."

"It's nothing against you," she said, realizing that he might think she'd quit because he'd gotten the promotion she wanted.

"I never thought it was. Take care of yourself."

He eased out of the car. She grabbed her cell phone

thinking she should call her father but she didn't want to give him the pleasure of doing that. Yet this was one time when she couldn't let him ignore her wishes. She dialed his office number and got Jean.

"Is my father available?" she asked.

"I'm sorry, Tempest, but he isn't. Can I take a message?"

He was playing this through third parties and she'd be happy to let him continue on that way.

"Yes, Jean, please tell my father that I'm not coming back to work for him. Also please advise the HR department to take me off the payroll."

Jean sighed. "Umm…"

"Jean, he can't rehire me without even asking me to come back to work for him."

"You have a point. I'll make sure he receives your message."

"And the HR department?"

"Yes, I'll do that, as well."

"Thanks, Jean," she said, hanging up the phone. It occurred to her that she'd probably had more conversations with Jean than her father over her lifetime. But she refused to dwell on that.

Instead she thought about the coming evening. Staying in was out of the question. She wanted to go public with Gavin in a big flashy way. In a way that would garner the attention of every media outlet. She wasn't just doing it to annoy her father, this would help Gavin, too.

* * *

Tempest e-mailed him a PR plan for changing his image within the local community. He glanced at the first few items then put the plan out of his head. He was a businessman who focused on the bottom line and didn't give a damn what anyone thought of him.

The first thing on the list was to buy art for the lobby of his building. She'd put a little smiley face after that one and a note that said just kidding.

She was the only one who did that. Joked with him, well except for his brother but that was simply because he and Michael had relied on each other and only each other for the majority of their lives.

"What's that?"

"Nothing," he said, fighting the urge to minimize his Outlook e-mail box. He hadn't heard Michael enter but then the door between both of their offices was often left open.

"Nothing?" Michael leaned over his shoulder for a closer look. "It looks like an e-mail from Tempest Lambert. I thought you said there was nothing going on with her."

"Who are you, Katie Couric?" he asked, taking the mouse from Michael's hand before he could open the e-mail.

"Ha, very funny. Why is she e-mailing you a PR plan?"

"Michael, did you come into my office for a specific reason or just to be a pain in the ass?"

"I did have a reason. Being a pain in your ass is just something I throw in for fun."

"I'm pretty sure Mom wouldn't miss you if I relocated you to our Alaskan office."

"We don't have an office in Alaska," Michael said with a small grin.

"We will if you don't get to the point."

Michael leaned against the desk, crossing his legs at the ankles and his arms over his chest. "Our inside source at Tempest's Closet said there was a lot of rumbling going on today in mid-to-executive level management. Did you know Tempest no longer works for Tempest's Closet?"

"She mentioned it." She'd come to him for a job as soon as her father had shown her the door. He was beginning to believe there was more to her unemployment than met the eye.

"Well the inside dirt is that she quit when Charles Miller was promoted to the PR vice president opening," Michael said.

Gavin leaned back in his chair away from his brother and the desk. He hadn't asked about why she'd left Tempest's Closet. Hadn't really wanted to know the details because then he might sympathize with her. Might have a real reason to trust her and then he'd have no barriers to keep between them.

"Who's Charles Miller?" he asked. He was as familiar with the Tempest's Closet organizational chart as he was with his own. He knew all the players in the company and the name Charles Miller wasn't ringing any bells.

"We're checking him out. Seems like that picture of the two of you caused a stir, as well."

He didn't give a crap what people thought about him. He had made himself stop caring the day his parents had moved them out of their large family home just off of Main Street and into a mobile home park. It was the same day that the local Tempest's Closet announced record sales and plans to double the size of their store.

But he didn't like the fact that anyone was speculating on what was between him and Tempest. What he felt for her was too raw. Too protective and possessive for him to want to share it with the world.

"We dealt with the picture, too," Gavin said, not wanting to give the situation too much weight.

"You didn't give Tempest an ultimatum, did you?" Michael asked.

"No. Why would I do that?" Then again, she'd left his office to go to a meeting. One with her father? Tempest didn't have it in her to be a corporate spy, did she?

"August wants her to come back to work for him."

Gavin didn't want to ask if she'd said yes. A minute ago he'd been certain she'd say no to anything her father asked of her. Now he wasn't. He realized steamy hot attraction and one kiss weren't nearly enough to constitute a working knowledge of her.

"Don't you want to know what she said?"

"How does your spy get this information so quickly?"

"We pay him really good money and he's highly placed."

Seriously he wondered if they had any property in Fairbanks that would make a nice office. They didn't do a lot of business in Alaska but Michael would be out of his hair for a while. "You're on my last nerve."

He chuckled. "But we're blood so you'll forgive me, right?"

He shrugged. "What'd she say?"

"She told him no."

Relief and a kind of sadness moved through him. He was glad she hadn't gone back to work for her dad but the sensitive woman he was coming to know had to have been hurt by that situation.

He would look at her PR plan and see if she really knew her stuff. If she did, maybe he'd find a way to hire her in one of their subsidiaries. She couldn't work in the corporate offices or he wouldn't get any work done from lusting over her.

"Was that it?"

"No. The Tempest's Closet stockholders are antsy and several of them put out feelers to sell blocks of shares."

Tempest had been more of a help to him than she could ever guess. Not just because she'd acted the way he'd hoped she would with her father today.

"Did you make an offer?"

"Yes, I'll know something tomorrow."

"Keep me posted," Gavin said reaching over to turn off his laptop.

"I will. Where are you going?"

"What are you my social secretary?"

"You never leave the office before eight."

"Then maybe it's time I started."

Michael didn't say anything as Gavin pulled on his coat and gathered his briefcase.

"You okay, bro?"

"Yes," he said and walked out of the office. But he wasn't so sure that he was okay. Everything in his life was changing. And it was all to do with one woman. The daughter of his enemy.

Tempest wanted nothing more than to stay in for the evening but she knew it would be construed as hiding out so she got dressed for her date with Gavin. He hadn't responded to the e-mail she'd sent him earlier. She'd left a message with his secretary letting him know that she was expected at a new club downtown later tonight.

The celebrity deejay was the brother of one of her oldest boarding school friends and she wanted to lend her support to him. But she was tired and deep inside where she didn't lie to herself she was one mass of aching hurt.

She didn't know what Gavin expected from her other than sex. She didn't know why she still allowed her father to hurt her. And she knew that going back to work for Tempest's Closet would change absolutely nothing. Her father would still treat her with the same disdain he'd held her in for her entire life.

She reached for the pitcher of margaritas that her housekeeper had left sitting on the bar. Getting drunk or a least a little buzzed seemed like just the thing to insulate her from the worries in her head and the aching loneliness in her heart.

But she thought of Dean struggling to stay sober in a safe house in Italy. And knew that too easily she could slide back into the party lifestyle that had almost killed him.

The doorbell chimed and she sank down in one of the gilt Louis XIV chairs that faced the fireplace. She set her margarita on the end table, then reconsidered, thinking it might look as though she'd been waiting desperately for him. She heard his footsteps in the hallway leading to her sitting room a second before she decided to pick up the drink. She took a sip and tried to look…

He was gorgeous. He stood in the doorway in the light of the setting sun and she forgot about the worries in the back of her mind. Forgot that she wasn't sure she trusted him. Forgot everything except the slow physical awareness that was spreading through her body.

Her pulse picked up and her breathing became a little shallower. He still wore his suit jacket but his collar was open and she saw that he didn't wear a T-shirt underneath. His skin was tan and she wondered if he was muscular. She wanted to see what was beneath that shirt.

"Good evening, Tempest," he said.

Just hearing her name on his lips was enough to make her stand up. She had to stop this. This was ridiculous. She wasn't even sure she trusted the man; was she really going to let this attraction take control of her life?

"Can I get you a drink?"

"What are you drinking?"

"Margarita."

"I'll have one."

She fixed his drink a little nervously. She knew what she wanted and had no qualms about going after it. But the scene with Charlie this afternoon when he'd told her about her dad kept replaying in her head. What if Gavin found out and thought he couldn't trust her?

She handed him the drink but his fingers lingered on hers. Trapping her hand in his grip. She glanced up at him and felt the world drop away. Felt it narrow to just the two of them. She no longer heard the sounds of Maria in the kitchen or the ticking of the grandfather clock in the hallway.

It was just her and Gavin and nothing else mattered. And she wanted life to stay that way. Suddenly it didn't seem like a good idea to go out tonight—she wanted to be all alone with this man, with no outside interference whatsoever.

"That's a big pitcher for one person."

She knew that. She'd never had a problem with alcohol so she used it when she needed to. But now that Gavin was here she realized how it might look to him. "I was hoping to have help drinking it."

"Not getting drunk?" he asked.

"I did think about it," she admitted. There were so many rumors about her that she tried to never tell lies. Not even ones that would help her.

He raised one eyebrow at her.

"It hasn't been the best day for me," she said reluctantly.

"Because of the picture?" he asked.

"Sort of." No way did she want to go into all the sordid details of her pathetic relationship with her father.

"Want to talk about it?"

"No—yes."

He drew her over to the loveseat and sat down, sprawled his large frame on the piece of furniture. It made her realize how big he was as he settled in next to her.

"Talk."

She stared up at him wishing she'd never opened her mouth. He seemed so immune to the doubts that plagued her, above such petty worries as what someone else thought of him.

"How do you do it?" she asked, taking an absent sip of her margarita.

"Do what?" He set his glass down on the table, stretching one long arm along the back of the loveseat.

She stared at his hands instead of at him. No lies, she thought. Realizing that with Gavin that rule was going to be much harder to keep. He made her feel so vulnerable and she hated that.

"Stay so cool," she said. She really wanted to know. She could fake it for a while and people never seemed to notice the falseness of her smile but inside she died a little each time. And she was so incredibly tired of feeling empty.

When she was with Gavin she felt more than she wanted to, which was a double-edged sword. She craved the attention and the emotions he effortlessly brought to the fore but at the same time she was afraid of him.

He reached for his glass and took a sip of his margarita. "I don't"

"It looks like it."

"Appearances can be deceiving."

"Yes, they can."

Tempest tried to push it from her mind but the thought weighed heavily there. Appearances could be deceiving. What was Gavin hiding, and was she really going to try to figure it out?

# Six

Appearances were a tricky thing, Gavin thought as he watched Tempest move through the crowded club. Anyone seeing her now would never have guessed at the vulnerability he'd witnessed in her home earlier.

He'd ached to draw her into his arms and just hold her but he knew he was just as much to blame for her current troubles. He'd been thinking about it all night how the one that'd come out looking bad in the entire photo-lost-job situation was Tempest.

Her father had gotten the sympathetic he's-done-everything-for-her treatment and Gavin himself had gotten the businessman-led-astray-by-a-beautiful-woman thing. It wasn't fair, he thought.

But then he'd learned early on that life wasn't fair. And usually he didn't dwell on that.

She was incandescent tonight, glowing with a light from within, as she moved among her high-society friends, the groupies who followed the deejay from club to club and the paparazzi that seemed to follow her everywhere she went.

Gavin leaned against the wall in the VIP section and just watched her. He still had absolutely no idea what he was going to do with her other than take her to his bed. He knew that if he wanted her there tonight he should be a little more sociable but night-clubs like this left him cold. And pretending to be something he wasn't simply wasn't his way.

"Are you going to stand here all night?" she asked, coming up to him. Her hips moved in time with the driving beat of the music.

"Probably."

"Why?"

"This isn't my scene."

"No kidding. Why don't you give it a try?"

"I'm not really social."

"I am."

"I've noticed."

She glanced up at him. He wished he could read what was going on inside her head because he knew something was off but had no idea how to fix it.

"Why don't you like this scene?" she asked.

"There's no point to this."

"The point is to have fun…is that something you've heard of?"

"Ha, ha, smart-ass. Of course I've heard of fun, it's just so pointless to hang out in a club when you know there are people waiting to take your picture and write down everything you've done."

She pulled him further into the VIP section to a small booth in the back that was shrouded in shadows. She scooted in and then glanced up at him. "Sit down."

He slid in next to her. Giving into the temptation to put his arm around her shoulders and tug her up against the side of his body.

"Why are we back here?" he asked.

"No one can hear us back here or see us."

"If you wanted privacy, why'd we come here?"

"Because my doorman at home is on the payroll of at least two tabloid newspapers. He always tells them when I have visitors of the opposite sex and how long they stay. This way he won't have much to report."

He took a strand of her hair in his hand swirling it around his finger. "How do you stand it?"

"It's my life."

He added this complication to the matrix running in the back of his mind. It wasn't enough that she was August's daughter. She was someone who was used to living in the spotlight.

"Seriously, Tempest, how do you stand it?"

She stared down at the table. "I'm one big fraud.

I smile at strangers and chat up acquaintances and pretend that they are friends."

He heard more than her words and knew that deep inside these kinds of situations took a toll on her. And he wasn't going to add to it. He had the money and the manpower to shield her.

He let his fingers slide down her neck, tipping her head back so that she rested on his arm. He traced the lines of her face, trying to ease the stress that he saw there. Then he leaned down and brushed his lips over hers. Just felt her in his arms, where he'd wanted her since she'd left his office hours ago.

She opened her lips and he felt the brush of her tongue against his. Her hands caged his face and she lifted slightly so she was pressed more firmly against him.

Deep inside where he'd been hiding for the majority of his adult life he felt something melt. Some part of him that he planned to ignore, but all the same that part knew that this woman was his.

*His.*

He took control of the kiss, changing it from a sweet gentle meeting of mouths, to an all out claiming of the woman. He wanted to make sure there was no doubt in Tempest's mind that she belonged to him.

A flashbulb illuminated them and he lifted his head, pushing to his feet, but Tempest stilled him with her small manicured hand on his arm.

"Want to dance?"

"No."

"Gavin…"

He stopped walking toward the velvet ropes and the photographer who'd snapped their picture.

"What?"

"I'm sorry my life is like this."

He glanced back at her, turning to face her. "I am, too. Let's get out of here."

"I wanted one dance with you," she said.

"Ah, hell, you know that guy is still out there," he said.

"Yes, I do."

He wasn't much of a dancer but couldn't pass up the chance to hold her in his arms. She'd changed into a skirt that was so tight and short, he couldn't keep his eyes off her legs, which were long and slim, accentuated by the heels she wore.

"Why don't you have a bodyguard?"

She shrugged but he wasn't going to let her evade the question.

"Tell me," he said.

"I did have one but he worked for my father. When I left finishing school my dad and I had a falling out so he cancelled the contract with the company that provided my bodyguard. My father said if I was going to court trouble then I deserved to get myself out of it…I've just kind of never wanted to give him the satisfaction of knowing I couldn't take care of myself…so no bodyguard for me. I can handle the paparazzi without one."

"Give me a minute," he said.

"What are you doing?"

"Hiring a bodyguard. And it's not because I think you can't handle yourself."

"Why then?"

He didn't answer her, refused to say out loud that he needed to protect her. Instead he dialed the private investigating firm that he used in researching company CEOs before he decided to invest in their businesses. He had a short conversation with the owner and the promise that a bodyguard would be along shortly to ensure their privacy.

She grabbed his hand, tugging him toward the dance floor. He pulled her into his arms and realized dating this woman was more complicated than a million different mergers but that didn't deter him from going after her.

Tempest watched the street lights and shadows go by as Gavin drove. He wasn't going in the direction of her condo and she was pretty sure she was going to get an up-close and personal tour of his place.

The bodyguard he'd summoned to the club was following behind them making sure they weren't followed too closely. She wasn't sure that the press would stay away from her, but it was nice for tonight to have this sense of anonymity. It was something she'd never had

"Thanks," she said, at last. Needing to talk, needing to get out of her own head before she started crying about her life. God, how pitiful was that? She had a nice home, food in her kitchen and a roof over her head. There was nothing to be so sad about.

"For?" he asked, his voice low.

She shrugged, wrapping one arm around her waist as a chill spread through her body. "The bodyguard thing."

"It was nothing. Cold?"

She shook her head but he adjusted the air conditioning making it warmer on her side. But it wasn't nothing to her. Her father always said she brought the intense scrutiny on herself. That if she'd acted like a lady they would never have been interested in her. Ironic that when she cleaned up her act and started behaving like a lady, he was the one who became more indifferent in her.

Gavin wasn't indifferent. But he was still holding a part of himself back from her. Not that she necessarily blamed him. She'd read the *Page Six* dirt on herself and knew without a doubt that anyone with a nice normal life would think twice about getting too involved with her.

But Gavin didn't have a normal life. He had a life where he was gunning for Tempest's Closet. Why? Even her father had never said exactly why.

"Can I ask you a question?" she asked into the silence. She wanted to unravel Gavin and figure out what made him tick. And a big part of who he was, according to rumor, involved the take over of her father's company.

"You just did," he said wryly.

"Are you trying to be funny?"

"I don't know, is it working?"

"No."

She turned in her seat to face him. His stark features were illuminated by the dashboard lights making him seem more of a stranger than she wanted him to be.

"Why are you fixated on taking over Tempest's Closet?"

He glanced over at her and then back to the road. "It makes good business sense."

"There seems like there is more to it than that."

He turned off the highway and entered an exclusive neighborhood. "Maybe there is."

"If you don't want to say then just tell me it's off-limits."

"I don't want to say anymore about it," he said, pulling into the garage of a large McMansion. There were two other cars parked in the three-car garage. One low, sexy sports car and an SUV that looked like it had been taken off-roading.

"Why not?"

"Tempest, it's private."

"And I'm only allowed to fall into a certain part of your life?"

He shrugged.

"I'm not into anonymous sex."

"Neither am I. I like you and I'll share parts of my life with you."

But just the parts that he wanted to share.

"I can't do this," she said. She'd had affairs in the past that were short and frivolous but she couldn't do that with Gavin. She wanted to know more about him. He made her feel safe and real.

And she was so afraid that if she slept with him, she'd be in over her head.

He glanced over at her his features illuminated this time by the garage lighting and she knew this was a crossroads for them. Either they'd continue on in a relationship or they'd part ways.

Gavin rubbed the back of his neck, He had known this moment was going to come—he should have been better prepared for it. And he'd already decided she was not a corporate spy. Was it possible that August didn't know why he was coming after him? Or was it only his daughter?

"Come inside and we can talk. If you still want to go home…I'll take you. The bodyguard is yours no matter what choice you make. Everyone deserves privacy."

"Thanks for saying that. A lot of people believe I deserve the attention. That it is some kind of punishment for my actions."

"People?"

She shrugged and he knew that she meant her father. She'd said as much earlier but now she wasn't going to say anymore. He opened his car door and pocketed his keys. He escorted her into his house.

As the door closed behind them he felt a sense of rightness. She belonged here.

He could talk her into anything on his home turf. But he didn't want to persuade her to stay. He wanted her as hot for him as he was for her.

He led her into the living room with the plasma screen TV on one wall and the tropical fish tank on the other. There was expensive art hanging on the wall that his decorator had purchased and the floor was made of marble he'd had imported from Italy. He didn't want to acknowledge it but he knew that he'd been working hard his entire life for a moment like this one.

He wanted her to know that he wasn't some poor kid who'd lost everything and lived on government subsidies. He didn't want to acknowledge that part of him, not in front of her. But he was going to have to. There was no way to talk about his focus on acquiring Tempest's Closet without talking about the past.

And standing in this opulent room even he felt the distance between who he'd been and who he was today.

"Can I get you a drink?"

"No, I'm good," she said, drifting around the room and settling on the couch.

He walked over to the well-stocked bar in the corner and poured himself two fingers of scotch before turning back toward her.

She looked like a sexy angel in the dim lighting. And he didn't want to let her go. Even though he knew deep inside that he wasn't going to get to keep her. The past was too much a part of the man he was today for her to every really be a part of his life but he wanted whatever time they had.

"Am I pushing too hard?" she asked. "I know what it's like to feel like you're being hounded."

"Ah, honey. You humble me." And she really did. She was selfless in a way that he knew she wouldn't recognize. She was constantly thinking of others and though she had a reputation for being a party-girl and going after only what would make her feel good, he was coming to realize that making others feel good was what did it for her.

"Come sit with me, Gavin."

He sank down on the sofa beside her and she turned toward him, slipping off her shoes and curling those long legs under her. The hem of her skirt rose to a dangerous level. He couldn't tear his gaze from her thighs until she put her hand on his forearm. Stroked her fingers up and down his arm.

She stared up at him with those wide-blue eyes of hers. Seeing past the successful man he was today and straight into the heart of him. Straight to that little boy he'd all but forgotten about.

He tugged her into his arms, until her back rested against his chest and she faced away from him. He wrapped his arm around her waist and lowered his head to the top of her hair. Breathing in that sweet clean scent that he associated only with her.

"Tempest's Closet industries took my life from

me," he said, softly. And realized he wasn't going to be able to do this. He didn't want to sound like some kind of sap whose life was ruined. Because he really couldn't imagine living another way. He was happy being the man he was today. And grudgingly he realized he owed that to August Lambert.

"How?" she asked, tipping her head back on his shoulder. Her silky hair slid against his skin.

"The same way they did so many lives in this country. Tempest's Closet came to my home town and the small merchants in the town slowly went out of business."

"Tempest's Closet brings a lot of money into the communities that it develops in. You know a lot of local governments solicit Tempest's Closet to get them to come to their towns."

"I thought you stopped working for Tempest's Closet."

"That doesn't mean I'm not still proud of what my father has done."

He pushed to his feet and walked away from her. This wasn't something he could ignore. "For every job that Tempest's Closet brings into a community at least five are lost. And a way of life is compromised."

She sat up. "A way of life? Tempest's Closet isn't going in and making these communities into company towns that they run. They bring fashion and style to places where such things weren't even talked about before."

"We're never going to agree on this."

"I know," she said, quietly. She studied him for a long moment and then stood and walked over to him.

"Did your family lose everything?"

He nodded.

"We owned the general store. You know one of those small old-fashioned ones that carried everything from clothes to hardware to groceries."

"Tempest's Closet shouldn't have affected the hardware and grocery part of your business," she said.

"No, but the other large retailers that followed Tempest's Closet to our town did."

"I'm sorry."

"Don't be. It made me who I am."

"I like who you are," she said, wrapping her arms around his waist and resting her head against his chest.

He tugged her up against him. There was no room for any other thoughts. He didn't want to dwell on the past or think about business. He just wanted to relish the feel of her.

To focus solely on her and the now. The part of his life that she could be in. He danced her around the living room. Just enjoying the feel of her in his arms.

He lowered his head to hers and kissed her again. Rekindling the desire that was never far from the surface when she was around. She responded instantly, tipping her head back and thrusting her tongue into his mouth.

He lifted her in his arms and walked out of the living room toward the stairs and his bedroom.

# Seven

Gavin's bedroom was different than she expected it to be. Done in warm earth tones with a large Ansel Adams' photograph from the Mural project but it wasn't a poster it was the real thing. She moved closer to it when he set her on her feet. The stark black-and-white photograph called to her as nothing else could.

Gavin put his hands on her shoulders and drew her back against his body. Just holding her while she examined the photograph to her heart's content. She felt the subtle movements of his body rubbing against hers. Felt his erection against the small of her back and knew in a few minutes that passion would take over and they'd be making love. But for this one moment she felt something she'd never expected to feel. Something she'd long ago given up searching for. A kind of welcome and peace.

She closed her eyes and turned in his arms, resting her head over his heart and wrapping her arms around his body. He lowered his head over the top of hers. The warmth of his breath stirred her hair before he cupped her face and tipped her head back so that their eyes met.

She tunneled her fingers through his hair, drawing his head down. Their mouths met, his lips rubbing lightly over hers. Touching her gently...so gently. She knew she'd never get enough of tasting him.

Then the dynamic of the embrace changed. His tongue thrust deep into her mouth as his hand swept down her back. He cupped her butt and drew her closer to him. His erection rubbed against her belly. She moaned deep in her throat and moved closer to him.

Her hands clutched at his shoulders, her body craving more. She felt his hands at the hem of her short skirt. Sliding up underneath it and rubbing random patterns on her skin. She shifted her legs, craving his touch higher. But he kept up the subtle caresses.

"Gavin…"

He nibbled his way from her mouth to her ear biting the lobe. When he spoke his words were a strong puff of air in her ear, felt as much as heard. "What?"

"Touch me," she said, breathing the words against his neck. Damn, he smelled so good. She wanted to close her eyes and lose herself in the sensation of him. The feel of his big hands on her skin. The white-hot tingle that followed his touch. The sweet craving for more that was permeating her bloodstream.

He moved his hand higher cupping her butt cheek and holding her in place as she undulated against him. She moaned deep in her throat, trying to stand on her toes and feel his erection where she wanted it. Needed it.

She lifted her leg trying to wrap it around his hip but he gripped her thigh in his hand, his long fingers holding her so close to where she needed his touch.

"I am touching you, Tempest."

But it wasn't enough. She shifted again in his arms but it was futile. She wasn't getting closer to him until he decided she was. "I need more."

"Not yet," he said.

She realized then that he was playing her. Not in a malicious way but in a power way. One that made her submissive to him and his desires. He'd give her what she wanted but only on his agenda. She didn't understand what his agenda was here. But she felt that he did have one.

She stepped away and looked at him. His gray eyes were cold and flat. She saw the passion in him in the flush of his skin and the erection straining against the front of his pants. But she saw that he kept a part of himself locked away from her and this moment.

"What are you waiting for?"

He reached out then, taking a strand of her hair

in his hand and drawing it through his fingers. She tipped her head toward him and his thumb found her lower lip. She knew her mouth was swollen from his kisses and it tingled as he moved his thumb over it.

"Just waiting," he said.

She couldn't follow the conversation anymore. Her world had narrowed to his hand in her hair and that thumb rubbing over her lip. She caught it gently between her teeth, sucking him deep into her mouth and his hand on her hair stilled. His eyes narrowed, his breath hissing out in a rush.

He drew her closer again, wrapping her hair around his hand. He pulled his thumb from her mouth and ran it across her lips and then down the side of her neck. He stroked her pulse there at the bottom of her neck before moving down the edge of her blouse. Caressing the skin left bare there.

His features were harsh and strained in the light, yet very sensual as he focused on touching her. And she realized what he was waiting for. He didn't want to rush this moment and neither did she.

He brought his mouth down to hers. His one hand burrowed deep in her hair, holding her still for his possession. His tongue delving deep, leaving no inch of her mouth unexplored.

His thumb stroked over her skin, down beneath the silky fabric of her summer weight top. Finding the lacy edge of her bra with his thumb, moving lower and flicking around the edge of her breast. She shivered as he came close to touching her where she needed it most. Her nipple tightened in anticipation but he just kept moving down her body. His knuckles brushing the underside of her breast.

He sucked her lower lip between his teeth and bit down delicately on her flesh before drawing his head back. "Take your top off."

She shivered again as the rough growl of his voice played over her skin. She drew her shirt up over her head tossing it to the floor.

"Now your skirt," he said.

She took a step back but his hand in her hair kept her bound to him. "Do it here."

She trembled at the command in his voice. She'd never had a man treat her this way in the bedroom. Moist heat pooled between her legs as she reached behind her back and loosened the button and then drew down the zipper. With a swivel of her hips the skirt slid down her legs and pooled at her feet.

"Now take off your underwear," he said.

She undid the bra and slid it off her arms. She leaned against him for a moment, letting the tips of her breasts brush against the crisp linen shirt he wore.

She hesitated to remove her panties. She'd be naked and he was fully clothed. He seemed to sense her hesitation and leaned down to capture her bottom lip between his teeth. He sucked on her lip until shivers ran down her body. Being naked while he was fully clothed no longer mattered. He lifted his head and she reached for her panties, sliding them slower down her legs until at her knees they fell to the floor.

Gavin stepped back to look at her. "Go lay on the bed."

In the lamp light her skin glistened and it was clear to him that she was too fine to be in his bed. In that moment, with her lying there waiting for him, he knew that he wasn't good enough for her. He was too rough—still the boy who'd had to fight for everything he owned—despite the millions he'd made.

He was too demanding and she was too…out of his league. There was the slight hint of shyness in her eyes as she settled in the center of his bed. And there was a part of him—granted it wasn't a big part—but a part of him that demanded she prove that she really wanted him.

"I'm here," she said, her voice soft and tentative. This wasn't the same nervy woman who'd confronted him in his office demanding a job.

He should walk away from her. Tell her to get dressed and make her leave. There was no good way for this to end, this affair they'd talked themselves into. His need for revenge was too great and as he looked at her lying there he wished…ah, hell, he wished he were a different man. The kind who could walk away from the past because he had a glimpse of what the future could be.

"Gavin," she said, lifting her arms toward him.

Walking away was no longer an option. Not when

she watched him with those wide vulnerable eyes and stared up at him like she really wanted him. Like her heart was empty without him. And God knew his heart was empty without her.

He sank down on the bed next to her hip, tracing the curves of her body with his hand. Her skin was porcelain and perfect. He traced a line down the center of her body over her sternum right between her two perfect breasts. Her pink nipples beaded as he moved his finger. He stopped and leaned over, breathing on her nipple, watching it tighten even more before he lowered his mouth and tasted her.

She moaned, the sound a symphony in his ears. Her hands moved restlessly, falling to his shoulders. Her nails scored his skin through the fabric of his dress shirt as she tried to draw him closer. But because he couldn't see a way to hold her in his arms forever, he wanted to make this moment last. He wanted to ensure that she never took another man to her bed and didn't think of him.

He caught her delicate flesh between his teeth as jealousy pounded through him. No other man would touch this woman the way Gavin would. His hands slid down her body gripping her hips as they lifted toward him. He pinched her other nipple and heard her gasp as he did so.

He lifted his head, making sure she was with him. She drew his head back to her breast. Lifting her shoulders so that the tight bud of her nipple brushed against first his cheek then his lips.

"More," she said.

He lowered his head to oblige her, working her nipple with his lips, teeth and tongue until her legs were moving restlessly on the bed. His body was so tight, so aching for the sweet release that she promised, that his entire being echoed with his own heartbeat.

He felt the blood pounding beneath the surface of his own skin. Felt the pulse pounding at the base of his spine and in the flesh between his legs. He attended her other nipple and then nibbled his way down her body, lingering over her flat stomach. He sucked the skin around her belly button and delighted when he skimmed his fingers lower to find the moist proof of her desire for him.

He traced the edge where the smooth skin met her curls and then ran his finger up one side of her and then down the other. The small bud in the center of those two lips was red and swollen, begging for his touch. But he ignored it. Shifting to his knees, he pushed her thighs apart.

She let them fall open making room for him between her legs. He looked down at her. Her skin was flushed with a slight pink tinge. She held her breath, everything in her body tensing as he lowered his head between her legs. Her hips rose toward him as he reached down and licked her once.

The taste of her was addicting. He pulled the flesh into his mouth, careful to treat her delicately.

She grabbed his head, pulling him against her as her hips rose with each tug of his mouth.

He bent lower to taste her more deeply. She was delicious and he knew that he'd never forget the sensations of this moment for as long as he lived.

She moaned and said something—perhaps his name or a demand—but he was lost in a red haze. He was surrounded by her and he could think of no other place he wanted to be.

He could feel her body starting to tighten around his tongue, and shifted back to see her at this moment. He wanted to watch her face as she went over the edge.

This was something that her money couldn't buy and her family name couldn't control. This was about Tempest and Gavin, he thought. He relished the sound of their names linked in his mind.

He pressed one finger inside her, then added a second finger, pushing deep and finding that spot that would bring her the most pleasure. He leaned down over her, taking her nipple in his mouth again, sucking her deep into his mouth.

She was panting, his name falling from her lips in between pleas that made no sense. He drew her out until finally he touched that bud between her legs and brought her to climax. She called his name and grasped his head, holding him to her like she'd never let go.

Shivers still rocked her body as she came back into herself. She couldn't believe Gavin was still fully dressed from the fine linen shirt down to his wingtips.

She shifted on the bed, reaching for him to draw

him down to her. He hesitated for a second and she wondered what was going on in his mind. She knew there was more to this than simple lust. Oh, God, please let it be more than lust.

She'd never had a man make her forget…forget everything except him. In the past sex was something she'd had because it was convenient or expected. But this was the first time in her life that she was with a man just because she wanted to be with him.

For the first time who she was—Tempest Lambert—was actually a strike against her. And he still wanted her.

She felt tears sting the back of her eyes and she turned her face against his chest, reaching for the buttons of his shirt. She undid them slowly, taking her time, revealing the masculine chest slowly.

Gavin wasn't waxed; she doubted it would even occur to him to do something like that. And she liked the feel of his chest hair against her fingers. She slipped her hand under the shirt and found his flat nipples. His breath caught as she scraped her nail over his flesh. She knew he wanted her.

She could feel him straining toward her through the clothing. It was a costume he wore, a façade of sophistication. She realized the real man beneath the clothing was rougher, needier and not at all sophisticated.

That very realization was exciting. She slid the shirt off his shoulders and pushed him back toward the headboard. She wanted to take her time and explore him. She wished she was brave enough to order him to take off his clothes and lay on the bed. But she wasn't.

"Why are you staring at me?"

She shook her head. No way was she going to say what she was really thinking. "You're gorgeous."

"Ha. I think we both know I'm not model material."

"No, you're not," she agreed. Because she'd been with model-type men. Men who were too picture perfect to be true. But there was something so real about Gavin. Something that made her feel real by association.

"You should at least have argued."

"Models aren't real," she said, tracing the delineated pectoral muscles on his chest. "They are airbrushed perfection."

She bent to taste his skin, licking a path over his chest. He tasted salty and his skin was warm and she closed her eyes wanting to lose herself in him again.

He turned in her arms, pinned her under his body. His mouth found hers, his tongue thrusting deep inside. The feeling of his muscled chest against her breasts was exquisite.

He reached between their bodies and freed his erection. She felt the scrape of his belt against her inner thigh as he pushed his pants down.

He hesitated as he was about to enter her body. "Are you on the pill?"

It took a second for her to understand what he was

asking. She just wanted him to drive into her and take her. Birth control. She'd never thought of the consequences of making love before…not really. But suddenly, staring up at his face in the dim lamp light, she did. She'd always vaguely wanted a family. A real family and kids. She bit her lower lip.

"Tempest?"

"No. I'm not on the pill. I'm not as promiscuous as the tabloids make me seem."

He cupped her face in his hands, leaning forward to kiss her. "I know."

Those few words made her wish they were different people. Or maybe that she was a different woman. One who would be strong enough to pull Gavin off his quest for revenge because deep inside she sensed that he'd never give up going after her father for her.

He kissed her so tenderly before moving away to put on a condom. He came back down on top of her and she put her hands on his chest, holding him back from entering her body.

Bending down, he captured the tip of her breast in his mouth. He sucked her deep in his mouth, his teeth lightly scraping against her sensitive flesh. His other hand played at her other breast, arousing her, making her arch against him in need.

"Now, Gavin. I can't wait."

"Not yet."

She reached between them and took his erection in her hand, bringing him closer to her. Spreading her legs wider so that she was totally open to him. "I need you now."

He lifted his head, the tips of her breasts were damp from his mouth and very tight. He rubbed his chest over them before sliding deep into her body.

She wanted to close her eyes as he made love to her. To somehow keep him from seeing how susceptible she was to him, but subterfuge had never been one of her strong suits. Gavin was essential to her in ways she was only beginning to comprehend.

She slid her hands down his back, cupping his butt as he thrust deeper into her. Their eyes met. She felt her body start to tighten around him, catching her by surprise. She climaxed before him. He gripped her hips, holding her down and thrusting into her two more times before he came, loudly calling out her name.

Disposing of the condom, he pulled her into his arms and tucked her up against his side.

She wrapped her arm around him and listened to the solid beating of his heart. She wanted to stay here forever wrapped in his arms. He made her feel safe and complete and she wished he didn't. She felt vulnerable to someone other than her father and that made her angry because until this moment, she'd been able to keep moving on and never look back. But now she was going to be looking back.

She understood Gavin so much better now than she ever could have before. And because she had her own weaknesses, she didn't want him to feel vulnerable with her. Plus, he had given her back something she wasn't sure she could have found on her own.

"Are you sleeping?" he asked.

She felt the vibration of his words in his chest and under her ear. She shifted in his embrace, tipping her head so she could see the underside of his jaw.

"No." This had been one of the most tumultuous days of her life. She felt that if she went to sleep she might wake up and find out that Gavin had really washed his hands of her and this had all been a dream.

"Thanks for taking care of the birth control. To be honest I wasn't thinking of anything but you," she said.

"You're welcome." He pulled her closer in his arms. "I want to take care of you, Tempest. To watch over you."

His words warmed the long cold part of her soul. And she knew then that she was starting to fall for him. How stupid was that? She'd spent her entire life trying to win her father's love and she was falling for the one man who'd make his acceptance an impossibility.

She propped herself up on his chest, looking down at him in the shadowy night. He made her feel safe and she knew it wasn't an illusion. He'd provided her a bodyguard and he held her in his arms tonight. She'd seen the same thing with his brother. The way he always protected those around him. What had happened to make him do that?

"What are you thinking about?"

"The way you take care of me. No one has ever…" she trailed off as she realized how vulnerable those words made her.

He slipped on a condom and rolled over so that she was under him. Her legs parted and he settled against her. His arms braced on either side of her body. He caught her head in his hands and brought his mouth down hard on hers. When he came up for air long minutes later, he said, "I will always."

She believed him. Gavin wasn't the kind of man to make promises lightly. When he gave his word he kept it and she wondered if she should ask him how he felt about her. If he thought he could ever love her enough to give up his vendetta against her father. But those kinds of words weren't easy to find and she was much too scared to find out that he couldn't love her to ever say them aloud.

Instead she lifted her hips toward his and felt him slip inside her body. Their eyes met and held again as he took her.

# Eight

Tempest glanced at the alarm clock, afraid to move in case she woke Gavin. The illuminated dial read 2:30. She had always been a bit of an insomniac.

She felt too vulnerable lying naked in his arms. She'd shown him too much of who she really was and now he had the power to hurt her. Really hurt her and she wasn't sure she trusted him not to. Oh, he wouldn't do it intentionally. He was too caring to deliberately hurt her but she was still…afraid. She tipped her head back, staring at his beard stubbled jaw in the dim light of the moon. She wanted to touch him. To explore him now that he was sleeping and not watching her. She wanted to memorize all the little details of his body so that she'd be able to pull them out later when she was alone and remember them. So that any time she saw him at social functions she'd have a secret knowledge of the man beneath the suit. The man behind the image.

Turning in his arms she reached up and touched his jaw. She ran her finger along the edge of it and felt his breathing pattern change. She closed her eyes and held herself still. She didn't want to disturb him, wake him up and maybe remind him that she wasn't supposed to spend the night with him.

What if he asked her to go? To be honest it had happened before and nothing made her feel worse than having to put her clothes on in the middle of the night and leave. But everything with Gavin had been different. Please, God, let things still be different.

"What are you thinking about?" he asked, his voice a sleepy rumble.

"Nothing," she said, softly.

"You're tense."

"I am," she said. No point in lying.

"Why?"

She struggled not to smile. There was no artifice in Gavin. He had no time for small talk and always cut to the chase.

She shrugged, very aware that she didn't want to reveal anything else to him.

He cupped her jaw and tipped her head back so that their eyes met. In the dim light it was easy to pretend that she saw something more in his eyes than was probably there. She wanted to believe that she really did see caring, affection and then the narrowing of his eyes and lust. But she didn't want to deceive herself.

"Tell me."

"It's nothing and everything," she said. There was no other way to say it.

He shifted on the bed, pushing the pillows behind his back against the headboard and drawing her into his arms. She liked that feeling that came as she lay there. It was safety and security but more than that it was belonging. However false it might be, for this night she belonged in Gavin's arms. And there was no place she'd rather be.

"Tell me the everything part."

"I don't sleep much at night. Never have. So that's the everything. Just my normal habits."

"Why don't you sleep?"

She shrugged, reluctant to tell a bold-faced lie and say she didn't know. Her therapist and she had gone over every detail of why she didn't sleep for years. Tracing it to the night her mother had died. Being woken up by her nanny in the middle of the night and informed that her mother was asking for her. Being rushed down the hall to her parent's big dark bedroom to hold that cold limp hand. Her father sitting in one corner not even glancing in her direction, while the machines made scary noises. The nanny watching her as if she knew more than she would tell.

"Why, Tempest?"

"My subconscious thinks bad things happen at night but I want to focus on now."

"Tonight?"

"Yes, just tonight. You and I together," she said. The words should be a reminder to her that she and Gavin didn't have forever.

"We don't have much in common," he said.

She'd like to pretend that the comment was apropos of nothing but she knew he was trying to warn her in his own way that this couldn't last. She knew that she should try to guard her heart but was very afraid that it was too late.

"I don't know about that," she said, so very afraid that he was going to use that as a reason to never see her again. She didn't want that to happen. She no longer cared if she got a job at his company, just wanted to stay with him. To have a legitimate reason to stay in his life.

"Name one thing we have in common."

"We travel in the same social circles."

He tightened his arm around her shoulder. "Yeah, but I'm a fraud there. I don't belong in high society."

"You aren't a fraud, Gavin. You earned your place in that circle. So many just find themselves there because of the circumstances of their birth." People like her. If anyone was a fraud, she knew it was her. She'd spent the first part of her adult life being exactly the kind of thoughtless heiress that gave the wealthy set a bad name.

He tipped her head back and leaned down to kiss

her. It was a sweet kiss that demanded nothing and gave everything. "You've paid a high price because of the circumstances of your birth."

"So have you," she said, shifting in his arms. Turning more fully into his embrace.

He lifted his head staring down at her and she realized they both had this in common. This past shaped by their parents. Those long ago events shaping the people they were today.

He lowered his head again. This time his kiss was demanding. She tried to caress him, to draw him over her, but he held her hands in his grip. He lifted her onto his lap and he pulled her hands up behind his neck. She let him. She hung there in his embrace, letting him control her. Hoping that he'd take her again and give her the release she desperately needed to find in his arms.

Tempest was exhausted and totally able to sleep now but didn't want to miss a moment of this night. Her skin felt as if she'd been branded by him. There was beard burn on her breasts and her neck. She fingered the base of her neck where he'd sucked on her skin the last time they'd made love.

She'd never had a man so obsessed with her body. Even now while he was sleeping his hands moved down her back. Tracing the curve of her hip and then moving slowly back up. She was drowning in a sea of sensation and didn't care to be rescued.

She'd never realized how alone she'd been surrounded by the hoards of people that populated her life. But she had been lonely and it was only now that she recognized it.

"Baby, go to sleep," he said.

His voice was a deep husky murmur that made her toes curl in a good way. She lifted her thigh over his legs, curling herself around him. More fully into his arms and into his embrace.

She felt him stir against her and shifted her hips to rub against him. He rolled her under his body, taking her wrists in his hands and stretching her arms up above her head.

"What is it?" he asked.

She stared up at him, his features barely illuminated in the dim light. She ached—pleasantly from the hours she'd spent in his arms, but inside she still craved more. She had no words for what she wanted. For what it was that was keeping her from drifting to sleep.

Instead she lifted herself up, leaning on her elbow and tracing his features in the dim light. He lay still under her and let her explore. He wasn't like the pretty boys she'd grown up with. The soft boys who'd matured into fine-looking men who graced the pages of fashion magazines and society gossip columns.

He had a scar in the middle of his left eyebrow. She traced it over and over again with her finger before bending down to brush her lips over it. She found another small scar just under his left eye and then further down on his jaw and neck. "What happened?"

"Skateboarding accident."

"Skateboarding?" she asked, shifting around to rest her arms on his chest. It was the least likely thing. She couldn't picture him doing anything other than running a multi-million dollar investment group.

"I didn't grow up in a bubble."

"I know. But skateboarding?"

"Yeah, I liked it. Skateboarders don't care about anything but your board and your skills."

He didn't say anything else but she sensed there was more to it then that. She let her mind roam over what he said and suddenly it came to her. "Is that when you realized that you could make your own dynasty?"

He shifted under her, pulling her over him like a blanket and then rolling her under him.

"I'm not into dynasty building."

He wouldn't be. Not with his quest for revenge. Revenge was focused on the past. On avenging wrongs done a long time ago. Dynasty building required a forward vision—something she realized that Gavin didn't have. "Don't you think it's time you started looking to the future?"

He took her wrists in his hands and stretched her arms over her head. Pushed one thigh between her legs until he nestled between hers. Then he held her under him.

"A future with you?" he asked.

She turned her gaze from his. She hadn't been fishing for that and wasn't even entirely sure they could have something permanent together. "I don't know. I just know that you're not happy living the way you have been."

"And my happiness matters to you?"

A day ago she would have said no. That it didn't. He was just a means to an end. A way of striking back at her father. But lying with him naked in his bed having been in his arms and felt the protectiveness that was so much a part of his nature, she knew that his happiness did matter. It mattered more than she wished it did.

She tried to free her hands, wanting to touch him but he held her in an unbreakable grasp.

"Tempest, I asked you a question."

She bit her lower lip. "Yes, your happiness matters to me. Don't ask me anything else, Gavin. A man afraid of the future won't like my answer."

"I'm not afraid, honey."

He lowered his mouth to hers. His kisses overwhelmed her. They should both be sated and not interested in making love again.

Yet as he thrust his tongue deep in her mouth, she felt the rekindling of her own desire. She wanted him again. She tried to angle her head to reciprocate, he held her still.

This was his embrace and she felt the fierce need in him to dominate her here. God, he made her feel like she belonged to him. She tried to remind herself that Gavin had made her no promises, but his body moving over hers felt like a promise.

# Nine

Waking in Gavin's arms wasn't something she was used to. Even after two months of quasi-living together on weekends and even during the week once and a while, she was afraid to open her eyes each morning. Afraid that somehow the relationship with him was another fantasy like the vivid dreams she sometimes had of her mother.

But the big warm hand drifting down her back and drawing her more fully against him wasn't a lie. She opened her eyes and realized that once again she was on top of him.

"Sorry," she said, trying to shift to his side.

"No problem," he said, holding her in place.

He stroked her back and shoulders until she relaxed against him. "Is this normal for you?"

She shook her head, refusing to look at him. The comforting sound of his heart beat under her ear. She wasn't sure she could explain to him why she always ended up on top of him during the night. She only knew that…heck, it felt more real when she held on to him.

"You're not exactly normal for me," she said, softly.

"Good."

She leaned up on her elbows again and noticed he was smiling. He rarely smiled, something she'd observed over the last few months but this morning he seemed…happy, content and she liked to think she had a lot to do with that.

"I'm starting to receive invitations for the fashion shows in New York next month. Do you want to go with me?"

"No."

"It would be a nice getaway."

"I can't. I have a project at work that I'm hoping to close then."

"What project?" she asked He never talked about work, which she suspected was because he was in a fierce competition with her father to take over Tempest's Closet.

"A big one."

"Involving Tempest's Closet?"

He rolled to his side, dumping her on the bed and sitting up. "I don't want to discuss it with you."

She bit her lower lip knowing she should just let it go, but the thing was they couldn't move forward as they were. They were lovers and the world knew it. The tabloids had taken to labeling her the high-society mistress. Sleeping with her father's fiercest competitor. And in essence that was true but she felt like there was so much more between the two of them.

"I think we have to." The last thing she wanted was to force this confrontation but she felt like his business with her father was always between them. It was the reason why the press were so interested in them as a couple. The reason why he wouldn't hire her at his company. The reason they lived together in a seclusion of sorts.

"Are you threatening me?" he asked, his voice a low rumbled.

Never, she thought. She was way too afraid to lose what she'd found with him. But she'd been operating on a level of fear for most of her life. All of her relationships had always been driven by that fear and she hated that. Everything about Gavin had been different and this had to be too. She took a deep breath.

"No. That would be silly. How could I possibly threaten you?"

"You have something I want very badly."

"What?" she asked, aching inside at the thought of what he might say.

She knew that Gavin wanted her in stark physical

terms. He told her every night. But she…oh, man she'd been hoping there was something more between them. Something…

And to be perfectly honest no one had ever wanted anything she had but her father's money. Oh, God, don't let him say her shares in Tempest's Closet. She thought she'd wither and die on the spot if he said that.

"Your body."

Oh, that hurt. It really did. In a way she hadn't anticipated. And now she felt small and alone. Where just a few minutes ago she'd felt powerful and sexy and wanted.

"I'm sure you can find another lover."

She wrapped her arms around herself wishing she could curl into a ball and disappear. Why exactly did she decide she wasn't running anymore? She'd had some brief thought that he was different. But this felt so painful and very familiar.

"Not like you."

She glanced up at him. "I don't want to fight but I think we need to find a way to move past your business with Tempest's Closet or else…"

"Are you going to ignore what I just said?"

"I don't know how to take that."

"You make me want to be a different man, Tempest. I wish there were a way for me to give up this thing with Tempest's Closet but it has shaped my life for too long."

She nodded understanding. Her outrageous press antics had been the same kind of thing. But she liked the life she'd made for herself once she'd stopped behaving that way. "The past is going to suck you down and leave you with nothing. You have to move on."

"I thought you said you liked who I was?"

"I do. But this thing with Tempest's Closet is…"

"Is what? We're having an affair."

She gave him a hard look. "Fine."

She turned and walked away going into the bathroom and turning on the shower. How could she have read him so wrong? How could she have misjudged the man he was? How could she possibly go back out there and face him without giving him a good piece of her mind?

There was rap on the bathroom door. Gavin entered, looking tired. The stubble on his chin darkened his features and made him seem almost menacing.

"I'm not good with this kind of thing."

"Let me take a shower and get dressed. Then we can talk."

He nodded and turned to walk out, stopping on the threshold. "I don't want to lose you."

Gavin's housekeeper Mrs. Stanton had Sundays off, which usually didn't bother him. He liked having the time alone with Tempest since she had started spending the weekends at his house. But this morning when things were so screwed up and he had no idea what to say to make them right he wished Mrs. Stanton were here.

Since she wasn't he busied himself making coffee and breakfast for Tempest. Cooking wasn't something he'd ever learned to do. He could work a grill and a microwave but breakfast wasn't exactly grilling time. Luckily Mrs. Stanton had left a breakfast casserole and some fresh fruit already cut-up in a bowl.

He put the casserole into the oven and tried not to dwell on the fact that he was losing Tempest. It was inevitable that she'd start to want more than he could give her. But then again he'd always been a hollow shell inside. The only time he didn't feel empty was when he was at work, and that had never bothered him before.

He suspected that Michael knew this, and that was why his brother spent so much of his time trying to involve Gavin in outside activities. Anything to get him away from the office.

Hell, he thought rubbing the back of his neck. He prayed that those few words he'd given her before he'd left the bathroom would be enough.

But he knew they'd held a tinge of desperation. How could Tempest miss it?

He turned on the music, filling the house with sound so he wouldn't feel so alone. But the Beastie Boys didn't work their usual magic. Didn't energize him and make him feel unbeatable. The music just made him realize how alone he truly was as he stood on the oriental carpet in the family room and stared at the electronics equipment that any man would envy.

He glanced around his opulent house. Seeing the things—instead of people—in his life. Even Michael was rarely a guest here. His mother had never visited him here. This was his inner sanctum. The place he hid from the world and ah, hell, he really couldn't imagine the place without Tempest.

He saw the ghost of her curled up on the couch next to him as he'd watched the basketball game last night. He heard her laughter in the hallway leading to the kitchen when he checked on their breakfast. He smelled that unique scent that was only Tempest. That blend of expensive one-of-a-kind French perfume and something else that was just Tempest.

He glanced over his shoulder to the other doorway and saw her standing there. Her hair was perfectly styled, her makeup flawless. She had on a pair of capri pants, a scoop neck sleeveless summer top and stylish sandals. She was the picture of casual glamour standing there.

And he saw them both clearly. Him with his stubbled jaw wearing only his boxers. Her so clearly perfect….

There might be a reason why he couldn't find the words to make her stay.

"I'd kill for a cup of coffee," she said.

She was trying for sassy but the sadness in her eyes made it impossible to pull off. He realized then that this was going to be his gift to her—this hollow emptiness he brought to all of his relationships.

Some gift. One that she'd remember long after he'd left her life. And he didn't want that for Tempest.

She should be sassy and happy. Teasing and laughing the way she'd been with him every morning until this one. But he didn't know if he could give her what she wanted.

"Gavin?"

He shook his head and pulled down the coffee mugs she'd bought for them at Starbucks, after insisting that using his company logo mugs wasn't going to cut it. They were big cups since they'd both discovered that neither of them could face the day without an extra-large-extra-strong brew. The green background with white flowers always reminded him of Hawaii.

He poured her a cup, added a splash of fat-free half and half and handed it to her. He poured his own and left it black.

"Breakfast should be ready in thirty minutes. Want to go out on the patio?"

She nodded and followed him outside. He sat down on the double-lounger and drew her down beside him. She held her coffee mug in both hands and took a tentative sip before tipping her head back against his shoulder.

She sighed but didn't say anything. His confidence rose a little when he heard that sound. She wanted to stay here with him, too. Maybe they were both in unchartered waters.

He'd always disliked August Lambert, okay, he'd

actively hated the man for years but at this moment he wasn't thinking of the past. He wanted to keep business matters out of this embrace and not let work affect his time with her.

He put his coffee mug on the table next to him and took hers and did the same. He turned and pulled her flush against his body.

She wrapped her arms around his neck and pulled herself closer to him. He held her in his arms hoping this would be enough. Hoping that somehow she'd be able to determine from his embrace that he needed her in his house, needed her in his bed, needed her in his life. Only now, when he felt like he might lose her, did he realize how intensely he wanted to keep her here.

"I can't say the words you want me to."

"I don't know what words I want you to say."

"Something about giving up going after your father's company."

She shrugged but he saw in her eyes that he was right. "Why can't you give it up?"

He didn't want to talk about that but he saw in her eyes that she did need the words and if she were any other woman he'd say "screw it" and walk away. Instead he sat up and grabbed his coffee mug, using the drink as a distraction until he could figure out what to say.

Tempest watched Gavin as he pushed to his feet and paced around the patio. A part of her really wanted to just let this go. She was used to taking only what the men in her life wanted to give her. Scrambling around for any bit of attention and then gratefully basking in it until they tired of her and moved on.

But she couldn't do that with Gavin. She was falling for him. Who was she kidding—she was already in love with him. He was the kind of man she'd always wanted in her life.

So why the hell didn't she just keep her mouth shut and let things ride? Mind her own business about the Tempest's Closet takeover, hard as it might be. She shook her head and reached for her coffee mug. Taking a small sip, she realized that settling with Gavin wasn't enough. She'd never really loved any of the men she'd been involved with before. She loved Gavin and that made all the difference. She didn't want to be a tabloid footnote to the merger or takeover with Tempest's Closet. They needed to clear the air about it to stand a chance of staying together.

"Gavin?"

He cursed under his breath and turned back to her. He watched her carefully and she saw him searching for the right words to say. That gave her hope as nothing else could. He wanted this relationship between them to work, too.

"I don't want to talk about business with you," he said.

Was it really just business? She doubted it since he'd brought it up this morning. From the beginning of their relationship he'd been careful to avoid conversations about her time at Tempest's Closet and he never talked about his own work, except to continue to turn her down when she asked him to hire her. To be honest she'd pretty much given up working for him.

"I don't think this is about Renard Investments and Tempest's Closet. There's so much more going on here than that."

"Yes, there is. But it's personal. And I don't want you to know that side of me."

She saw the concern in his eyes. The anger and the fear. Did he really think that hearing him admit to things she already suspected would make her leave?

"I'm not going to look at you differently."

"You will."

His confidence shook her own and she worried about what he might say. Maybe this would be the morning he walked out of her life. Oh, God, she really hoped it wasn't.

"Just say it. Don't worry about how it sounds, just say it."

He ran his hand through his hair and then sat down in one of the arm chairs across from her. He was muscled and lean sitting there looking for all the world like a man who had it all. The kind of man who clearly could have anything he wanted because he wasn't afraid of hard work.

"I want revenge on your father."

"Revenge?" She'd guessed there was something more to the take-over than just business. But revenge?

"Yes."

"Why?"

"He took everything from us. And I want to do the same to him."

"Does your family feel that way, too?"

"My mother doesn't. But Michael does."

Of course his mother wouldn't. A mother would know that revenge was too destructive. A mother would weep for her son and the fact that he could never have a future without letting go of the past.

Tempest felt a knot of ice form in her stomach. She'd expected something tied to pride. Something that she could combat. Something that she could find a way to fix so that they could be together.

"Tempest, just know…I wish it were different."

She saw him then. Heard the rap music still pulsating from the stereo in the family room. Saw the beautiful but empty house and the lush retreat he'd created for himself. And she sensed that he didn't know any other way to be. That he'd spent his entire life focused on one thing.

Taking over her father's company. Ruining her father. Her heart ached because her father was just like Gavin. He lived for his business, nothing could interfere with Tempest's Closet as far as August was concerned. Certainly not her.

But from the beginning Gavin had always had time for her. Granted she'd arrived in his life amid scandal but he'd always been there for her. She thought of all the things he'd done for her and how he'd filled her life in ways she'd never expected another person to.

She wasn't going to walk out on him now. She put her coffee mug down and went over to him. Sitting down on his lap she wrapped her arms around his shoulders and tucked her head under his chin.

His arms came around her and he held her so close and so tight that she knew her instincts were right. Gavin wasn't playing with her to get at her father. She imagined at first he'd had some sort of intent to that end but not now. He held her with the same intensity that she was holding him.

Both of them needed each other in a significant way. Maybe in a way he hadn't experienced before. Or allowed himself to experience before.

"There's only one question I need answered," she said, turning things over in her head until she had the kind of sharp clarity that made all the inconsequential stuff drop away.

"What is it?"

She tipped her head back and looked up into his diamond hard gray eyes.

"Do you want me to stay with you?"

"Hell yes."

"I need a commitment from you, Gavin. More than this temporary arrangement."

He buried his head in her neck and didn't say anything for a long time.

"Gavin?"

"I'm giving you more than I've ever given another woman. Can't that be enough?"

She thought about it, wanting to say yes of course she'd take whatever he had to give her. But she knew that once she started settling she'd never be able to convince him that she was worth more. That *they* were worth more.

"No, it's not."

He lifted his head, looking down at her with those startling gray eyes of his. "I don't know how to build anything," he said.

She knew that. Had seen the truth in those words more times than she'd wanted to count. "I do."

"I'll try," he said, as his mouth captured hers in the kind of kiss that left no room for thinking about anything other than Gavin.

# Ten

Michael stood in the doorway leading between their offices, clearly excited about the report he held in his hands. But this was a moment that Gavin had come to dread in his mind. He knew that it was only a matter of time until August over-extended himself far enough that Renard would be in a position of power. A position that they'd maneuvered and planned to be in for over ten years, one which would enable Renard Investments to come in and take over the company.

It was what he'd focused on for years, but now that he had Tempest in his life, he was no longer confident that it was going to bring him the same sense of pleasure he'd expected it to.

"He did it. Took the bait just like you said he would. Tempest's Closet is most definitely over-extended. I just got off the phone with Hugh Stephens in Orlando. He's going to make the loan offer."

"Great." Hugh Stephens worked for one of Renard Investments subsidiaries that was connected through so many other companies that the trail was hard to trace. And knowing how desperate August's finances were as he clung to old ways of doing business, Gavin's gut had said that Hugh could get Lambert to commit to another loan. This was the final nail in the financial coffin that Tempest's Closet had been heading toward for a long time.

"Great? What the hell's going on? You've been planning this since we opened our doors and all you have to say is 'great'?"

"It's business, Michael. We knew he'd make too many mistakes eventually and Tempest's Closet would be ours. I'm not going to dance around the office."

"Given that you can't dance that's not surprising. But something's off here, bro. I figured you'd be breaking out that bottle of scotch you've kept in the wet bar for years. This is the moment we've been working for."

"I'm happy."

"But not like I thought you would be. If this isn't enough for you, what are we going after next?"

"We'll find another company that needs us."

"Gav, talk to me."

Gavin rubbed the back of his neck and refused to look at his brother. Was he having some kind of meltdown? Was he really letting a woman affect him this deeply? Did he honestly think he had any kind of control over what he felt for Tempest?

"Hell, I'm ecstatic, Michael, you know that. Let's open the Glenlivet and drink up."

Michael smiled at him and Gavin realized that his brother had been waiting for this moment for a long time, too. That even though Michael always seemed so open and jovial a part of him was waiting for this retribution against the man and the company that had so altered the course of their lives.

He poured two fingers of scotch into both of their glasses and turned to face his brother. They looked into each other's eyes. Michael's were the same deep brown that their father's had been and for a moment Gavin stood frozen in time.

He remembered what his father said all those years ago—the Renard boys were wily as foxes and twice as smart as the competition.

Michael's mind must have gone down a similar path because he said, "To the Renard boys—"

"Wily as foxes—"

"Twice as smart as the competition."

They clinked their glasses together and each of them swallowed the scotch. Gavin savored the feel of it burning down the back of his throat.

There was a knock on his office door and he

glanced at his watch. He was having lunch with Tempest today.

Just the thought of her standing on the other side of the door tinged his happiness with something sour. He put his glass down and excused himself from his brother. He opened the door and she smiled up at him.

"You ready?"

"Not yet."

"No problem. I'll just sit out here and wait for you."

But he didn't want to discuss the take-over of her father's company with his brother while she sat in his outer office.

"Michael, can we talk about this after lunch?"

Michael's shrewd gaze didn't waver as he put his glass on the counter of the wet bar. "Sure thing, bro."

"Hey, Michael. I'm going to fashion week next month, do you think your girlfriend Melinda will want to join me?" Tempest asked.

"What is fashion week?" Michael asked.

"You're kidding right?"

"No. I'm not. Will Melinda know what it is?"

Tempest and his brother continued to banter back and forth about fashion and men's ignorance of such things as Gavin turned back to his desk and logged off the network.

It felt strange to know that the end of his quest to take over Tempest's Closet was in sight. That finally the company that he'd lusted after for all these years was going to be in his hands.

Tempest's cell phone rang and she excused

herself to take the call, going out of his office. Michael closed the door behind her, pivoting to face him.

"Have you changed your mind about Tempest's Closet?"

The question was unexpected coming from Michael. "Why would you think I have?"

"Because if we go through with this take-over you're going to be destroying the company that her father named after her."

"August barely pays any attention to her."

"It doesn't change the fact that he's her father."

"My personal life is none of your business. Our company is doing what we do best. We've found a shaky investment and we're going to ride in and rescue it from failure. The investors will be happy."

Michael nodded and walked toward his own office, pausing in the doorway to glance back at him.

"Sounds perfect, Gav. Really it does, but you and I both know that nothing is perfect."

"What's your point?"

"I don't think you're going to be as happy about this as you've always thought you would be."

"I'm not the only one who wanted it."

"I know. I'm not saying this is only about you, but I do think you've changed. And taking over Tempest's Closet has never been my goal."

"The hell it hasn't. You just toasted his downfall the same as I did."

"You're right. But when Tempest walked in, I

realized that no matter what we do we are never going to get Dad back. He's dead and maybe it's time we started thinking about living our own lives."

Michael walked away and Gavin just watched him leave. Those words lingered in his ears as he stepped into the outer office and saw Tempest smile up at him. He didn't want to sacrifice his chance to have a life with her.

Gavin was too quiet during the lunch. It had been two long weeks since that morning on his patio where they'd had that tentative talk. She'd been careful of everything she said to him. Trying to keep the peace and hoping that maybe they really were building toward a life together.

But something was off today. She didn't know what it was. Maybe it was the whole fashion week thing. It was kind of silly and kind of frivolous but she loved it. It was one of the few memories she had of her mother. Even though Tempest was supposed to be in school in October her mother would always pull her out and take her to New York for the week.

They'd stay at the Plaza hotel back when it used to be a hotel. She smiled to herself. Then glanced across the car to Gavin's harsh features. She put her hand on his thigh.

"Are you upset that I brought up fashion week?" she asked, as they drove back to Gavin's office.

"Why would I be? I know that it's something

you've been planning on. I'm sure Melinda will be thrilled to go with you if she can get the time off."

"I know but it can be kind of…I don't know… trivial."

"Considering you've been talking about trying to write for *Vogue* I think it would be foolish to skip going. Have you heard back from that editor?"

The relief she felt unnerved her. Maybe it was because he'd been so quiet during lunch and she had the impression that his silence had to do with her.

"Yes. She wants me to write an article on Tempest's Closet and its tradition of bringing haute couture to the masses."

He glanced over at her and she saw something in his gaze that she couldn't define. But it caused a chill to run down her spine.

"That sounds right up your alley."

She realized she'd touched a nerve from his past. The past that had shaped him and driven him to become the man he was today. She knew that he didn't think the masses benefited from Tempest's Closet coming into their small towns. Maybe her article would change his mind.

"I don't know how it'll turn out. I've never written anything other than press releases before."

He signaled to change lanes and then looked over at her. "It'll turn out good like everything else you try."

She flushed at the compliment and at the confidence and pride she saw in his eyes. He pleased her on so many levels that sometimes she woke up afraid that this was all a dream. The fragile bond they'd formed two weeks ago should have made her feel more sure of their relationship but it had only made her realize how vulnerable they were.

"I was thinking about staying in for dinner tonight. Kali's hosting a birthday party for one of her coworkers but I thought a quiet night would be better."

"I'm going to be later at work tonight than I thought. Why don't you go to the party and we'll catch up later?"

He hadn't mentioned that earlier. She didn't want to go to the party by herself. She was slowly coming to realize that socializing wasn't what she really took pleasure in. She'd come to really enjoy the evenings that she spent home with him. Just curled up on the sofa while he worked or watched TV.

"Oh. Okay. I'll go to her party."

"You don't have to go if you don't want to. I thought you might not want to stay home by yourself."

"You're right. What kind of socialite stays in when there's a party?" She tried for a flippancy she didn't feel and knew she'd failed miserably when he glanced over at her.

"What was that tone about?"

"Nothing."

"Tempest…"

What could she say that wasn't going to make her

sound like an idiot and make him tense up on her? She knew better than to confront him with anything to do with Tempest's Closet and her father. Yet it was so much a part of her life—she couldn't ignore her heritage any more than he could.

"I don't have to write the article. I know you don't really agree with everything that Tempest's Closet has done."

He didn't say anything but pulled the car into a parking lot and turned to face her. "I'm not bailing on dinner because of an article you're writing."

"Really?" she asked, doubting him. There was something going on here. Something more than he'd ever admit to. She wondered if it had to do with Michael and whatever the two of them had been discussing when she'd arrived in his office.

He nodded. "I'm proud that you're going to do an article for *Vogue*. I think it'll be a great career transition for you. A way for you to stand on your own and show everyone that there's so much more to Tempest Lambert than a high-society heiress."

The relief she felt was so intense she thought she might cry. What the hell was wrong with her? Her emotions were taking her on a roller coaster ride and she wanted off. She wanted to find a nice safe place in her relationship with Gavin and had the feeling that it would never happen.

"A high-society mistress," she said. That phrase always made her feel a little smarmy. Like she wasn't good enough for Gavin to consider her as anything other than a mistress. She knew it was just a scintillating title that the magazines used to entice readers. But it did tarnish a little of what they had together.

"I've talked to my lawyer about suing the tabloids but he said that would only add fuel to the fire."

"I wish there was some way to make them back off. Should we stop seeing each other?"

"No, baby. Move in with me permanently."

Throughout lunch all he'd been able to think about was what Michael had said. He was going to tear apart Tempest's heritage. *Her legacy*. But it was too late to swerve from that course of action. His entire life would be a lie if he broke the vow he'd made at sixteen.

The vow that someday August Lambert would fall to him. There was no way to stop everything he put in motion. By the end of October when Tempest's Closet held their annual shareholders meeting, Renard Investments would be the majority shareholder and he would demand that August step down as CEO.

And he didn't want to lose Tempest. The only way to keep her was to get her into his house now. To enmesh their lives so tightly together that when the changes happened at Tempest's Closet she would have something else. Something with him.

Oh, hell, she was staring at him like he'd lost his mind. Maybe he could have phrased it better. He should have waited until they were out of the car at least. He was acting like the animal he was beneath his Turnball & Asser designer clothes. The animal that he tried time and again to hide from her.

"Are you sure you want me to move in with you?" she asked. Her fingers were twisted together in her lap. She'd spent a lifetime by herself. Since her mother died she'd been on her own. Would she want to live with him? They were both loners, he thought. Of course with him it was obvious but only someone who'd really gotten to know Tempest like he had would recognize the solitary way she moved through her scores of friends.

"I wouldn't have asked if I wasn't," he said, but he sounded angry. And she was looking at him like he'd lost his mind.

"I'm making a mess of this."

He was known for his cool demeanor and had convinced more than one hesitant investor to go with an investment based solely on his word. He could convince Tempest to do this. He hadn't made himself into the man he was today by vacillating.

"You are. This isn't like you."

But he realized that it was like the man he wanted to be. This was the answer he thought he might have been searching for since that first night he'd made her his.

Reaching across the seat he cupped the back of her head and drew her forward until their lips met. He felt her surprise but her mouth opened under his. He thrust his tongue deep inside her, tasting her completely.

Hell, he really wanted to marry her. To legally make her his but he knew he couldn't do that until he had taken control of Tempest's Closet and that mess was behind them.

Her hands crept around his neck and her fingers slid beneath his collar getting closer to him, touching his skin. He wanted more. But this wasn't the place for seduction.

He pulled back, brushing his mouth over hers because he didn't want to stop kissing her. He never wanted to stop tasting her.

"Say yes," he said.

She stared up at him and in her clear blue eyes he saw all of her hopes and her dreams. And he hoped that he was man enough to live up to them. He was so afraid that he couldn't. Because he knew that he'd been doing the ultimate snow job on her. Convincing her that he was a whole man when inside he was empty. When inside he'd been eaten up by that long ago vow. And only now that she was in his heart did he feel like he was starting to be someone completely whole.

"I'm not an easy person to live with."

"Neither am I."

"My phone rings all the time."

"That's okay. I bring my work home with me every night."

"I can't cook."

"Mrs. Stanton takes care of that."

She was throwing up things that were inconsequential but he sensed there was more to her arguments. "What's this really about?"

"I've never lived with anyone. Not since my mother died."

He hadn't realized that. "You mean as an adult, right?"

"No, even as a child. When mother died, my father kept me at boarding school or summer camps. We'd meet at hotels for different holidays."

This was her legacy, he thought. This was what August Lambert had left her with. Suddenly he felt a hell of a lot better about his plans for Tempest's Closet. A man with priorities that screwed up deserved to have the rug jerked out from under him.

"Those things don't matter to me. We're practically living together every weekend. I think we do okay."

She looked into his eyes searchingly and he wondered what she wanted to see in his gaze. He really hoped she'd find it.

"Are you sure?" she asked. He recognized the hope underlying her words.

"I am very sure. I've never really had much of a home, either, but I want to try to make one with you."

She nibbled on her lower lip and then took a deep breath.

"Yes," she said at last. Her voice was so soft he

was afraid he'd misunderstood but he knew he hadn't.

"Great. I'll call the movers when I get back to my office."

"There's no hurry," she said. "I know you're busy."

"Not too busy for this, Tempest. I'm not too busy for you."

"I never thought you were."

He would do everything to make her feel like an integral part of his life. To make her see that even though he couldn't give up his revenge, he wouldn't give up on her, either.

# Eleven

Tempest had been to the Shedd Aquarium more times than she could remember for different functions and events. But tonight felt just a little magical as she entered on Gavin's arm. It could be that this was the first function they'd attended since she'd moved into his house. Or maybe it was just the fact that they'd been together for three months.

Earlier this evening, Gavin had made sweet love to her on his king-sized bed when she'd come out of the shower. Her entire body was still tingling. He glanced down at her and she blushed, thinking of the way she'd begged him to take her.

He raised one eyebrow. "What are you thinking about?"

"Nothing."

"Nothing, hmm, I'm thinking about the way you felt when I—"

She put her hand over his mouth. "Stop it, don't say that out loud."

He waggled his eyebrows, kissing the inside of her hand as he pulled it from his mouth. "Well, I am."

Someone cleared their throat behind them and Tempest glanced over Gavin's shoulder, meeting her father's disapproving gaze.

He wore his tuxedo with panache and ease. He'd always seemed so well put together that she felt she'd never measure up. But with Gavin's arm around her waist…she didn't feel like she was lacking.

She'd found her place in the world after a lifetime of searching. She wished she were alone with Gavin because she'd tell him right now. She'd confess the love that she'd been carrying as a secret in her heart. What good was love if it was kept inside?

She slid her own arm around Gavin's waist and leaned closer to him. He squeezed her hip.

"Good evening, Tempest."

"Hello, Father," she said. Gavin turned so they were both facing August. He looked tired and a little tense but then the retail business was a stressful one. She smiled at her father though she sensed an underlying tension between the two men.

Her mind was a total blank, which didn't surprise her. Her father unnerved her as no other person could. She always felt like she was thirteen years old and trapped between being a child and an adult. She felt awkward and gawky.

"Father, you know Gavin Renard, right?"

Her father nodded and held out his hand.

Gavin shook it. "Evening, August."

An awkward silence fell among the three of them. Tempest saw Kali over her father's shoulder trying to get away from the people she was with and come to the rescue.

"Doesn't the aquarium look nice tonight?" she said, desperate to overcome the awkwardness of this conversation.

Gavin glanced down at her. She hoped he realized that this wasn't the place for the conversation he wanted to have with her father.

"Yes, it does. But then it is always spectacular."

"Yes it is. Renard, will you excuse us? I'd like to speak to my daughter in private."

Gavin excused himself and her father led the way to one of the small quiet alcoves that had been set with cocktail tables.

Her apprehension about dealing with her father was stronger than ever tonight. There was something almost solemn about him and she just couldn't put her finger on what was wrong.

"What did you want to talk to me about?"

"About your being Gavin's mistress."

She wrapped an arm around her waist. Was he concerned for her? She cautioned herself not to read too much into his attention. The last time she had…well she'd been more than disappointed. But this was the first time since her mother died that he'd engaged her in a private conversation that had nothing to do with Tempest's Closet.

"I'm not really his mistress. The gossip columnists just keep saying that. But we are actually living together now. I think he might be the one." She hoped her father had gotten beyond believing what he read about her in magazines and newspapers.

"The one what?" August asked.

"The one I marry."

"I doubt that."

"Why?" she asked. Her father didn't know Gavin like she did.

"He's after Tempest's Closet."

"Dad, that's business. Gavin would never let that affect his relationship with me."

"What makes you so sure?"

She didn't know. She could say that it was her gut but she knew her father wouldn't accept that answer.

"I just am."

"Don't set yourself up for disappointment, Tempest. I'd like to think I raised you to be pragmatic if nothing else."

He turned to walk away and she almost let him go. "Father?"

"Yes?"

"You didn't raise me. Boarding schools and nannies did," she said, brushing past him. "And you don't know the man Gavin is away from the business world. He'd never hurt me the way you have."

He stopped her with a hand on her arm. "He already has. He's taking over Tempest's Closet and forcing all the family out. That includes you."

"What are you talking about?"

"Maybe you don't know your man as well as you think you do," he said.

"Just tell me what's going on," she said.

"Maybe we should let Renard do that. Tell her, Gavin."

Gavin stepped out of the shadows, coming to stand next to her and her father. She looked up into his eyes willing him to laugh and make light of her father's comments but he was too somber. There was more than a kernel of truth in her father's words. She shouldn't have been shocked by that. Her father never joked around when it came to business.

Gavin hated the way Tempest stood with her arm wrapped around her waist. His instincts had said letting her go off with her father had been a bad idea. But he wasn't about to shelter her from the truth.

"Tell me what exactly?"

"I'm not sure," Gavin said. He didn't know how much information August already knew.

"Something about your buying up shares in Tempest's Closet and forcing the family out."

August's information was complete. Gavin wondered if he had a leak in his own organization or if the boys at Tempest's Closet had finally gotten smart.

"I didn't buy up the shares; Renard Investments did on behalf of a consortium of investors. I've only just spoken with our investors this afternoon and we haven't made any decisions on what we will be doing with Tempest's Closet at this point."

Tempest was watching him with those wide blue eyes of hers and he had this sinking feeling that living with him wasn't going to be insulation enough from the shock brought in by his ruthless business maneuverings. That somehow she was going to slip through his fingers tonight.

"You are Renard Investments. Whatever you recommend to those investors they will do."

"That's true."

"Put my father's mind at ease, Gavin. Tell him you're not going to tear the company he built apart."

He stared at her and knew that this was going to be the moment when he lost her. Because he couldn't do what she was asking him. He wasn't going to put August Lambert's mind at ease.

He wanted the older man to spend as many sleepless nights as his father had. He wanted the older man to be forced to come begging to him for his job. And then he wanted—oh, hell, he craved—the opportunity to tell him no.

"This really isn't the place to discuss business. Call my secretary in the morning, August, and I'll try to squeeze you in."

"I'm not going to come to your office."

"That's your decision. But I think we both know that you are over-extended and I know I hold all the cards."

"And my daughter," August said.

Gavin nodded. He would have preferred to do this away from Tempest. To keep her out of the seedier side of what he did. The fact was hostile take-overs were never pretty. They were down and dirty fighting. The kind he was best at.

And she'd always seen him as something more than he was. Maybe this was for the best. Let her see the man he really was so that she'd know exactly what he had to offer her.

Except with Tempest he was a different man.

"I'm with him because I want to be. Our relationship has nothing to do with Tempest's Closet," she said.

"I'm not so sure about that. This is a man who has the money and power to control the media and yet he still allows them to refer to you as his mistress. He's not the one for you, Tempest."

She glanced at him and he saw the doubt in her eyes. But he wasn't about to defend himself against these ridiculous accusations. Tempest herself asked him not to bother with the stories the scandal rags had been running.

"I asked him to leave the media alone. These kind of stories blow over."

"You always were good at believing whatever lies you told yourself."

She visibly recoiled from her father and Gavin reached out, pulling her to his side and tucking her up against him. "You direct your anger toward me, Lambert. Tempest has nothing to do with this business between us."

"She has everything to do with it. You placed her squarely between us."

"Even I can't control who I fall for."

"Are you saying you care for her?"

Gavin wasn't sure he wanted to do this now. Do this here. But not confirming his feelings for her wasn't going to help anyone.

He glanced down at Tempest. Leaning close he whispered into her ear. "Yes."

She wrapped one arm around his waist, holding him tightly to her. "Me, too."

He wanted to pick her up and carry her away from this place. Away from the crowds filling the aquarium and away from the man who was watching them.

"If he really loves you, then he won't destroy the only legacy I have to give you."

"Of course, he isn't going to destroy it," she said. "That's not your intent is it, Gavin?"

Destroying Tempest's Closet had been his goal for far too long. There was no way he could give it up even for Tempest. Her legacy wasn't a chain of retail stores. Her legacy was the writing she'd be doing. Sharing her past with readers and talking about a unique point in fashion history that her father established.

"I'm not at liberty to discuss this right now. We can talk either in my office tomorrow, Lambert, or at the stockholders' meeting in two weeks."

August gave him a tight smug smile. "That's exactly what I thought. You'll never let my company stay as it is."

"It is a failing business," Gavin said.

"It's an institution like Macy's. You can't close us down."

"I'm not sure what course of action we will take. And I'm not discussing it further tonight."

"Why not? Afraid Tempest will see the real man she's involved with?"

"She already knows exactly who I am."

"Does she?"

"Yes."

"Then tell her the truth of what you plan to do with Tempest's Closet."

"Okay then, I will. I'm going to sell it off piece by piece. Are you satisfied, August?"

Tempest watched her father walk away and then she pushed out of Gavin's arms. Surely he wasn't really going to ruin a company that employed so many people. Surely his hatred of her father and Tempest's Closet didn't go that far.

"Did you mean that?"

"Yes."

The music started in the other room as the party got into full swing. But she felt less like partying than she ever had before. She didn't know how to reach Gavin. She knew that her father represented something dark and dangerous from his past. Something that had shaped him.

But the man she'd fallen in love with wasn't the kind of man who'd take away the livelihood of so many.

"You'll be little better than he is if you do this."

"It's not about him or you. Don't worry about it, Tempest."

"I'm not worrying. I just think that you haven't thought this through."

"I assure you I've thought it through. I've been running a successful company for more than a decade. I think I know what I'm doing."

"You're wrong."

"Wrong?"

"Yes, you're too emotional about my father—"

"Stop right there. I'm not emotional about this. Taking over Tempest's Closet is just another day at the office to me."

Except it wasn't and she knew it. Tempest's Closet represented something to him that no other company could. She took his hand in hers.

"Think of the families that will be put out of work if you do this. Families that have been making a good living—"

"Tempest I care for you, but I can't and won't change my mind on this."

She pulled back. "I'm not trying to manipulate you."

"Good because you can't."

She dropped his hand. "You're life will be empty, Gavin if you do this."

"Are you threatening me?" he asked.

She remembered the last time he'd said those words to her. And they'd come out of that moment stronger in their commitment to each other. She knew she just had to find the right words to say.

Find the thing that would relax him and once he got some distance from the confrontation with her father maybe he'd calm down and be able to talk to her rationally.

"I asked you a question, Tempest."

"Don't speak to me like that," she said. "You know I'm not threatening you."

"Really?"

"Really."

"The consortium has already agreed to tear the company apart and sell it off. It's the only way to make a profit. Are you still going to stay with me?"

"You're acting like a jerk."

"No, I'm acting like a man whose woman is trying to get him to make a business decision that makes no sense."

"I'm trying to get you to see that there's no prospect for a man who can only destroy things. For a man who doesn't see that only by building things and creating new opportunities can there be a real future."

"A real future with you?"

"With anyone, Gavin. You have to let go of the past."

"Would you be so concerned if my past involved any company other than Tempest's Closet?"

She stared at him for a long moment and realized that she had fooled herself into thinking that he really wasn't the man the media made him out to be. That he wasn't the man *Forbes* had called a 'cold-blooded profit maker.' Because the stories written about her were never true.

"The sad thing is that you have to ask me that."

"Sad because it's true. You know you like the money you make from Tempest's Closet. You haven't had a job for the entire time we've been together."

"I don't have to work because my mother left me a trust that pays me an annuity. I don't live off the profits I make from Tempest's Closet. They are re-invested in the company."

"Whatever you say."

"I don't have to explain myself to you."

"Neither do I."

There was a finality to his words that made her realize he'd anticipated this sort of ending for them. And it was an ending. She saw it in his eyes and in his stance.

"I wasn't asking for an explanation," she said, pushing a tendril of hair back behind her ear and re-alizing her hand was shaking.

"What were you asking for?"

She had no idea. This argument had gotten totally out of her control. To be honest she no longer was angry at him. Instead she was sad because she couldn't see a way around this situation. Couldn't find a way that she and Gavin could have something lasting. Ever. It wasn't about Tempest's Closet or the small town that he'd grown up in.

She had a moment of true clarity seeing Gavin as she'd never seen him before. He was an emotionally damaged man focused only on business, one who'd taught himself to hide away from the world.

She recognized that because she did it herself. She hid behind fashion and the paparazzi. But she'd always craved a man like him. A place like his arms where she could curl up and forget the outside world existed.

"I was asking for you to let go of the anger and bitterness that's controlled your life so long and take a chance on love."

"I'm not bitter," he said.

She just shook her head and walked away. Not knowing what else to say to him.

# Twelve

Tempest left the Shedd Aquarium and caught a cab out front. But she had no idea where to go. She couldn't go back to Gavin's place and she had no interest in going to her empty condo. She wanted to find a quiet place where she could just break down and cry.

She felt tears stinging her eyes but she forced them back. Actually she didn't want to cry. She wanted to find a nice numb place where she couldn't feel.

What was it about her that she couldn't see the men in the life for what they were?

The cabbie was looking at her, waiting for an address, and finally she sighed. She had no idea where to go. She thought Kali would take her in but that would be humiliating beyond measure.

How could she have been so wrong about Gavin? Her cell phone rang and she glanced at the caller ID display before answering the call. *Gavin.*

"Where are you going?" he asked.

"I don't know," she said. She hated the way her voice sounded thready and weak. She didn't want him to realize how deep his rejection had cut her. As if there were any way she could hide that. Gavin had always seen straight through the masks she wore to fool others.

"I'll crash at Michael's tonight. Go back to my place."

There was no way she was going back to his place. Not even to get her things. She didn't want to remember the illusions she'd bought into while she'd been there.

She didn't want to remember what it had been like to be happy for those few short months. It was almost the way she'd felt about her father's house on Lake Shore Drive. That big mansion that she'd lived in when her mother had been alive but had rarely set foot in after her death.

"Thanks but I don't think I'll do that. I can find a friend to stay with."

That weird sound of silence buzzed on the open line and she bit her lower lip hoping...what? That he'd somehow say he was an idiot and that he was going to give up making a huge profit just to make her happy.

She sighed, missing him more than she should, considering he'd just told her taking revenge on her father mattered more than she did. But her heart didn't care about Gavin's revenge. All her heart cared about was that she'd be sleeping alone in a big bed without him by her side. She'd be waking and reading the newspaper by herself. Her life would go back to its busy but empty schedule.

"Goodbye, Gavin."

"Tempest?" There was a note of pleading in his voice that made her hope. Was he going to alter his plans for Tempest's Closet?

"Yes."

"If I could change…"

"You can," she said, believing it with all her heart.

"But not on this. In the future I can be a different man, maybe start building things instead of buying them and then selling them off piece by piece."

She knew that it would be too late. Too late for them because, whether Gavin knew it or not, putting all those families who relied on Tempest's Closet for their livelihood out of work was going to affect him.

"I hope you do change," she said, softly.

"But it's too late for you. Is that what you are saying?"

She wished she had a different answer but she didn't. "Yes."

"I thought you cared for me."

"I do. More than you'll ever know but I can't keep shifting who I am to please you."

"I've never asked you to do that."

"You did tonight when you said that Tempest's Closet wasn't part of my legacy."

"This really is over?"

It broke her heart to say it but they both knew it was true. "Yes."

"Take care, then."

He disconnected the call and she hugged her phone to her chest. The cabbie was still looking at her and she figured she was making a fool of herself. "The Ritz-Carlton at Water Tower Place."

Her family had long kept a suite at the hotel. She'd crash there tonight and in the morning make some solid plans. One thing was—she needed to get a job, start working to get her mind off things. The article for *Vogue* was something, but not enough.

The sites of the city she'd always called home flashed by the window as the driver wove through traffic. She realized she was going to have to leave Chicago. Not just temporarily, but forever. She needed to get as far away from the men in her life and the humiliation she felt at having tried to make them love her. To make herself more important than their business machinations. More important than their workaholic schedules. More important than their game of one-upmanship. She'd lost but good and it was time to leave.

She wished the decision was an easy one, but inside she felt a tearing deep in her heart and she knew it was going to be a long time before she forgot Gavin Renard.

It started to rain as the cab pulled to a stop in front of the hotel. The doorman opened the cab for her and she stepped out, forcing a smile on her face. Time to start pretending she was Tempest Lambert, happy-go-lucky heiress.

The heiress who didn't care that the world knew her business. She made sure that she lingered in the lobby, chatting with a couple she knew from her childhood. She was careful to keep the smile and lighthearted banter foremost until the door to her 30th floor suite closed behind her and she sank to the floor leaning back against the wood door.

Gavin went to the table he'd reserved for the event and sat down. But he was scarcely aware of anything going on around him. He knew he should be making plans. Now that August knew he had enough shares to force him out there was a chance the other man would try to manipulate the stock somehow.

But he couldn't focus on that just now. Where was Tempest going? Why had he let her leave like that?

He just wasn't willing to give into any kind of ultimatum. It didn't matter that she hadn't really been telling him he had to choose between her or Tempest's Closet. He knew in his heart he couldn't have both.

And he'd only known Tempest for a few months. He'd been focused on Tempest's Closet since he was sixteen years old.

"Where's Tempest?" Michael asked as he seated Melinda and then took his seat.

Gavin hoped that he'd never have to answer that question again. But since it was Michael he knew he couldn't ignore it. In fact, considering that they'd become friends he was probably going to have to endure more than one question. "Gone."

"What? Is she okay? Melinda had a sinus headache earlier."

"Tempest's health is fine. August is here."

"Did he say something to her?" Michael asked. "You know he's the most arrogant men I've ever met. When I called him with your offer he said he'd rather rot in hell than do business with us."

Because of Tempest he had asked Michael to put together a package for August that would give the other man a figurehead position with no power but at least would let him hold on to his pride. And more importantly, to ease the shock and pain for Tempest. But that cold bastard had found another way to twist the knife in.

"He knows we have purchased all those shares that were available and somehow he knows that we're behind Hugh Stephen's loan, too. I think we need to go back to the office and look for a leak."

"Tonight?" Melinda asked.

"Yes," he said. Yes, definitely tonight. He needed to get to work. Work had been his salvation once and it would be again.

"Gav, are you sure about this? Shouldn't you go after Tempest instead?"

Michael was right—and it really pissed him off.

He wasn't going after her. Not now. He'd have to beg her to come back and he wasn't into begging.

"When have I ever asked you for advice?" Hell, he hated asking for anything.

"Never, but maybe you should start."

He admired Michael more than any other man he'd ever met but that didn't mean he was going to listen to him when it came to Tempest. Michael couldn't begin to understand that complex woman. Hell, half the time he didn't.

"You're not exactly a great example of success when it comes to relationships," Gavin said.

"I asked Melinda to marry me," Michael said, turning to her and drawing her into his arms.

A future. This is what Gavin should be planning instead of how to make August squirm. This is what he should be focused on instead of a quest for vengeance that would never bring him peace. "Wow, that's big. Why didn't you mention it to me?"

Michael ducked his head, rubbing one hand over his chest. "I wanted to make sure she said yes first."

"Congratulations, bro. I'm happy for you. Welcome to the family, Melinda."

Michael reached across the table, his hand falling on Gavin's shoulder. "You could be happy, too."

Not anymore. Not now that he'd seen the way Tempest had so easily believed the worst in him. Granted he hadn't tried that hard to convince her otherwise. Not that her opinion of him was what stopped him from going back to her. What really kept him in his seat was the pain he'd seen in those glittery blue eyes of hers.

Beyond the anger had been the kind of soul-deep pain that he wasn't sure he had the right to ask her to forgive him for causing. And the root cause remained, because he sure as hell wasn't backing down from August. The one tentative olive branch he'd offered had been rebuffed, and to be honest, he wasn't interested in trying that hard to win over her old man.

"You should get out of here and take Melinda some place nice to celebrate."

"I'm going to. We're just dropping in for a few minutes. I'm taking tomorrow off."

"Enjoy yourself."

His brother hesitated before walking away and Gavin forced a smile to reassure him. He was happier for Michael than he could express. The table filled up with business associates until there was only one empty spot left. The chair that should have been Tempest's.

He talked with those around him, functioned as close to normal as he could. He had the feeling that this was the life he'd made for himself. That there'd always be that vacant chair in his mind that should be filled with her.

Ah, hell, he was getting maudlin. Was he really letting her go? Was there really no way to keep her?

He left as soon as the dinner was served. Instead of driving home he cruised the city finding himself on Lake Shore Drive. He slowed at the gated mansion where August Lambert lived and glanced up there.

For Tempest's sake he knew he should at least make an effort to smooth things over with her father. He wasn't going to give in to her old man. But he was a shrewd negotiator willing to do whatever it took. And he wasn't going to leave the Lake Shore Lambert mansion until he and August had hammered out a deal that gave him what he wanted—a way back into Tempest's heart.

Revenge wasn't as sweet as he'd always hoped it would be. And seeing Michael get everything that Gavin had secretly dreamed of having with Tempest had twisted the sword of her leaving in his gut a little bit.

Sitting in his luxury car and watching August's house he realized that maybe it was time that he did become a better man.

He pulled up to the gate and rang the bell. He didn't know if August had left the Shedd yet or not. But Gavin could wait. He would wait as long as he had to and use the time to figure out a way to make the situation with Tempest's Closet right. August was going to agree to his terms because if he didn't the old man would really end up with nothing. And if he accepted Gavin's deal to remain part of the company then he'd still have not only a job to go to each day but also a chance at a relationship with the daughter he'd never had time for.

Then once Gavin was finished with August, he

was going after Tempest. Because even a few hours without her in his life was too long.

The bed was too big and the halls too quiet. After nearly a week at the Ritz she realized that her old habits were back. She was sleeping maybe two hours a night. No matter how she tried she couldn't get comfortable in her sleep, she kept rolling over and searching for Gavin.

She tossed and turned in the king-sized bed one more time before finally getting up. Wrapping herself in a robe she went to the windows and glanced down at the streets. Unlike Manhattan that was busy 24/7, Chicago did sleep in the wee hours of the night.

She pushed her hair to one side and wished that she could calm the voices in her head. The ones that warned her that maybe she'd overreacted and that she should go back and try one more time to make Gavin see reason.

She wandered around the room filled with a feeling of nothing, of that emptiness that made her want to do something crazy. Finally it was a six o'clock and she changed into her workout clothes and went down to the gym.

While she was running on the treadmill, everything coalesced. She didn't need to leave Chicago, she needed to find her place here.

She realized no matter how hard she ran or how far she moved away, the past would always be with her.

The past defined who she was today in a way that she'd never realized before. Asking Gavin to give up his revenge was like asking him to stop breathing. She'd heard his sparse tales of the past. Understood that her father and Tempest's Closet had changed the course of his life—and given him something to drive toward.

She left the gym, grabbed a bottle of water and headed for the elevator. She stepped into the car. After her shower she was going to make some real plans for the day.

"Hold the door."

She put her hand out between the doors to keep it from closing. She never could figure out which icon button meant door-open.

Gavin stepped into the car. He had on jeans and a rumpled Harvard T-shirt. His hair was mussed and he had stubble on his jaw. He looked tired but so good to her that she wanted to jump in his arms. She'd missed him more than she'd wanted to.

"What are you doing here?" she asked. Their last conversation had felt so final that she'd never expected to see or hear from him again. And clearly dressed the way he was, he wasn't here for a meeting.

"Looking for you."

"How did you find me?" she asked. The only people who knew she was here were the hotel staff and Kali. Kali had come over the first night she'd arrived.

"Kali."

"I can't believe she told you where I am." Kali had been as angry at Gavin as Tempest had been.

"Um…she didn't. I had to go to Michael and ask him for Melinda's help to call Kali."

"What?"

"Can we talk about this in your room?"

"Sure."

She couldn't believe he was here. Or that Kali had given up her location.

She led the way down the hall to her room with Gavin following closely behind her. He hadn't said another word on the ride.

She opened the door and stepped inside, seeing the mess she'd made of the room. The open box of chocolates on the table, the empty tea mug and the robe she'd left lying over the back of the couch.

She walked to the window and leaned against the wall next to it. The city was just coming awake.

"Okay, so explain to me what you're doing here."

"I wanted…I mean you were…ah, hell, Tempest. I don't know what to say."

She wrapped an arm around her waist and stared at him. He'd never really been too vocal about what he felt. But the fact that he was here meant something. But she was afraid to speculate on what it meant. Afraid to hope that he was here because he wanted a future with her.

"Start at the beginning. You went to Michael?"

"Kali wouldn't take any of my calls, well, except for one."

"And you asked her where I was?"

"I never got the chance. You should know that you have a really good friend in her."

"I do know it. I also know she has a bad temper."

"So I found out," he said.

She wanted to smile at the way he said it. "After that you went to Michael?"

"No. I called every hotel in the city but no one would give me any information about you. I checked the airlines and you weren't listed on any flights out. Same with trains so I had a pretty good hunch you were still in the city."

"Why did you do all that?" she asked, no longer caring how he found her.

"Because I need you."

"You need me?"

"You were right when you said that I couldn't keep living my life the way I always had. I treat everything like its temporary and try to insulate myself from disappointment. But when you left…there was no insulation."

"I never meant to hurt you."

"I know. I didn't mean to hurt you, either, but I did."

He crossed the room to her, pulling her away from the wall and into his arms. And though she wasn't sure she should, she wrapped her arms around his waist. He crushed her to his chest and she held him back just as fiercely.

Cupping her face in his hands, he tipped her head

backward. "I don't want a life without you. I like the man I am when you're around me."

Her heart sped up at his words and she saw real affection and caring in his eyes. "Oh, Gavin, what are you saying?"

"I'm saying I love you and I want you to marry me."

He kissed her then before she could say a word in response. His tongue thrusting past the barrier of her teeth and tongue. His hands sweeping down her back and holding her molded to the front of his body.

When he lifted his head, she started to speak but he rubbed his thumb over her lower lip. "I should have said this first. Your father and I are working out a plan for Tempest's Closet—it's not the role he's used to and he'll have to work for our new CEO but I think he's considering it. The consortium has agreed to allow Michael to step in as CEO for a year. Michael has a solid plan to get Tempest's Closet back on track."

"Dad agreed to that?"

"He didn't really have a choice. It was take the deal or walk away with nothing."

She stared up into his gray eyes finally believing that he really did love her.

"I love you, Gavin."

"And you'll marry me?"

"Yes."

He kissed her hard and carried her into the bedroom. Making love to her as if it had been years since they'd been together instead of just an incredibly long week. Knowing they had both found the home they'd been searching for.

# Epilogue

Her father's chauffeur-driven Mercedes arrived promptly at 7:35 p.m. Tempest nervously smoothed her hands down the simple lines of her white satin wedding dress. The last nine months had flown by and her new life was everything she'd always dreamed it would be.

Her father climbed out of the back of the car while Marcus, his driver, stood holding the door open.

Tempest stood at the top of the steps looking down at her father. Their relationship was still a little awkward but he'd been making an effort to get to know her and she was getting to know him, as well. He said that Gavin's take-over had forced him to realize there was more to life than Tempest's Closet.

So here she was trying not to smile too brightly but when her father glanced up at her, she couldn't help it.

"You're so beautiful, Tempest. You look just like your mother."

"Thank you, Father," she said around the lump in her throat, her nerves melting away at the compliment. This was her night. The night when she and Gavin were going to be married at her father's estate.

The tabloids had stopped referring to her as a high-society anything.

The drive to the Lake Shore mansion was quick. There was a silence between her and her father that wasn't exactly comfortable but it wasn't as strained as it would have been in the past. "Thanks for agreeing to let us have the wedding here."

"Your mother would have wanted you to be married in her gardens."

"She did love her garden," Tempest said.

"She also loved you, Tempest. Every night before she went to sleep she'd remind me how lucky we were to have you."

Tears burned the back of her eyes. She had so few memories of her mother, and her father had never spoken of her before. This small nugget about her mom was like a precious gift.

She blinked rapidly, stopping the tears that threatened.

"Are you sure about marrying Renard?"

"Yes," she said. She wasn't nervous about marrying Gavin.

Flashbulbs exploded as they passed a knot of paparazzi who were clustered around the gated drive of her father's mansion. She and Gavin had agreed to letting *Vogue* magazine—and only *Vogue*—do a profile on their wedding. After all, she had now made a full-time job of writing for them about the fashion industry from the inside.

Her father nodded once as they came to a stop in the drive. Marcus opened the door to the car, and her father came around and took her hand, escorting her through the house and into the back yard.

There were close to a hundred people assembled there. She glanced at the sea of faces not really seeing them. Her father walked down the aisle ahead of her and took a seat up front. She'd decided against asking him to give her away since he'd never really had her. Instead she glanced to the right and saw Gavin waiting for her.

"You are gorgeous," he said, coming to her side and kissing her passionately on the lips.

"So are you," she said, feeling the love he felt for her flow through her. Feeling surrounded by the love she felt for him.

"Even though I'm not model material?" he asked, making her smile.

"Even though."

He dropped another quick kiss on her lips.

"Can't you wait for the honeymoon to do that?" Michael asked coming up behind them.

"Mind your own business, bro."

"I guess I finally can now that Tempest is in your life."

Michael winked at her. "He needs a lot of advice, Tempest. Are you sure you want to take him on?"

"Very sure," she said.

"You messed up her lipstick," Kali said, stepping up beside Tempest. "Give me a minute to fix it then we can get this wedding started."

Kali fixed Tempest's lipstick and then hugged her. Leaning close to her to whisper, "I'm so happy for you."

The wedding fanfare started and Kali and Michael walked up the aisle in front of Tempest and Gavin. They had decided on a simple wedding with only Kali and Michael as their attendants.

As the Wedding March began to play, Tempest glanced up at Gavin and knew he'd given her the kind of happiness she'd always thought she could never find. She couldn't wait for the ceremony to be over so that they would be legally bound, though in her heart she knew nothing would ever take him from her side. They worked hard to build a future they'd both be proud of. And Gavin had been talking about children and building a dynasty together. She thought about what her father had said to her long ago about choices—and realized she'd made the right one when she'd approached Gavin.

\* \* \* \* \*

*When business is pleasure…*

*Turn the page for a sneak preview of*

The CEO's Scandalous Affair
*by*
*Roxanne St Claire,*

*the thrilling start of* THE GARRISONS *series,*
*available from Mills & Boon® Desire™*
*in September 2008.*

### The CEO's Scandalous Affair

#### by

#### *Roxanne St Claire*

"We've reached our cruising altitude, Mr. Garrison. Would you care for the usual?" The lone flight attendant on the G5 that the Garrison family routinely rented for business travel smiled benevolently at him. Her prematurely gray hair was, as always, pulled back into an elegant bun, her simple dark suit unmarred by even a fleck of lint.

"Thank you, Christine, I would. Anna?"

Across the small expanse that separated the two widest leather recliners on the plane, Anna had already lined a granite-topped table with a sea of manila folders and papers, and she had a laptop open and fired up for work.

"It depends," she said. "What is the usual?"

"Tomato juice and Tabasco."

She made a face. "Coffee, please."

"Come on, Anna," he urged. "Live dangerously."

He hoped for a clever quip, an easy smile, but got only a shake of her head.

"Just coffee, thank you." When the attendant nodded and moved toward the galley, Anna lifted a paper and held it toward him. "I've compiled a list of pending open items for your attention, Mr. Garrison."

He didn't remind her to call him Parker. Anna Cross was back to business in a big way. It was as though she'd been wearing a sign that said This Is Work, Not Fun ever since she'd arrived at the executive airport and climbed out of her little Saturn wearing her most staid suit selected from a wardrobe that couldn't be called anything but *ultraconservative*. Navy jacket, shapeless trousers, flat shoes.

Where was the girl who felt pretty in pink underwear?

Parker took the list, and reminded himself that he was the one who'd suggested she accompany him to *work*. He'd made that clear. At least, that was how he rationalized what was, at the moment, an impulsive idea brought on by the not-so-semi state of arousal the bathroom encounter had left him in.

He knew why he'd suggested Anna accompany him to London.

But did she? Sure, she was a terrific, grade-A, indispensable administrative assistant. Sure, she was attractive, classy and intelligent enough to make small talk with the high rollers at the hotel gala. And best of all, he trusted her. She had no gold digger's interest in his money, ready to translate one weekend in Europe into a lifetime of luxury like so many of the women he knew.

But, to be honest, not one of those was the real reason he'd made the unorthodox suggestion. The real reason was simple: he liked what he'd seen in that bathroom. And he wanted to see more. And seeing, he knew as sure as he breathed, wouldn't be enough.

Under any other circumstances, he'd make his move and he'd make it in about five minutes, launching a romantic, sex-charged weekend with champagne and hot kisses at thirty thousand feet. Seducing a woman was an art and a pleasure he took seriously. And often.

But something indefinable held him back. Something oddly unfamiliar had him waiting for a clear invitation, a straightforward cue from her.

Maybe she'd take off her jacket, playfully taste his spicy tomato juice, unclip her barrette and give her hair a sensual shake. That was what other women would do. They'd throw in a head-tilting giggle; slide their bare, pedicured feet on his lap and let the games begin.

But not Anna.

She pulled a pair of butt-ugly reading glasses out of her purse and slipped them up her pert nose. She tightened the clip that held her hair severely off a face devoid of anything but lip gloss and maybe mascara. Then she took her copy of his agenda, pointed to item number one, cleared her throat and said, "You mentioned the Nassau property. I have the files."

Not only did she refuse to send a single cue of feminine interest, she doused his low simmer by mentioning the biggest headache in his life.

He took the file and flipped it open.

"Is there something in particular you're looking for?" she asked.

There sure was. Dirt. Problems. Issues. Anything that could get rid of the half sister who'd just been named his equal partner at Garrison, Inc. "Just want to see how the business is doing."

"Last quarter's financials are on the left side, including occupancy rates and banquet revenue," she told him. "On the right, you'll see information about new resort programs and key employee files. The manager of the resort, Cassie Sinclair, seems to be running things quite smoothly."

At the mention of her name, Parker sucked in a slow and disgusted breath. He flipped through the pages, immaculately ordered and filed, frowning at the excellent revenue stream and the strong outlook for the next season based on advance reservations.

"Is something wrong?"

Yes, something was very, very wrong. He wanted the property to be a disaster. Wanted something he could hang on Cassie Sinclair to prove she couldn't be a Garrison.

"No," he assured her.

"Oh, I thought I might have misfiled something."

"Have you ever misfiled anything, Anna?" he asked with a teasing smile.

A soft blush rose in her cheeks. "If you're asking if I ever make mistakes, I think you, of all people, know that I do."

Mistakes like lingering in his shower a little too long? He held her gaze, still hoping for a spark of connection, but she looked away—as she always did—just as Christine returned with the drinks, some fruit and freshly baked muffins.

Parker returned his attention to the file. "The place is turning a nice profit," he said, half to himself.

"You make it sound like that's a problem."

Should he confide in his assistant? Maybe a little shared confidence would loosen her up. At least get her to slide out of that straitjacket she wore. Plus, he needed someone to talk to. Someone he trusted.

He lifted his tomato juice and took a long drink before he dove in. "Cassie Sinclair, it seems, is more than just the manager of the Garrison Grand-Bahamas."

"She is?"

"She's my half sister."

Anna's jaw dropped an inch. "No way."

He gave her a bittersweet smile. "Evidently there is a way. It's called an affair and my father had one for a long time, resulting in the birth of a woman who is now, according to his will, my equal partner in Garrison, Inc. and—" he held the file up "—the owner of this hotel."

"I don't believe it," she said, dropping back into her seat.

"Neither do I. But that's why God invented lawyers," he said with a shrug. "And why I have to make an appearance in London this weekend."

"Will she be there?"

"Oh, I doubt it. But it's only a matter of time until this gets out to the very small and incestuous hospitality industry. It can't help my business. I'm attending this event for visibility and positioning. More of a PR move than one that will impact the bottom line."

"So that's why you were talking about DNA testing and contesting the will," she said. "Oh, and why…your mother…" Her voice drifted off.

So the rumor mill had already started churning.

"My mother has her way of coping." He picked up the drink again. "And I'm afraid it's not Tabasco in her tomato juice."

She gave him a sympathetic look. "Your family is strong. You'll weather this storm."

"I hope you're right."

"You just have to stay focused and keep running everything the way you have. You can't let this distract you."

The unsolicited—and amazingly accurate—advice took him by surprise. "You're right, Anna. Very astute." He smiled and leaned forward, inexplicably drawn to her. "Thank you for being so understanding."

She held his gaze just long enough to give him hope that the cue he wanted was right around the corner. But she just handed him another file.

"When you're ready to go over the agenda for the marketing-firm meeting, it's all in here. And I'm able to take any e-mail dictation now," she added, tapping the open laptop. "I'll download it and send it when we arrive in London."

Oh, yeah. Anna Cross was all business today, and being a smart CEO, he ignored the urge to reach across the space that separated them and unclip her hair just to see what she'd do. She was way too valuable an asset to him to let hormones screw it up.

\* \* \* \*

*Don't forget to look for*
**The CEO's Scandalous Affair**
*next month.*

## MILLS & BOON
# *Desire* 2-in-1
## On sale 15th August 2008

### Scorned by the Boss *by Maureen Child*

This millionaire thinks he can win his assistant back with seduction. Then she discovers his ploy and shows him two can play his game!

### The Texan's Secret Past *by Peggy Moreland*

Mandy knew that *working* for charming rancher Jase Calhoun would lead to heartache, so why'd she gone and *slept* with him?

✸

### The CEO's Scandalous Affair *by Roxanne St Claire*

This Miami millionaire had dated his way through almost every eligible woman in the city… Could his unpretentious assistant make him rethink his policy on romance?

### Seduced by the Wealthy Playboy *by Sara Orwig*

Brittany Garrison needed his help to rescue her sinking business… but didn't know millionaire Emilio Jefferies' price would be her seduction.

*Series – The Garrisons*

✸

### The Kyriakos Virgin Bride *by Tessa Radley*

Zac Kyriakos was the definitive alpha male – bold, powerful and passionate… So how could innocent Pandora resist the wealthy Greek's charms?

### The Billionaire's Bidding *by Barbara Dunlop*

Hotel magnate Alex Garrison wants her family's business, and he's prepared to do anything for it…even propose!

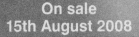

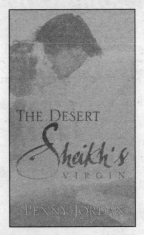

# *Celebrate 100 years of pure reading pleasure with Mills & Boon®*

To mark our centenary, each month we're publishing a special 100th Birthday Edition. These celebratory editions are packed with extra features and include a FREE bonus story.

Plus, you have the chance to enter a fabulous monthly prize draw. See 100th Birthday Edition books for details.

*Now that's worth celebrating!*

### July 2008

**The Man Who Had Everything by Christine Rimmer**
Includes FREE bonus story *Marrying Molly*

### August 2008

**Their Miracle Baby by Caroline Anderson**
Includes FREE bonus story *Making Memories*

### September 2008

**Crazy About Her Spanish Boss by Rebecca Winters**
Includes FREE bonus story
*Rafael's Convenient Proposal*

Look for Mills & Boon® 100th Birthday Editions at your favourite bookseller or visit
www.millsandboon.co.uk

0108/CENTENARY_2-IN-1

# FREE

## 2 BOOKS AND A SURPRISE GIFT!

We would like to take this opportunity to thank you for reading this Mills & Boon® book by offering you the chance to take TWO more specially selected 2-in-1 volumes from the Desire™ series absolutely FREE! We're also making this offer to introduce you to the benefits of the Mills & Boon® Book Club™—

- ★ **FREE home delivery**
- ★ **FREE gifts and competitions**
- ★ **FREE monthly Newsletter**
- ★ **Books available before they're in the shops**
- ★ **Exclusive Mills & Boon Book Club offers**

Accepting these FREE books and gift places you under no obligation to buy; you may cancel at any time, even after receiving your free shipment. Simply complete your details below and return the entire page to the address below. You don't even need a stamp!

**YES!** Please send me 2 free Desire volumes and a surprise gift. I understand that unless you hear from me, I will receive 3 superb new volumes every month for just £4.99 each, postage and packing free. I am under no obligation to purchase any books and may cancel my subscription at any time. The free books and gift will be mine to keep in any case.

D8ZEE

Ms/Mrs/Miss/Mr.......................................Initials ..............................

BLOCK CAPITALS PLEASE

Surname .............................................................................................

Address ..............................................................................................

............................................................................................................

.....................................................Postcode ...................................

Send this whole page to:

The Mills & Boon Book Club, FREEPOST CN81, Croydon, CR9 3WZ